# Fight Night
## on a Sweet Saturday

# Fight Night
## on a
# Sweet Saturday

★    ★    ★    ★    ★

*a novel by*

MARY LEE SETTLE

New York ★ The Viking Press

*In memory of my father*
*who loved the river*
*and with grateful thanks to my mother*
*who taught me response to the land*

# Fight Night
## on a Sweet Saturday

★　　　★　　　★　　　★

# Chapter One

GOD, my brother Johnny and I were bright! We wore it over a mild bodily undertow of Anglo-Saxon sadness, and we treasured it like a tribal tattoo.

So when the telephone rang in my apartment in New York on the Saturday night before Labor Day in 1960, I didn't want to answer it. I was in bed with somebody. Now, I am ashamed to tell this, not because I was in love, or felt ecstatic or savage and wanted to protect myself from prying, or even sinful or afraid of getting caught. No, it was worse than that. It didn't really matter. That's how Johnny and I were, three years ago. It just didn't make a damn bit of difference, and I was proud that it didn't. Johnny and I were far too bright for that.

But the timing was bad. It was embarrassing to lie there listening to that intruding ring. I let it ring five times, while we both watched the light from the crooked street lamp outside my apartment washing the ceiling, and wished whoever it was would give up. Eduardo held my hand as if that could stop me, held it harder until he hurt me, but I finally drew it away and turned on the lamp, as we both knew I would.

Even then, just for a second, I wasn't going to answer. The phone kept on ringing, insistent, demanding. I stopped it with my hand and then was against its receiver, drawing a sheet around me to hide myself from the light, because at that hour on Saturday I knew it would be Johnny, and whoever refused him?

I counted the quarters tolling, eight quarters. He called, "Hello there, fellah," sounding far away, turned away from the telephone, wherever he was, all alight with Saturday-night speed, taking the fact that it was I for granted. At my sinking back, smiling, into that trance no one could break, Johnny's voice engulfed me from five hundred miles away over the mountains and in the nest of Canona.

Eduardo said, "Oh, for Christ's sake, Hannah."

I held the telephone in my palm to protect it from his intruding noise and whispered, "Shut up."

He got up from beside me. I heard his bare feet shuffling across the floor. I didn't see him leave my room, but I heard him put on a record of Eric Satie. It sounded thin and pure from the living room.

Johnny said, "Hannah, are you asleep?"

I asked first, as we all had a thousand times, "Are you all right, Johnny?" I had been asking that since I was six and had already begun the mother-worry of a trusted little sister. Even at twelve years old, Johnny was as elusive as a grouse.

He just laughed and answered, "Come on down here," as if the possibility were like sense and memory, needing no space or time, or decision. Five hundred miles away in West Virginia, Johnny was commanding me from a telephone booth. When I knew which one, I would know just how far he had gone in his night, that hot night where in the high Manhattan buildings no air moved and the stillness inside the room was fetid with city breath.

"Where are you?" I asked softly, partly to keep my voice away from Eduardo's disapproval. I heard him go into the kitchen. I could hear ice rattling, whether from Johnny's drink in the booth or from Eduardo's I neither knew nor cared. The sounds met in my head.

Now, in the kitchen, I knew I was becoming "us," rolling in Eduardo's angry mind toward "they." At such times he hated us. Usually he loved me as you love in spite of. Sometimes I knew he was feeding one of his dark red Brooklyn furies by sleeping with "an upperclass American bitch." That pleased Eduardo, but it made me feel like a can of beans. Seduction is, after all, one of the ways to kill an enemy. Eduardo had said the time before, "Jesus, Hannah, they always call you back. I even hate your body when they do. Your damned brother, dancing down there on that ridge. Don't answer!"

The door to the refrigerator shut.

"You should have seen me in my bunny suit. I was yum yum . . . !" Johnny was at the time of night when he broke into the middle or the distillation of a story, expecting me to see the rest for myself. Usually I did. We had traveled for so long through the same past. But this story of the bunny suit he would have to be drawn to earth to tell.

"What bunny suit?"

"Hell, honey, you know." It annoyed him to be reminded that I was not always there, like an imp on his shoulder, watching and whispering, as he was imp on mine. I sensed in his voice the wit at the edge of despair that showed he had reached a stage of urgency in his drinking—in his trying to tell what he had to.

There was a long silence. The connection sang a single, thin note. I waited.

"I have"—his thin voice at my ear was factual—"a hat full of quarters. A goddam Chipp straw hat full of quarters."

"The bunny suit?" The bedroom door opened. Eduardo tried to catch my eye. The music was loud in the room.

"What in the hell is that?" my brother demanded.

[ 5 ]

"Oh, come on—the bunny suit." I ignored the question, not, at that night minute in the heat and being drawn back toward Johnny, knowing or considering why.

Eduardo closed the door, carefully.

"Hey, you know how I spent the goddam morning?" Johnny was getting ready to tell me, share his hatful of quarters and his Saturday night—religious holiday over America, "Irish" night, "nigger" night, "fun" night, the night for a man to fight free to the surface of his life, not caring how he did it or how much hate he dragged up and let fly.

"Your three minutes are up," the soft mountain twang of the operator interrupted.

"Wait a minute, honey," Johnny told her, flirting, forgetting me. There were more bells of quarters. "Now for God's sake don't interrupt me," he commanded coldly.

"You know what today is, Hannah? It's Operation Spaceman. I'm telling you the God's truth, fellah. Operation Spaceman. We all had to wear space helmets to talk on the goddam telephone. Cover a lot of space through space. Telephone—get it? At nine o'clock this morning I was sitting in the goddam office with a goddam baby helmet, so help me, made out of blue sateen with a couple of wire rabbit's ears for antennae with little redwood knobs on the goddam ends."

I laughed, obedient.

"Ten of us on the telephones with these little old red balls bobbing every time we got in there butting our heads against some guy in a company store didn't have any customers left anyway. Special sales today. Jesus, Hannah, ten grown men hooked up like that to make us get in there. Sell. Get in there . . ."

His voice faded as he leaned away from the mouthpiece.

"Charley!"

I knew where he was then. He had reached the Wayfaring Stranger, that juke joint crouched under Canona bridge where you could get sour bourbon in small dirty glasses and Custer's Last

Stand was on the wall, courtesy of Budweiser. Charley, the fat ex-GI owner, tended his own bar and listened to all of us. He told me one night how at forty-five he was going through college in the daytime because his schoolteacher wife from upriver kept calling him a slob every time she got mad. "Man, does that dry hillbilly bitch get in my thirsty craw!" he had ended his story. "Man, did she loosen up while the war was on. Fooled the hell out of me."

Johnny wasn't drunk enough yet to call him "student," which Charley took from him with professional good will.

"Hannah, you still there?" Johnny came back, knowing I was. "So there I was this morning talking to this guy to keep him from hanging up on me. I could hear my voice and see myself and it wasn't my voice and it wasn't myself in the goddam cheap obscene blue sateen. I could see myself . . . oh, hell, good-by, honey."

He hung up, ignoring the time he had paid for. I sank the little Princess of a telephone into its cradle and lay there, dull, not either place. Heat lay over me like an incubus.

From the living room the nervous little control of Satie still twinkled from my hi-fi. I knew that any movement would be toward quarreling of one kind or another. The heat and then the telephone had set a charge. We both waited, I so near asleep, so not caring that I won the waiting, and Eduardo came in, swimming through the heaviness.

Out of heat and need he said, "Don't answer it again."

"I won't," I told him, but we both knew I would. Then I said, "Come here to me," like a good sport, with that habit phrase women use to call all hurt children to be petted, all bad children to be whipped, a phrase for children out of a woman's mouth, but a woman disguised in a thin boy's body, a 1960 body—still providing the demanded bone and flesh. In another time I would have had larger breasts, great thighs, the pink bite wounds of whalebone stays. Eduardo caught my urchin, pale honey-dyed hair as if it were weeds.

[ 7 ]

He was diving down, holding my hair, head up from my neck to breathe once, and reflect the light in his dry hard eyes. He struggled against me, heavy and impersonal, then back into the killing safety of my water, at the erect point of fear, striking out, making love to me, drowning, not giving a damn for that minute that I wasn't there.

One night in my parents' house set sentinel on the hill above Canona, at the persistently polite time of dinner, that daily acted scene with the family where no one spoke the truth at table, it being, by the rules of my mother's whip-run house, a "peaceful, pleasant interlude" for all of us, Johnny and I had met eyes through the yellow candlelight across the table, and I knew he wanted to get over the genteel wall, away from the arid faces we assumed as if there were a disapproving guest watching us all. I knew he wanted me to tag along, saying nothing. I never knew when he would go. He had been down the talking mouths of easy men and women when he wandered, down to jukebox chapels below the main street of Canona, up long narrow stairs to bars unrecognized during the blue-plate, busy working days or in my mother's house. Those accepting, yawning, secret dens, the Raccoon Club, the Wildcat, the Wayfaring Stranger, drew him in, becalmed him, as more intense men with less laughter are becalmed by easy sex. He was away, with me tagging along after him as I had done all my life, a little sister as trained as one of the dogs. The loveless dry people we saw in the light at the dinner table, their lips pinched, then closed, as if even a childish yawn let the devil in, made him feel dirty, depraved. This I caught from him, how they fouled and hurt the angel in us; he never knew, as I would have to learn, that it was partly his own evasiveness which had long since dried their mouths. He would slip secretly toward freedom, diver too, quick killer, deep, isolated regretter.

"Oh, Jesus, oh, Christ," Eduardo whispered.

The telephone rang.

I sobbed with laughter.

[ 8 ]

It rang again. Eduardo ran back to the living room and slammed the door as if the telephone had questing eyes.

Of course I picked it up, and heard the quarters plunk, Johnny knowing I would be there and answer, dependable.

"Hey, fellah." The thin, faraway voice of Johnny was as close as my ear. "I've got a friend of ours here. Wai' minute." He turned from the telephone and I could hear a swish of a late-night car passing and knew he had wandered by now into the booth under green fog of lights of River Street.

"Broker!"

I could hear them arguing.

To find Broker Carver, he would have been down to the river. By this time Johnny's movements through the town of Canona were as formal as a ballet. He had gone up on the bridge to watch the black river shining between the street lights on its banks. Long snakes of mirrored light in the water stretched away in the distance toward high mountains he could not see but only sense by the cool breath that came down from the eastern gorge even on still, hot nights. He could trace the river from the streetlights, all the way up to its great bend above Canona where they turned, hidden by rising hills near the water. From his center on the bridge the pinpoint glow of Canona's night houses splayed out through the valley and up the hills to either side of him. In the town behind River Street, the flood-lit white thin tower of the Methodist Church thrust up above the black roofscape. Nearer the river loomed the dark monolith of the Coal Trust Building where Johnny had sat that morning, trying to sell televisions, or dishwashers, or what electric dreams he could, in his blue bunny suit. At Christmas twenty stories of its windows were lit to form a gold cross that dominated the winter sky above the valley and swam huge in the flowing water. Now the building was a dull shadow moved by the current.

But after he stood there for a while, the river drew him nearer, down the long steps where if he lurched and fell the black water would claim him. It was as if for a priceless minute the shadow, the neglected beer cans, even the river, could suspend their meaning and be there, to be watched with the same unfearing love and as deliberately as when he was a child, ready to swim in the dirty water against our father's express command. At the times of his wanderings when I wasn't with him, I would wake in the night, at school, abroad, shut in my bedroom, dreaming as vividly as if I were awake that he had fallen, seeing the water close and hold him, and dream myself under it, drawn down, downriver, through the tunnel of darkness. I would wake up, tears bursting from my eyes; wherever I was, I would wake up and be back there with him on those steep concrete stairs.

Once at their base he stooped down, where the water was no longer black but rich undulating purple and blue, heavy with coal wash and smelling of it. He forgot me and watched his face, so like mine we could have been in that darkness reflections of twins. He was intent on his face forming and re-forming in the water, now dancing, a grotesque parody, now destroyed by a floating beer can; once a catfish surfaced the water into his reflected eyes. My face was mirrored, high over his shoulder, smaller, worried, waiting for his mood to bring him back away from the bank.

On that Saturday he had already been there if Broker was with him. I could hear them arguing. Broker's voice called out, "Hell, she don't want to talk to me, son."

Once I had come across a picture in an old album of my mother's, taken when her family still lived twenty miles above Canona on the farm at Beulah. It was a hammock where a smiling girl, her little face plump under a wide pompadour, gazed at a young man who wore a wide-brimmed Panama hat and was lolling against a column of the Mansion's porch, looking as though he owned the girl. Aunt Annie had changed so, grown in a double growth of wit and rich casualness that hinted of a wish to be as blowzy as an old whore, that I had to be told the girl was she. My brother, not my mother, told me the boy was Stuart Carver.

He had gotten the name Broker in the 20s when, riding high, wide, and handsome on the Carvers' coal money, he had gambled on wildcat gas wells, as if it took too long to mine the black gold for his needs. Those quick strong geysers of fortune the killing country offered to men who would take flyers let him down time after time. Where luckier men had tapped gas, Broker had tapped salt water—brine, once the fortune of the valley, now a disaster. He had turned from gas to the stock market, his money had swelled, grown huge, burst one Monday in 1929 when he was staying at the Biltmore after a Princeton football game. The burst had taken his sisters' money too, and he had gotten off the C & O train at Canona depot four days later, drunk. He never was sober again, but suicide by alcohol lasts for years. His giant, frail frame still carried life and hard-earned prejudice we once thought of as wisdom. One Carver sister ran the library and didn't speak to him. She still lived in the Carver house on River Street. On the wall of her bedroom was a framed yellow letter from Carrie Chapman Catt.

Every year the other sister, Aunt Eliza Wilson, would clear her house on the hill of friends and family and invite Broker to dinner. She had married too carefully for the loss to ruin her. We, who had been taught as children to call her aunt though she wasn't kin, would find out and hide in the bushes to watch Broker shamble up the walk across her glossy lawn to see how drunk he was. One night he fell into her swimming pool, the first ever dug in Canona, and Johnny fished him out and took him to the door. When Johnny saw Aunt Eliza's face he switched to a hatred of her which never left him but which he hid from her, as he hid his hatred from most people, under a mask of politeness that had made him her favorite beau for her daughter Kitty Puss. Aunt Eliza flirted with him and said he was "gal-*ahnt*"—that gallant contemptuous ridicule he already carried as protection. She said he was just like Jeb Stuart.

Until the knowledge of Canona's one door-slamming sin was brought in on us by experience, we didn't know what it was that made Broker like a man already dead, shut out of people's minds. Money disaster had a phrase: You ran through with every last thing. I could see people fleeing down River Street, running through it, shoveling money, until they threw the last thing, the last dollar, and having at last committed the unpardonable sin, they were stripped as if they had shed their clothes, left naked, turned away from, cut from the minds, except in moral stories or in late-night memories. Money could be joked about, but if mentioned seriously —a breach of form all the way to the soul—it was in low tones of awe or disaster, sending the room temperature down as once the admonitions of Jehovah had, or the defeats of war in the same houses. But on the whole we were taught that money didn't matter compared to the more important things in life. What those things were we were left to find out for ourselves.

I could hear Johnny still arguing with Broker.

Eduardo started the Satie record again in the living room. I held both sounds and was with Broker and Johnny, when I was eighteen, Johnny and I in evening clothes, lolling on the pissed-on weeds of the riverbank under Canona bridge, where Broker and his friends drank wine and threw the bottles at imaginary fish in the strong, dirty river. He told us the belly side of the whole town's history with that incisive bitterness of a man with no more to lose. He wore a suit of Johnny's—what we called a cad check from Brooks. Wine stains and dry snot decorated its curled lapels.

"Now, here's what they ought to do." He looked at Johnny, and the foglights caught the deep runnels of his face. "They ought to bring the National Guard in here and take over. Just take over, lock, stock, and barrel. They ought to drain the coal out of this river. There's a fortune in this river—a goddam fortune. They ought to just string a hydraulic net across, up around Beulah, easy as taking candy from a baby. Nobody knows how to run this damn valley." He hawked and spat in the river.

"I sound like a Red. Goddammit, I am a Red. They ought to just march in and take over." His dull eyes glistened, and he looked

[ 12 ]

up at the Wilson house against the sky in the distance on the opposite hill, shining with the lights of a party Johnny and I had run away from. "Bunch of Wop rednecks, union bastards." He forgot he was a Red. "I told 'em so at Princeton in 1910 . . ."

"And about this here space program." He dropped into the language he had spoken for thirty years below the bridge. "They ought to . . . You believe in flying saucers? By God, I do. Them little, green fellers are goin' to land right on this here river and take over."

Now the music of Satie was louder. Eduardo had opened the door and looked into the bedroom. I started to hang up but he slammed the door again.

"Broker can't come to the phone. He has to pee," Johnny told me.

"Aw, don't tell Hannah something like that, you son-of-a-bitch, that's dirty." Broker's graveled voice was hollow in space beyond the telephone.

"Johnny, where have you been?" I wanted to know what had started the drunken search through Saturday night, which would end as blankly as it always did—what flick of yearning, which wrong memory, the clanging of what doors against his freedom.

"It's Labor Day weekend, honey, and we're all in labor. Old Dan Tucker he got drunk, fell in the far, and he kicked out a hunk . . ." Johnny deflated. "Hell, *you* know where I've been. Goddam club dance."

When the strip-mining beyond the north hills of Canona had got too near Slingsby Mansion, which had been the country club as long as I could remember, the members began to complain of the sulphur fumes from the great slag heap three miles away down one of the hollows, which by some ironic trick of prevailing wind would send its smell to permeate the terrace and the ballroom. Every morning the Negro servants would wipe coal dust off the white window sills and the gilt chairs, muttering to themselves.

So five years before, the country club had been moved across the river to what the women called with bright-eyed garden-club excitement, the unspoiled section of the southern hills. I always wondered if the women knew what they were saying.

Now the new golf course stretched in long fingers across the razorbacked ridges. In the center, at the high head of a long hollow with a running creek which emptied into the river, a new clubhouse had been built. It was the first "modern" building in Canona. Looking out of its huge glass front or from the wide terrace, you could see in the distance a vague star cluster of Canona's lights between the dark hills.

Everything was brought over—oh, not the gilt chairs or the fine marble and mahogany bar, which were sold because, out of fashion with the Canona clubwomen, they were already in fashion again in New York, where I had to sit in an expensive night club as if they, like all the other ghosts, were following me, and look at the mark on the fine mahogany bar where my cousin Wingo Cutwright had fallen into it, chipping the carving and his arm. No, what was brought were the table arrangements for dinners, for dances, the mark of people, sets, crowds, adding, fusing, subtracting sometimes out of a quarrel or a marriage unsanctioned by the women, but with a still unchanging center made by accepted barriers of age and kinship.

That never altered. Years should mean growth, the chipping, marring, reordering of change, but the face of Canona Country Club, like the faces of some of its women, seemed only to weather and shrink. I had been there so often. Going back for Labor Day the year before, I had been shocked, as always on returning, at the aging without changing.

My sister Melinda Cutwright, and her best friend Haley Potter, whose closeness was made up not of a meeting of minds but of wills, had arranged their table and everyone around it. No one had ever cared or fought. Anyone who had fought Melinda had long since stopped. Certainly we had. On weekends she and Spud, her husband, entertained friends—whom Johnny and I always called "important people from Ohio." I never knew Melinda and Spud to entertain anyone without some reason. Their guests were always important, and we were always briefed ahead of time, as my mother had briefed us as children, on whom to "be nice to."

On that night the year before, Melinda had told me to sit at their table for a while, saying, "You can join your own age group later." My skin had crawled. Then I caught Johnny's eye. For some reason I didn't know, he wanted me with them.

The men moved easily in white jackets and the women in the expensive wide-skirted dresses they had bought so carefully for the last dance of summer, new but looking always the same. We swept in a noisy phalanx across the wide terrace, where the tables were lit with huge candles protected by glass cylinders. Our table overlooked the hollow to the valley and the floodlit pool below the terrace. It was all so much the same it hypnotized me for a while; we were lulled by the lovely night and the formal banter of the party, where over and over the men at the table were chanting, "Sweeten your cup. You can't fly on one wing." They looked so bland, well fed, the men. Then I was shocked awake to the real time again. In the candlelight someone lurched at my shoulder and whispered what he thought I would like to hear—"See, Hannah, we're still committing suicide in a cultural Sahara Desert"—and laughed, teasing me. By the time I turned around, whoever it was was gone. There was only perpetual Wingo, looking over the valley without seeing it, and beyond him George Potter—Plain George—flirting heavily with the important wife from Ohio, a form of hospitality for all female visitors. The remark had isolated me. I knew a new thing, that the men knew what was happening. They knew and let the women go on play-acting. In a conspiracy of silence they were letting the pretenses of the night flower to satisfy the women; they seemed not to give a damn.

At the end of the table Melinda, her hard forehead shining with whisky she could drink all evening without losing control, was instructing Haley Potter about Picasso. She was conquering Picasso

[ 15 ]

that year, between golf and Goren, with much the same drive and cold correctness.

"Of course you wouldn't want him in the *house*," I heard her say, glancing through the candle-light at me, "I mean you wouldn't want to *live* with him." Tall, awkward Haley listened and nodded, agreeing seriously.

Across the table my brother-in-law, Spud Cutwright was talking earnestly to the man from Ohio, who had sunk easily into his chair as if all the country clubs were the same in the same safe, groomed world.

There was a sense of something wrong, of demands stirring in the pines. Johnny had been put beside a new divorcee Melinda had picked up on Nantucket. He was being gallant, obedient to Melinda, who had whispered to me, "I think he's interested . . . Cornstalk Collieries." On that aging, drunk head in the candlelight, the floodlights from the pool catching her weathered skin, lay Cornstalk Collieries. I wanted to laugh—or run.

As if he sensed it, Johnny caught my eye again, begging me to sit still. He went on listening to her, wearing his expected face, teasing with his still, understanding watchfulness, hearing nothing she said.

Later in the night there were the usual gusts of quarreling between Plain George and his wife, Ann Randolph. Melinda's voice had a steel edge as she began to arrange where we would go. A fat man I didn't know took me aside and told me a dirty story about an impotent man and a whore in a motel. He told me because I had been away and so "would get this one," as if the world beyond the hills were compounded of easy sex and glittering free beds. It was a barbershop joke, the kind he wouldn't have told his wife. Under the lovely bowl of night in the candlelight under the dark trees, I felt sick with shame.

Johnny rescued me. "Linda says we're going there," he said. His eyes were haggard with boredom. I started to turn away but he caught my arm. "Oh, for God's sake, Sissy, don't rock the boat," he ordered me. Behind him the latest of Melinda's chosen women sat watching his back. She had dropped into hopeful, childish sadness and let her thighs yawn with need.

I knew I would go and not complain. Later I remember holding the divorcee's head while she was sick and moaning. In between retchings she told me about the "loss" of her husband; the whisky had made her too soft, too vulnerable, for any reserve. In a tired language none of the others spoke she was trusting me.

As if Melinda sensed it, although I said nothing (we never *said* anything), she pulled me out of her frail white bedroom, leaving the woman alone, and muttered, "Every time you come back you get Johnny all upset."

Things, I could see, were not moving according to her plan. They never quite had, but she had tried for years. "If you had listened to me," she would say when anything went wrong. Melinda was right. She was always right. I thought of Broker, who would end his stories, "It's not right, Johnny, but it's true." Melinda was right and Johnny and I were true, and in all our life we would never be able to tell her the difference.

I looked at the clock on my Japanese chest—one o'clock on Sunday morning—suddenly realizing that the record had stopped in the living room and that I could not hear Johnny.

"Johnny?"

"I'm here, Hannah." His voice was as soft and calm as morning, as if he had been sitting cold sober in the booth, waiting for me to speak.

"What are you doing?" I asked him.

"Oh, thinking. There's a twelve-barge stern-wheeler going by. Why didn't you come down, honey? I needed you."

Then it *had* ended with the need turning into begging from Melinda's trapped widow, that one or another one. There had been so many trotted before Johnny, with one thing in common, the smell of money. I had seen that supplication on the faces of wives, the yearning for the uncaught man, the demand of his secrets.

I had seen other men depraved by it—not Johnny. He never gave enough, but no one knew that except me.

"Ah, Sissy—you came down last year."

"Was it bad tonight?"

"Jesus, the usual bunch of damn women. Important . . ."

"People from Ohio." I helped him finish.

"I start out in a goddam bunny suit and end up a call boy." Suddenly he was drunk again. "Why the hell didn't you come? Up there with that bunch of perverts."

"Oh, for God's sake, Johnny, not chauvinism from you!"

"Wait a minute! That's a Monday morning word, this here's Saturday night. Sweet, sweet Saturday, not a woman in sight. Can't *nobody* find me. Mother and father are at Egeria . . ."

"Why?"

"Mother needed the rest." His voice was dutiful as if he were saying his catechism.

I wanted to yell at him, "You told me, oh, Johnny, you told me yourself. 'Little Sissy,' you said, 'get out. Get in my little Lincoln convertible prairie schooner and go West,' "—as if, that long ago, he had known something he couldn't tell me without having to tell himself.

I had been eleven, dressed in organdy for Melinda's wedding. Johnny at seventeen, in rented morning clothes, had already sneaked several drinks. I could smell Sen-Sen on his breath. He had lurched up to me, where I stood owl-eyed with pleasure and fear, waiting for the car to come for Melinda, and whispered that. He pointed to the new car mother had made father give him for his birthday because our cousin Brandy Baseheart had one, and because Johnny would "need" it to drive to Princeton in the fall.

It was my first wedding and I was willing it to be beautiful. Even at twelve I had to will it, and I wanted Johnny to shut up for once and let me do it, let me forget that the Cutwright mines and Beulah Collieries were fusing in blood as they had long ago in business,

[ 18 ]

as if Melinda and Spud were to meet and couple at the end of miles of rich black tunnel under the hiding hills, married by oily spirits Johnny and I had named coal trolls. I wanted only to see the wedding, the reception in the caressing summer sun on the manicured lawn on the old country club.

Johnny ran off before I could answer. Upstairs Melinda and mother were still looking together into mother's mirror. They had let me watch Melinda dress, hear the huge white taffeta skirt whisper as it settled over her dark, muscular body and her legs stringy from tennis. I stood in the corner of the room, out of the way, fidgeting in white organdy which scratched, dressed an hour ahead. Mother's dress—a yellow chiffon she still called georgette —looked as dry as her skin and sagged too much over her little taut body. She already had on her hat, that summer day in 1942; it was small, tipsy on her head; a white ostrich plume tickled at her neck. She kept swatting at it as if it were a fly, in her nervousness to get Melinda dressed. Out of the window of our house on River Street, through the frail, billowing white curtains, I could see our neighbor, Jim Dodd, sitting on the upstairs porch, waiting for Martha, his wife. I had a crush on Martha that year because she had given me my first nylon stockings for my birthday.

Finally Melinda stood before the mirror, my mother beside her. Fear or excitement had stripped Melinda's face of that ever-present tension in her jaw, and for a minute she looked so lovely that my nose tickled with tears. It was as if just for a minute the fantasy would work.

"Oh, Linda, it's all so *right*. Melinda Lacey McKarkle to James Donald Cutwright," my mother chanted, awed, looking at her in the mirror. She hugged Melinda's arm so she wouldn't disturb the froth of her veil and the sprigs of orange blossom in her black hair, then mother's eyes went far away and filled with tears, and I, at the time, thought she was trying to remember if she had forgotten anything.

[ 19 ]

"Something old, something new, something borrowed, something blue," I reminded her, cold inside at the thought of walking down the church aisle.

"Oh, Hannah, run on, dear. You're in the way," mother said, remembering me. She went on staring into the mirror. I knew better than to disturb that frozen stillness.

From somewhere deep in mother's dreams, which at eleven I sensed and feared with my skin but didn't understand, she had constructed a Melinda and a Johnny for herself. She had wanted to train one hard one to make up for the devil of a shyness she could never shake, land ghosts she never told about, which she had carried from upriver at Beulah, first to the big farm in the hills south of Canona and then to River Street. Melinda, with the silent Puritan will and the dark looks of my father's family, had taken on those bitterer dreams. Once she would have run a church, or managed the mores of hard sons and dim daughters, morally incisive and cold. Now she played games hard and well, managed, as mother trained her to, perpetual cocktail parties with an eye to the business of "keeping up standards." Even her engagement to Spud Cutwright had the air of a game well played. I, sneaking around and spying for romance, had heard of none. They had known each other too long.

With the same narrow zeal she and my mother had planned and furnished the houses on the hill. Since 1939 the nice people of Canona had been worried about the war, so when the new houses began to follow the cleaner air across the river and my mother's land became what she called with surprised awe "valuable property," she sold it in large restricted plots to our friends. I remembered the day the old sycamore stump which had dominated the ragged creek hollow was dragged from its ground by two caterpillar tractors. Its taproot had come out of the ground like an enormous snake. The trunk was hollow and bedded with leaves. Johnny and I hid in it when we played. English houses, Tudor, Georgian, and Queen Anne, sprang up like expensive mushrooms.

Mother told Johnny and me she was putting some land "by" for us. The two largest hill crests with a view of the distant water she saved for herself and for Melinda. It was the same arrangement that we had in the family burial plot in the cemetery, which, on clear days in winter, we could see across the hills north of Canona. The Methodist steeple seemed to point to the acres of white dots.

That year, because of the English, we worked for Bundles for Britain. Christmas presents all carried the British Royal Crest in gilt paper, and mother bought the *Illustrated London News* and started using Pears soap, which reminded me of locker rooms at camp. When the cake was thin you could see your fingers through amber. Mother made us soak the little pieces and put them in a wire basket to swish through the bath water, practicing at war.

So, of course, when the twin houses were being built, the mountain wood was shaped into exposed beams, the roofs rose steep, and the downstairs rooms were paneled, with holes bored into the fleshy new wood by a surly carpenter before they were stained. The houses had not been finished for Melinda's wedding. From the front window, as Melinda inspected her face for a last time in the house on River Street, I could see the two slate roofs.

I had watched mother and Melinda go through the agonies of choice and then end with a bedroom for Melinda's new home that was a replica of my mother's—the same kind of mahogany bed with a tester, the "old" chests, the billowing curtains, the bright slip rugs.

But if Melinda was cast into a hard dream mold, Johnny was cast as a rake; out of a fear as deep and unquestioned as taboo, a fear of hurting mother which they both thought of as love, he developed an insolent charm to please her and make her smile and say he was like her father, that ghostly dandy, mother's model of a gentleman, who, she said, could have charmed the birds from the trees, and who had been caught by a stray bullet from a drunken miner's gun in 1912 and left mother fifteen forever, inside the armor of her rigid body. On that point, as long as I can

remember, had been her tears. Touching it had brought a nameless twinge of panic to all of us. She seemed always poised on the
edge of another minute like it, and we were taught to respect that
wariness like a cocked pistol—an unknown miner's pistol, un-
cocked too late for some of us. Trailing that bloody shirt, "He
wore the *finest* linen always," she would say, she had solicited our
attention. With no one to blame, her blame diffused and spread.

Behind her, as she and Melinda stood in front of the mirror, was
the picture of the only other wedding I ever heard mother say was
"so right"; about her own she never said anything. The picture sat
among the Waterford scent bottles—which never held any scent
because it gave her hives—and the ormolu boxes for her jewels.
I could see it reflected in the mirror, framed in gold and flecked
with brown spots of age like the hands of an old woman. There
was President Chester A. Arthur, and my great-grandfather Senator
Daniel Neill looking as rich as God, with his heavy black, well-fed
beard, standing beside a beautiful, straight, sad-looking young
girl, my grandmother Lacey Kregg from Virginia, who, mother
said, had been sold to my grandfather, James Neill, by old General
Kregg as if she were a filly. Mother would point to the old man,
who stood behind his daughter, and tell us he had taken her to
Washington in clothes he'd borrowed money for, on the last useless
land at Albion in Virginia, after the War had ruined him, going
after Neill money as if the Neills had stolen it from him. I wished
then that Melinda could look a little sad, like my grandmother. It
seemed more fitting.

In the center of the picture stood mother's beloved "papa," who
had driven a four-in-hand through the streets of Washington;
she made us see him whipping the horses down Massachusetts
Avenue, chased by a longing bevy of eligible virgins of good family. He had the look of high heartlessness mother admired so. He
seemed amused at the wedding, which had begun so richly the
slow journey of his married life, ending at Beulah at the family
mine, in a time of trouble no charm could stop. After his death,

mother's family had moved "downriver" to Canona, for in that narrow valley no Rubicon of decision was crossed. It was floated down, rather, to Canona, the center. "Downriver" had a finality about it which still exists. People were carried by the river to a more fertile promise, usually dislodged by two extremes, need and hope.

But mother brought the ghost of her father with her and lodged it with Johnny. For me, she didn't have much of a plan. I think that I, like a wood's colt, was a surprise not provided for in dreams. She decided that I was "the artistic one of the family," and, having done that, she thought about me in guilty fidgets as if she had forgotten me before I was born and was trying out of duty to recall me. Johnny had been left to bring me up. We, bay-headed brats, saw Melinda being groomed over the years and ourselves fitted carefully into what a family should be, split so early, to please her, into perceiving one life and acting another at the same time.

On the day of Melinda's wedding I stole a last look at her in the mirror as I ran by to get out of mother's way. I held the picture in my head, as I still do, thinking I would never again see my sister so lovely. If wanting to love and loving ever are the same thing, I loved Melinda that day, so pretty and unprotected by her will for once, in her safe, planned life.

That was why Johnny's remark about running away jarred my pleasure at Melinda's wedding, and made me mad at him. On the way to church in the family car, I squunched away from him when he dug me in the ribs to make me speak and leaned my head like a dog out of the window all the way to All Saints. Later, at the reception, I had a wave of remorse, as I always did when I ignored him, feeling that I had let him down in front of others. I ran through the crowd on the old country club lawn. Polite noise hummed over my head. I passed mother and father standing with the rest of the bridal party and slipped behind the big pink bulk of Aunt Annie. Her voice in the air above me was going on as if she'd said it before and was running down. "It was simply beautiful." She looked down and caught me. "Wasn't it simply beautiful?" She asked me, I guess, because I was the only one of the wedding party who had sneaked away from the line and she'd already said it to everyone else.

I wandered down the long rope of people shaking hands as if they hadn't kicked the end out of the same cradle. They stood in a wavering line as though they were still having their pictures taken in front of the big stone columns of the country club porch. Father was standing beside mother, watching her with that concerned look he had which had creased his face into deep lines that never tanned even when he'd been playing golf all summer. You could see the lighter streaks when you caught him alone, his face relaxed. Mother kept talking to the moving line of people as if she were dragging her mind back to their outstretched hands.

"Thank you. Thank you," she kept saying. Once she said it to empty air in front of her.

As I watched, the line swayed, broke, and was lost among the scattered guests. I couldn't see Melinda and Spud for the crowd around them, but Johnny and Kitty Puss Wilson were meandering across the lawn together to the big tables with white tablecloths, made into a bar. Everything was white and glass and froth except Brandon's face, black above his laundered white jacket. Brandon was the best waiter in town. He knew what everybody drank.

I knew what I could do to make up with Johnny. I had been saving my money, as I always did, in that effort to wake mother's and Melinda's attention with Christmas presents. Money was hard to get your hands on. Johnny never had any. We had all the things we needed, but money in its virgin form was dangerous.

I knew what Johnny wanted more than anything in the world that June of 1941. He had a picture of Douglas Bader in his room and he snatched the papers in the evening and closed himself in there with them. Once I went in and he was standing in front of the mirror. It scared me for a minute.

He was not singing as he usually did, but speaking . . .

"A lonely impulse of delight
Drove to this tumult in the clouds."

He caught me watching him, and instead of chasing me out he told me it was a poem his teacher at Lawrenceville had taught him.

"Hey, Sissy, listen to this. It's a poem by Yeats: . . .

"I know that I shall meet my fate
Somewhere among the stars above;
Those that I fight I do not hate,
Those that I guard I do not love."

He buried his head in his arms among the silver cups and the kind of Christmas presents eighteen-year-old boys get and don't use. I couldn't make out the rest, but he was crying when he finished. I pretended not to notice.

"Sissy," he almost whispered into the telephone.

"I'm here," I said, but we didn't say any more. We could sit for an hour in contact through that night-air wire as if we were sitting in the same room or the same bar, without speaking, just letting the hatful of quarters tick away, thinking together silently like two mountain women on a party line.

We sang the poem to a hymn tune afterward, and neither of us could finish it without our throats hurting. We sang it to "When I Survey the Wondrous Cross . . ." sitting together on his bed with the door shut. He told me how to fly a Spitfire. Then he made me promise not to tell what he was going to do. When he saved enough money he was going to Canada to join the Royal Canadian Air Force.

Johnny and Kitty Puss had their champagne and were already going toward the hidden side porch of the club when I caught up with them. I pulled at the tail of Johnny's rented morning coat. He turned around with that insolent look he had when he was Kitty Puss.

"Johnny, I'll lend you the money." I stood on tiptoe and whispered at the air.

He didn't change his face, "Okay, Sissy, okay," he said. Kitty

Puss Wilson's face was already radiant, the way sweat is radiant when there isn't much of it. When she saw me she yelled, "Why, honey, I meant to tell you all the time, you look just gorgeous in that dress."

"It scratches like hell," I told her. I hated the word "gorgeous" coming out of her round red lips.

I thought Johnny hadn't heard me. He acted that way. Later, after I'd gotten into my bathing suit and was at the pool watching the people all bright across the grass, the ushers broke away and came pounding over the lawn, pulling Spud with them. I could hear mother calling, "Don't, boys," but she was laughing. She laughed at expected things. Spud acted as though he were pulling back but he was loving being the center of that wildness for once.

Johnny saw me and yelled, "Sit still, Sissy!" I sat still, feeling scared of the way they looked in those cutaway coats and striped trousers, running toward the pool, ruthless with joy.

"Clear her head. She'll sit still," Johnny called to the others as if they weren't running right beside him. They grabbed Spud up into the air and threw him over my head into the pool. Brandy Baseheart went in after him and then Johnny; they splashed the scared children who clung to the pool edges and watched.

Kitty Puss Wilson stood like a figurehead on the diving board, letting them cheer her from the water. Her dress caught the breeze and flattened against her body, swinging out behind her like the Victory of Samothrace. Then she made a neat swan dive into the water.

I did think Johnny had forgotten about my promise and I slipped to his room the next evening after dinner to tell him again. The door was shut and inside I could hear my mother. She was talking in her cold voice, the one we called her money and virginity voice.

"I want to exact a solemn promise from you, son," she was saying.

I couldn't hear Johnny answer.

"I know what's on your mind," she went on. "I always know, son.

Now your father and I have made every sacrifice for you to go on to Princeton. We are *not rich people* . . ."

I knew that mood. She said it about the Pears soap too.

I mooched on down the stairs to steal the paper and read "Boots and Her Buddies." I'd heard all about the sacrifices so I didn't bother to listen any more.

But the next day the picture of Bader was gone, and Johnny acted as if he'd forgotten the song. He just left it in my mind all summer. He borrowed the money, though, and promised he'd pay it back when he got his allowance for school, but he didn't spend it on going to Canada. He had the craziest summer he ever had in his new car with Kitty Puss Wilson. He spent the money on beer at the Wayfaring Stranger.

He got arrested for the first time a month before he went to Princeton. Father went down and got him out. Nobody said a word at dinner for about a week. Mother finally wrapped her mind around the fact and healed it for herself. She said she was sure Johnny had been made the scapegoat; the word "scapegoat" seemed to please her. The temperature of the house lifted and the summer gathered speed again. One night late I went downstairs, barefooted and in my pajamas, to raid the icebox. I heard Johnny and Kitty Puss murmuring in the dark sunroom. They must have heard me because by the time I came back they had gone and the sunroom still smelled faintly of chestnuts. When I was twenty-one I cried at the same sweet chestnut scent, my mind's eye slashed open at last to that night, unable to tell a scared boy why I cried.

Mother was set on Johnny's marrying Kitty Puss. "I think those children are made for each other," she said one evening to Aunt Annie as they sat in the porch swing, watching them drive away down River Street in the car.

"I wonder if they really love each other." Aunt Annie sighed and made the swing sigh too.

My mother jumped up and said in the piercing chicken

shriek she had when she forgot to "modulate" her voice, "Annie, you make me *sick*. You just make me sick with that mind of yours . . . tacky . . ." Her face was twisted and childish.

Aunt Annie made her remark about Southern women, which was usually touched off by such outbreaks from my mother.

"We Southern women only do things for two reasons," she said while mother glared at her, "because we're in love and because we're not." I had heard her say it a hundred times. That remark, which the family always said was "typical of Annie," reverberated and echoed down through the years of my growing up. I would know ahead when it was going to intrude into Aunt Annie's comfortable talk. It trained me to hypnotize myself with questioning. Incised with women's training in a world that dishonored and condemned it, I would long to be fair and would watch my dog self, salivating, waiting to know which bell had been hit. Such power to speak quite dumbly to the nerves gave Aunt Annie the family reputation for wit which, out of some basic disappointment and an inborn knowledge of her rape muscles, she honed until it was as sharp as a knife—a circumcision knife. Still, Aunt Annie seemed unique to me, in that she was a woman in a place where most of the female sex went from long, cute girlhood into tyrannous old age without an intervening period of responsive womanhood. Mother never spoke of her without a slight, teasing sneer.

Well, mother couldn't buck the United States Army. After Johnny was drafted she shrank inside her frail body and treated the rest of us like strangers. All through the war she talked about "my son" as if she couldn't remember Johnny's name. She wrote him two long, long letters to APO addresses I still remember, pouring out to him her pains of war and rationing. She said she couldn't bear to write any more, it upset her too much, but she wouldn't put a service star in our front window. She said that was tacky.

Once Sally B. Potter and I raced through the house and mother stood at the door, yelling, "You just don't *care!*" and calling my name over and over in a panic until we were out of earshot and safe.

If my father and I talked about Johnny she froze, and if we didn't she accused us of forgetting him. Dinner was long, silent, and lonesome.

"Hey, Sissy, hey, Hannah," Johnny called, finished with his own thinking in the telephone booth. "God, it was strange, honey . . ." He had the door open for the river breeze. I could hear River Street. He was letting the middle of a memory come out in words.

"It was a huge black shadow. I saw it crawling against the glass . . . the big window. Huge."

"When?" God, when in time was he?

"Tonight, honey, we were in the ballroom. I saw this *giant shadow* across the glass front of the clubhouse. It was like the woods fighting back. It looked so free. I had to get out of the place. You know?"

"Sure." I had to know. He always said "you know," taking for granted that I did.

"I ran out. I left Linda's visitor on the dance floor. Hey, you know what it was? This skinny bastard was standing in front of a flood-light on the hill beyond the pool. Just as I got out he ran down the slope and started pushing chairs into the pool. Christ, chairs and floats and crap. It was great. I didn't stop him. I wanted to help him.

"They heard the noise inside and old Spud ran out then. He was yelling, 'Hey there, hey there, man.'" He imitated Spud's busy voice. "Bunch of fat phonies raced out after him . . ." I could see the fat phonies flapping across the terrace. It was a twelve-year-old word and we were for a minute twelve years old, the children of light jeering and mocking the awkward, ugly children of darkness. "God, it was great! The skinny guy got away though. He just cut out through the woods and over the golf course like a coon."

I was helpless, laughing.

Johnny switched again; sober, casual. "You coming down when the quail season starts?"

"Maybe."

"Don't be that way. Remember that covey up at the hill farm above Beulah? We could go there. Hey . . ."

Oh, I remembered with quick tears. Johnny made me cry, there in my safe Manhattan hutch, but I didn't say a word to let him know. I didn't because his convenient drunken memory—his Saturday-night memory, not his Monday-morning one—had gone back to the hill farm as it had been when we first went there with father's youngest brother, Uncle Ephraim McKarkle, who was only ten years older than Johnny. We called him uncle as a private joke between us.

That day Uncle Ephraim never said a word all the way to the hill above Beulah. The woods were too fall beautiful to talk in. Through the green hollow where the creek curled over the rocks, up past the old graveyard with its nameless stones, we climbed to the edge of the abandoned hill farm. It belonged to Beulah Collieries, but they had let it alone. In the distance a gaunt house sagged, a big square clapboard, weathered and unpainted, its windows hollow-eyed. It reminded me of a deserted mountain woman, weather-brown, watching blankly across the neglected fields as if she wouldn't let anything but God Almighty stop her empty vigil. Around it, like hungry children, the well, the outhouses, and the corn crib leaned. Old gnarled apple trees still carried neglected late-fall apples. The whole huge field smelled of apples and ripe harvest.

Uncle Ephraim went on ahead, motioning Johnny and me to keep behind him. Away to each side the dogs quartered through the high weeds and the lespediza covering the huge forgotten clearing.

"You have to keep up," Uncle Ephraim warned, low in his throat.

We kept up, watching the feather-tails appear and disappear, flicking through the cover; from time to time the dogs tossed their heads up above the weeds to check back.

Then the whole field went still, or seemed to. Fan froze on point, and Jubel loped across and froze behind her. Uncle Ephraim ran without making a sound, with Johnny beside him. He motioned Johnny to stand still, then he walked in, and the covey whirred up ahead of him. Johnny shot, and I saw a bird flip over and plummet down. Jubel went after it and brought it back to Johnny. I saw him take the bird and put it to his mouth as if he were kissing it, but I knew he was biting its jugular vein. He'd told me that was what you had to do. When I got there he was kneeling in the weeds petting the dog. He threw me the bird to carry. Its feathers were silk-soft and it was still warm.

Ten years later we had gone back to the hill farm. We had walked up the coal-seamed hollow without a word to each other, not like Uncle Ephraim's mountain silence to keep from scaring up the birds, but stupefied. The mill creek was black. It ran sullenly along a ditch beside the dirt road grimed with coal dust. Where the old graveyard had been, the side of the hill was blown away to widen the lane up to the hill farm. There was just a blank wall of cliff rock, with a few trees still above it, their roots exposed where the cut had eroded in the rain. I don't know why we went on but we did, following the deep truck ruts up toward the old plateau. Johnny's new dog Calhoun hung his sad hound face down and stayed at our heels even when Johnny tried to hie him on ahead.

At the top of the hill we stopped. The hill farm had been sliced off and thrown down into what was now a dirty gully. The topsoil, weeds, apple trees, the house, the corn rick were gone. As far as we could see, to the line of trees marking the opposite hollow, there was only a vast dead-gray table. Nothing grew, or could grow, there. The farm had been exposed down to the coal seam, and that had been peeled away, leaving only an expanse of bare, dirty, level rock; there was not a clue of life across the great, abandoned, dirty strip mine. Calhoun loped toward the line of trees across the blasted space. We followed on. By the time we reached the center of the rock table there seemed to be no direction, no purpose to it. The place was dead. Not even a weed could find soil to lodge in and grow to cast a hopeful small pool of shadow. The hill farm had at last been harvested, down to naked rock.

When we got home we told about it—or I did. Johnny didn't say a word. Mother said it was too bad, that the garden clubs were discussing it. Then, excited, she told us about the blasting. She said that when the dust cleared, several coffins, hard as the rock, were jutting out beyond the cut. She said they must have been the "early settlers" at Beulah. Then she said, "Beulah Collieries and the Colonial Dames had them reinterred near the family plot here at Canona. We couldn't put their names of course, so we just put up a plaque to the first settlement on the Kanawha River." Her voice had lilted solemnly.

Johnny and I didn't mention it again. On that Saturday night I realized that he had neatly stepped away from it in memory.

"Johnny, I don't want to come down there," I cried.

"Oh, for Christ's sake, Hannah, what the hell's the matter with you?" Johnny sounded fed up and tired. Then he added to himself, "Jesus, I can't even go to . . . I'm still in this damned monkey suit." He remembered me. "I need a drink. See you . . ."

He hung up. I found pajamas and put them on and went into the living room. Eduardo was lying back on the sofa, looking at an abstract painting of his; he gazed at me as if he didn't know me, his eyes as sullen as a city stranger's. We both looked at the painting. Red streaks exploded apart, racing to protest against the confines of the canvas, escaping a dead black burn at the center. When I had bought it, speaking carefully about its vitality, Eduardo had smiled and told me to shut up. He had delivered the painting to my apartment, hung it on the wall, and stayed a week.

"He won't call back now," I apologized.

"I never know what's coming out of there," he told me evenly, without moving. I knew he had rehearsed everything he would say to me, and that it would be clever, because he was hurt. It had all happened so many times. "I just never know." He looked back at the huge, alive painting, swirling blood and coal and escape. "What do you hang on your walls for trophies down in God's country?" he asked.

Melinda had kept a fox head in the deep freeze until it leered sideways from being shoved against the game. She had it mounted anyway, and it grinned from the wall among the family photographs.

I went over to Eduardo, hiding my face to keep from laughing, wanting him to touch me. I could feel him looking at me as if I were far away instead of right beside him.

"I never know whether it's going to be your rich good sport or your violated Southern virgin or your boy. Who the hell are you anyway?"

I just lay there in my pajamas, still wanting to laugh. He looked so exposed, all bravely naked on someone else's sofa, safely hidden from his mama in Brooklyn, talking too easily and too much. "Oh, this time it's Tom Sawyer. Tom Sawyer in drag!" He took my shoulders and made me look at him. He didn't sound hurt. He had retreated into being objective, and I was the object, turned and inspected carefully. "This is the last time I'm going to paint your fucking fence. When I love a woman, I want her there. All there!"

"Sure—*when* you want her," I told him, ready to fight.

He climbed slowly over me, grinning, and disappeared into the bedroom. When he came back he was dressed. He leaned in the doorway for a minute. I thought he was going to speak, but he didn't. He just stared.

We could have quarreled. I could have teased him into playing Wop and hating me for a while for being what he called sometimes "a sleek American moneybag," but we were both too tired and we'd played that too often. I didn't see him shut the door.

It was lonely. Outside, the street sounds had died down so I could hear the moan of the city. The painting died as I watched it—died from being looked at too long and from being there with the twisted wire sculpture from Nico and the tin-can montage from Lou and the plaster imitation of a Giacometti from I didn't give a fuck who. I thought of the language of Buber, how he said that the Zulus had one word they used as we use "far away"; it meant "there where someone cries out, O mother I am lost."

I think I went to sleep. It was later—a space of time. I heard Johnny say "Hannah," as clearly as if he were in the room. I know these things aren't supposed to happen, but it did. For a second I thought he was there. In the bedroom the clock said four o'clock. I sat on the bed, willing him to call back, cold with a fear I couldn't name, remembering the dream about the river and wondering if I'd had it again. I knew then what was tugging at my late-night mind's edge. Johnny's night was not yet finished. He had not reached the last call, the point of turning homeward, drunk to the sober point of defeat for another week.

The telephone was silent. Through the thin walls of the apartment I could hear an unknown man crying as if he were nestled for comfort in his own arms. At five o'clock I called the airport.

★　　　★　　　★　　　★

# Chapter Two

THERE WAS no decision that morning. I just let loose, as if I'd been
clinging too long to a rock to stay grounded—let loose and let
myself take off skyward.

We cruised at seven thousand feet over the flat Virginia Tide-
water, with the morning sun behind us; then the tiny black shadow
of the Martin began to skim and dip over the rolling sun-green
Piedmont. It was a glass-clear morning, so clear that I could see far
ahead the faint backbone of the Blue Ridge. Virginia slid away
under us, surging up, undulating green. We flirted nearer and nearer
the mountain barrier. Over the foothills the Martin's winged
shadow danced. Here and there on the sky floor the white pattern
of a nestled town passed, the long-drawn lines of rivers cutting
east. Beyond the Piedmont we withdrew farther from the land,
higher in the air; we climbed to ten thousand feet above the currents, which tossed the air as the land below had been tossed into
hills aeons ago.

Johnny had told me the Royal Air Force pilots talked of height
as angels. He had heard their voices calling, during the war, "Fly-

ing at ten angels." I could see from ten angels the Blue Ridge rolling nearer, misty deep blue in the distance, as if their color reflected the bright morning sky. Patched with great blots, still waves of spruce and pine groves were night blue on the gentle eastern slopes. The summer rhododendron made damp black pools.

The first ridge passed under us. As far as I could see, the mountains to the west were giant furrows plowed north to south, row after row—a barrier backed by a barrier to the east which seemed endless. In between, little veins of rivers ran north, ran south, finding a stronger waterway to the eastern ocean. How empty Virginia looked that morning from the sky! We cruised over with Blake's "confident insolence" of angels.

That was what Aunt Annie had finally said to mother to calm her that day on the porch, the summer of Melinda's wedding, when we watched Johnny and Kitty Puss get into the car. They had had that confident insolence, mother gazing after them, with romantic safe-money eyes, seeing what she wanted to see, screaming away Aunt Annie's sentimental intrusion.

"They do look angelic," Aunt Annie had conceded. Then, her body senses always wiser than she ever allowed her conscious mind to be, she shuddered slightly. I could feel it through her dress as I sat beside her in the swing. She laughed and said, "Someone must be walking over my grave"—as if she were physically aware of something she thought it wiser not to tell.

The Martin's shadow leaped the high backbone of the western watershed. Below, I could see the new mountains, steeper, narrow-ledged, limestone jutting from pools of dark where the sun had not yet filtered through the thick mist of the woods. Johnny and I called it the mean side of the mountains, grander, more aloof, more secret, with more dangerous steep divides than the gently rising, evocative Virginia slopes. No wonder the tall, walking Scots who settled there moved more easily in that stern, familiar place than the genteel from the rolling east, who either died, retreated into fantasy, or

[ 36 ]

had to learn to walk again, grow longer, thinner, as jut-boned as the rock ledges and the harsh trees. There was no sign down in the narrow gullies that anyone had ever touched the mountains, much less lived in them. Far below, in the New River pass, the sun reached the thin ribbon of flying water and made it shimmer. I could see the bald patches of the strip mines circling the ridges; from ten angels they looked as formal as ancient rock battlements. The valley widened and we lost altitude. Down the stabbed sides of the lowering hills, shale from the shaft-mine entries flowed black. The river widened at the end of a still lake of brown water from the mountains. I could see the falls throwing a veil between us and the rocks.

We began to be tossed by the air currents eddying from the prevailing wind that blew downriver. The plane tipped, and I saw the right wing dip toward Beulah Valley, lying way below us as if some small hand had pushed down the hills, its palm lying along the bend of the river, its fingers splayed to form the hollows; the raw rock table of the Beulah hill farm was dead gray in the sun, but that was the only sign of people from so high. Hidden in its morning shadow by the eastern hill, Beulah lay blank and dark, as if it had never yet been found. The plane leveled. The whole of Beulah had been pinpointed for a few seconds at our speed, then was gone, as we turned south to make a wide arc for the Canona landing. My body begged the plane not to touch down in that wave after wave of western hills, not to commit itself to one point of dangerous ground.

Canona, long, narrow, on the right angle of its rivers, was below. I tried to pick out houses as we crossed the southern hills. I could see only the raw-looking new golf course, then the town's pattern and the exposed cemetery. The houses built on the rock ridges of the new suburb were hidden by carefully tended trees.

The trees rushed up at us. I could have reached out and touched their tops as I felt the Martin's wheels contact ground. The woman beside me, who had drowsed during the hour it took to cross Virginia and the mountains, jumped fully awake, seeing the treetops, scared.

Across the flat tarmac the small airport was already black with people. It could have been any modern terminal anywhere.

Johnny would let me go sometimes when he piled his car with boys and raced up the hill to the airport when it was new, to look at the girls perched on stools, waiting to be admired in the airport canteen, which was turned, until it got too familiar, into a hangout. There Johnny and his friends flirted with the town girls, who switched their shining long hair and drew in their waists with wide belts we weren't allowed to wear. They sashayed through the canteen, their backs arched with promise, seeming so sure of themselves. Johnny was in love with a girl called Thelma Leftwich —his face shone and softened when they sat together. But when mother and Melinda decided he ought to have a dance, she wasn't there. Whenever Johnny and I were alone in the house he talked to Thelma Leftwich for an hour on the telephone. I asked mother why she didn't come to Johnny's dance and mother said it wasn't quite fair to the girl, that it was unwise to make friends you'd have to drop later. Then she turned her head away and wouldn't talk any more. Johnny stopped going to the airport.

He made up a game there. When the planes came into sight the boys would chant in whispers, "Old thin old Nobodaddy aloft, farted and belched and coughed," and beat one another's arms until somebody identified the plane, Eastern Airlines, Capital, Piedmont. Johnny had learned the rhyme his first year at Lawrenceville. He brought me Blake as he was later to bring me Yeats, tossing them to me and then forgetting them himself.

One time, as we drove down the hill, the boys in the back seat dared him to drive through Carver Street, where the women hung out the upstairs windows and called out to the boys. He just yelled, "Shut up! For Christ's sake, shut up in front of my sister!" We didn't go.

[ 38 ]

On the two-story wall of the airport waiting room there was a safe, green, aerial view of the hills, and in front of it someone had once put a plastic sign, *Prepare to Meet Thy God,* with a box of tracts. It was the same sign the people from the Church of God painted with whitewash on the cliffs by the road. The airlines got so many complaints that the plastic sign was changed to *Jesus Saves.* It was still there that morning when I walked through the waiting room to get a taxi.

I caught myself looking through the Sunday morning crowd of mountain people who brought their children in jalopies to see the planes land. Even though no one knew I was coming, the child in me expected someone there, Johnny or my father, to meet me and let fall casually the temperature at home as we drove down toward the valley. They never knew they were doing it, but always by the time we had driven through the town and over the bridge I would know the neural state of home—what event, small or large, had tipped the scales off balance a little, so that I was expected to walk carefully, aware and upright, for it was the unexpected that tipped mother and Melinda, jarred the coiled tension they mistook for composure.

So I planned this time to slip in on Sunday morning when Johnny was asleep, mother and father gone to the spa, and Melinda and Spud to church, just to have the morning to myself and walk in the washed sun.

The taxi crawled through the clog of clean crowds gathering at the cluster of churches in the tic-tac-toe made by Lee, Jackson, Carver, and Neill Streets. Godly, righteous, and sober, they trekked in family squads toward church. In a minute of panic I could see them surging over the taxi in that slow Sunday march, not even seeing it, just trampling it down. Plain George and Ann Randolph Potter crossed the street in front of me, George looking as if he'd had a hard night; Ann Randolph's lips were folded for Sunday morning. I hoped they wouldn't look up and see me. Down the street the bells of the Catholic Church rang out for Mass.

"Church makes me feel so good," mother said on Sundays, when she came back bathed in the bland milk of an approving small-town God and flung down her white gloves. I wanted to pray, "If You'll forgive me, I will hereafter live a humble, sinful, exposed life to the honor and glory of Thy beautiful name," but I never said it. Through all the years, except in uneasy flashes, we were skimming people, leaving the taboos as intact as the unweathered gray stones of pseudo-Gothic All Saints, silent on matters better left unsaid.

Plain George turned at the corner as quickly as if I'd called to him and saw me. He ran over to the window. I thought he said, "God, Sissy, I'm glad you're home," but I couldn't get the window open in time and the taxi moved on. He stood looking after it and waved sadly. I thought then it was because of the hard, hot night he'd had and that he was always glad to see me.

In the eighteen years since the twin Tudor houses had been built, the lush gardens had grown up around them so that they looked almost as they were meant to, old, ivy-covered, correct clumps. The heavy, nearly ripe September leaves of the trees up the drive whispered, and along the slope of mother's garden the shrubs, in what she called her Cruikshank curves, moved in the late summer breeze. England as a fashion had been replaced by gardens and the ridge land was rich green under the trees, which, cleared for twenty years, had spread their branches out and lowered them quietly for great patches of blue shade. We drew up in front of mother's house. Across the lawn I saw that there was a car in front of Melinda's—a white sports car.

I was relieved. They had gone to church, taking their visitor to the beginning of the Christian Sunday: church, drinks, golf, all the children buzzing like bees around the pools. The hours stretched out ahead, formal, unthinking, and Johnny asleep upstairs, off duty at church because our parents were away.

Even so, I let myself in catlike and stopped to Indian read the signs, by habit, as Johnny had taught me to do, checking whether gloves were put away or flung across the English refectory chest, whether the silver tray was filled with unopened letters, if the hall had the dark, deserted atmosphere that sometimes my fingers could almost touch.

The morning sun caressed the polished floor. For a few seconds I had the illusion, the waking dream, of safety instead of the destroying dream of the night's pit I always carried and always rejected. Above the pine paneling of the hall the frigid green walls were grotto cool. Great-grandfather Neill's portrait dominated the entrance, as if mother announced ourselves at once to any stranger who came beyond the brass eagle of the door knocker. She never just pointed it and told about it. Senator Neill and great-grandmother Melinda hung stated in the air of the house as they hung in fact. The living room had, in mother's phrase, been built around great-grandmother Melinda, who had watched me coldly, so witch-beautiful, with great black knowing eyes that seemed to move in the firelight at night. She held a rosebud in her long, dead-white hand. She made me as awkward as if she had been calling me down ever since I was a child from over the fireplace.

The Senator's portrait had really belonged to my Uncle James, but when he died mother pointed out that it ought to stay in the family.

My uncle James had never been around when I was growing up. Once, hearing a car stop and thinking it was my father, I ran out of our old house on River Street. It was a taxi. Uncle James was sprawled across the back seat, both his eyes closed, black as old meat. He looked foul and frightening. He smelled like rotten food. I ran and hid behind the Dodds' boxwood trees next door, and saw my mother, green dollar bills flapping in her hand, walk out smartly, thrust the bills into his hand, and slam the taxi door. I watched her walk back up to our door slowly, her head down, exhausted, her tweed jacket drooping from her shoulders.

James's widow, Aunt Beulah, we never saw except at funerals, when she came in dressed like a starving blackbird, walking with alcoholic care, one of that row of dim black Eumenides that Southern families have, who would file into the pew to haunt times of truth with their presence. She had offered to sell the portrait to the state, but they didn't want it; Senator Neill had been forgotten by everyone but mother and her friends. Mother had had me drive her up Cemetery Hill to Aunt Beulah's rickety clapboard house with dangerous long, wood stairs, and I had sat while she persuaded.

After two hours Aunt Beulah had cried out, "For Christ's sake, take the son-of-a-bitch and leave me to hell alone."

Mother had told her calmly that she fully understood her grief, that she shared it; she said all this as she marched across the small room and lifted the portrait down herself, not even telling me to do it, clearing the way carefully over the plaster Spanish dancer and the china spaniel on the mantel. Uncle James had been dead a week.

On the way home she only said, "Of course it's so sad, but you have to be sensible. I couldn't just leave the Senator *there* . . ."

I didn't answer. I could see out of the corners of my eyes her white-gloved hands folded calmly in her soft fawn wool lap.

"Oh, Hannah, it's no use trying to make you understand the importance of your family. You have to have roots," she muttered, as if there was a choice to be made.

I was too young to be quiet. I didn't yet know it was like shouting in a canyon. "She's family too," I began.

"How dare you talk to me that way when I'm still suffering the death of my brother!" Mother's voice caught, strangled, tearless.

I stood for a minute in the hall that Sunday morning, looking again at the Senator's heavy face. He had sat, reared back and rooted, for his bad portrait with its false aging of a new "old master." He was as stiff as his mind must have been by the time he had had himself appointed Senator, because he thought it good for the children to grow up in Washington. I searched for evidence in his face of the gambler he had been, but there was none. He looked, instead, like a satisfied Presbyterian elder, cheeks red, eyes small piercing dots over his patriarchal beard; in short, as mother had explained in the small, awed tone she had for such matters, he looked very, very rich.

It was he who had provided both a fault and a strength in our family ore, that touch of protective aloofness that meant "there was money somewhere." In the crash of '98 he died, from what mother called extending himself too far. I could see him then as a great wave, stretched longer and longer over miles of hill land, until he broke and receded, losing his strength and leaving us, especially my mother, with one gold nugget of pride. The last extension he had made had turned out not to be the big safe deal he had staked his fortune on. Johnny said the Senator had at last been dealt a cold deck. There was nothing left of the fortune in land and paper but Beulah Collieries and the hill farm downriver at Canona, where we spent our summers before the new suburb took over and mother built the house I stood in, and placed the Senator, from whom she said "all this sprang," as honored as a Chinese ancestor, to confront strangers at the door.

I thought how Eduardo and his friends would have hated mother's correct, cold, rejecting hall, with the portrait, the green walls, the two "good" small sofas from Beulah, the English refectory chest; yet they, as rigid as mother in their intelligent, brutal disdain, had for a minute more in common with her than with me. I was glad that none of them was here and that only Johnny was upstairs, flung across his bed, snoring as he did when he had drunk like that; the room a jumble of clothes, letters, postcards stuck on the walls, photographs of a long history of girls that mother would say proudly just ran after him like the girls had after her papa, his boots still in the corner from last hunting season, puddles of brightly colored golf tees and change catching the sun, an old jug he'd found with a skull and crossbones on it—a room suspended at twenty-two, where Johnny and I both seemed to have stopped, with a man of thirty-six lying in it. I wanted to slip past it upstairs, to where mother kept my seventeen-year-old girl's room *virgo intacta* as she had planned it. Beyond the living-room door I could see a pair of too thin legs, feet in brown-and-white shoes, quite still, like a statue. The Tiffany lamp mother would never get rid of, no matter how much Melinda hinted and teased, was still lit at the height of the sunny morning, as if the people in the room had not yet noticed it was day. The house was as cold with the sense of climax as it had been when Johnny left Princeton after the war—cold and clear with the precision of detail that shock points out.

"Who is it?" Melinda's voice was as sharp as a knife. She leaned on the door frame, her face drained of its habitual decisiveness, looking as if she had been washed against the paneling. When she saw me there was no passing of love or of relief across her deadened eyes—not even the tightening of hatred I had seen in them so often. Melinda stared at me as if she didn't want to be reminded I existed.

Her face without make-up was dry under summer tan, her lips narrower than ever. She said, "How did *you* get here?" not even coldly, and then, not waiting for me to answer, "How did you find out?"

Seeing the sinewy legs beyond her, for one wild second I thought that Johnny had finally been shot down into their formal nest, and that she was facing the fact that he might marry with the same harshness she faced any fact of life. She and mother for years had coaxed him to prove his love for them by marrying a copy of themselves. I had to wait for her to tell me. Loyalty to Johnny and years of secrecy were too strong for me to tell her he'd called me.

"I *knew* you had something to do with this," Melinda said and started to cry mildly, as if she'd cried before and this was the last of it.

"What's happened to Johnny?" In that dim house my yell hit against the upstairs wall and echoed down the stairwell.

The feet beyond us moved. Melinda turned her back on me

and went into the living room. I could see her sagging spine stiffen under the fine baby-pink linen of her dress, as if she were calling all her training to help her.

"I believe you've met Katy." She mentioned vaguely. It was last year's widow by consent. She sat as if she had been hardened into a shell again; what seemed to be embarrassment at the atmosphere in the house, a flagrante delicto, chased over her face, shifting her eyes across me when she nodded, saying nothing. She had the ruthless concentration of a woman riding a perpetual point-to-point. My family's wave of irresponsible affection for her had receded with trouble and left her stranded in her chair, with the party that would never happen ready in the living room and the year's best friend, Melinda, standing lost, twining and untwining her thin muscular hands.

"I just can't stand any more." Melinda tried to run out onto the terrace above the river, but the long white table Minnie Mae had set for drinks after church was in the way. She stopped and clung to it as if it were a spar, her knuckles white.

"If I've told Minnie Mae once I've told her a thousand times— the silver julep cups have to be put in the icebox, not on the bar— in the *icebox*." She was sobbing.

Mother had bought the cups at Tiffany's and had them etched with the Kregg crest. They had long since become a part of the family silver "from Albion on the James." I concentrated on the cups as completely as Melinda did, knowing that I would have to break through a barrier against telling the truth as deep as the forbidden name of God. It wasn't that she wouldn't tell. She couldn't. She had never learned the language. I took her hard broad shoulders and turned her toward me. For just a pause we clung together.

"What happened?" I asked her and held her until she answered.

"Oh, honey, Johnny fell. I guess he fell."

"Oh God! Into the water, about four o'clock?"

She heard my whisper. "No. Sissy, he hit his head. Spud's down

there now. I called Ann Randolph and told her to call people not
to come," she babbled. "I told her to tell people not to come or call
up, we needed the telephone free for the hospital."

My hands dug into her shoulders. Johnny was alive. "How bad
hurt is he?" I, stripped to sorrow and hope, spoke like a mountain woman.

"The skull has been fractured over the ear." She retreated into
hospital abstractions as if all concentration were on an anatomical
head, not Johnny's.

"Hannah, you'll have to take Johnny's car and drive up to
Egeria." Finding something to tell me to do made her voice gather
strength again. "Mother can't be told over the telephone."

"I told you I'd do that." Katy's accent strode toward us from
Nantucket.

"No. I think one of the family," Melinda told her. The woman
looked as if her drained, aging, pale face had been slapped.

"Where is his car?"

"It's—oh, Hannah, the police have it." As if the last horror had
been exposed, Melinda wailed, "What are we going to tell people?"

"I'll drive you down." Katy got up from the chair. I couldn't remember what last name she was using.

The telephone rang. Melinda grabbed it and listened, then said,
"Oh, no, honey, we're trying to keep the phone clear." She hung
up and looked at me as if she'd just seen me for the first time. "Oh,
Hannah, why couldn't you and Johnny listen to me? Nothing like
this could have happened then." Melinda was right—nothing,
good or bad, would ever, ever happen. We would have laid away
our sex, our doubts, our lives, like toys to be outgrown. She wandered out of the room, through the door, and toward her own
house, forgetting us.

"Where's Spud?" I asked Katy, who was already striding toward
the little white car.

"At the hospital," she flung over her shoulder.

[ 46 ]

"For God's sake, tell me what happened," I begged her.

"He wouldn't stay with us. He had to go wandering off somewhere. You people . . ." She made the engine roar. I could see more of the night. This woman's body had been begging then as easily as she rejected us now. She sat stiff with fury and defeat, revving the engine hard with her brown-and-white shoe, her hands gripping the wheel.

"Where did it happen?" I tried again exhausted.

"In jail," she said coolly; the moving car had given her power back. She was ready again to travel. All the way back down the mile of winding road through the hill lawns she never said another word. If she had been a man careening in that car through the tree tunnel between the manicured gardens, she would have been called psychopathic, but being a well-groomed, thin American woman, she was as much a part of the road she ran on as a car ad—a mainspring, social ideal for what mother and Melinda sought, bought, and gave in to when they had a chance. Their hopes spun round such physically successful women, and she now was shrugging us off, without malice. She wouldn't have cared enough for that. It was simply that we were in the way of her light, fast, selfish road. I realized that for the first time in years I had thought "we" of myself and my family.

She drove on, almost physically jettisoning the burden of hope and choice. It was not despair; that would have given dignity at least to her hell. No, she had wanted Johnny for a little while, as she had wanted other men, men as hard and as easy as herself. For that she had been prepared to act any way she had to. Even the pathos I remembered, probably repeated at Johnny the night before so that he felt engulfed in it, was calculated so deeply that she had exuded a true momentary yawning need, but now that Johnny was out of the way, perhaps dying, she was dropping her pretense, putting us behind her.

I saw Melinda and mother as so sickeningly innocent that they infuriated me—so provincially vulnerable to any woman who fitted their parody of gallantry they called a lady, that cold irresponsible ease of privilege without responsibility that they could never understand but only copy.

"Where the devil is the place?" She swooped over Canona bridge. I pointed down Neill Street.

As I got out in front of the police station I leaned over toward her. She stared straight ahead, already bored and annoyed with my thanks.

"I want you to be gone by the time I get back," I told her quietly. She looked at me, unsurprised, all our language of understanding already spoken, then spurted the white car forward as if I had released her.

Five miles upriver from Canona she would forget us. She would shed her bodily fury by the time she took the eight-lane ramp over Beulah at a neat sensuous sixty in that car. She would concentrate on the mountain curves, enjoying their feel under her fingers. East of the mountains she would fade toward Aiken or toward Middleburg. It didn't matter to her. She was one who obliterated her past, her crashes into contact, as she did the smooth miles behind her, unless within it there was something or someone she wanted and could raise the emotional stud fee for.

Our exposure of organic grief had embarrassed and repulsed her as much as Aunt Beulah's had mother. Somewhere the reasons connected. We had shattered the American genteel rule of indifference, against diving deep, against tears, a rule most of us were prepared to protect with one another's lives.

The downtown empty Sunday street in front of the police station was still littered with Saturday night. There was not a sound. There were not even any men sitting in white shirt sleeves on the steps, leaning against its Greek municipal columns. I knew where to go. We all did though we never admitted it. The dirty corridor to the sergeant's desk was as familiar as All Saints or "the club." The sergeant on duty sat with his chair tilted back and his feet up, talking to a Negro policeman. A row of half-empty bottles stood along the wall behind him, confiscated the night before. The sergeant saw me but let me wait for a minute, not unkindly; I was just another of that long line of women who come in on Sunday morning after a hot close Saturday night to bring bail or to question, sometimes to cry.

The Negro cop was going off duty. He lounged against the heavy radio stand, drinking a last cup of coffee.

"Me and Sadie was just settin' down to watch Perry Mason," the sergeant finished what he had been telling. "I come in off the porch and seen the temperature reading ninety degrees. I said to Sadie, 'I'm glad I ain't on duty. It's a fight night,' I told her. Heat lightning. We sat there drinking beer and watching Perry Mason. Boy, I'm glad I wudn't on duty."

The Negro cop patted the radio. "This here never shut up from midnight on. One signal eight after another. Man, I tell you, two o'clock a call come in some guy was ridin' a horse in the post-office yard. There wasn't nobody but a signal eight half on the sidewalk, half in the street. Them bastards," he said with the annoyed affection of a Carver Street mother. The big public face of the clock above his head said eleven-thirty. I had been home for an hour.

The sergeant slung his feet down and swung round to the window.

"I just got here," I told him. That wasn't what I meant to say. He waited, watching me.

"I have to pick up my brother's car," I explained, fast sliding toward tears under that impersonal warmth.

"Now take it easy. Who's your brother?" He humored me. His kindness, after the passion, the anger, the long night, probed with the efficiency of a nurse.

"J-Jonathan McKarkle," I told him and cried, "Nobody will tell me what happened." Somebody touched me on my shoulder. I told the hand, "They think they've told me and they haven't told me."

The Negro policeman said, "Now, Miss Sissy, come in here and sit down for a minute. Everything's going to be all right."

"But it'll get rougher before it gets smoother." I wanted to tell him the answer that Johnny and I used. Then I recognized him. "Toey, I didn't know you."

He led me into the deserted, dirty courtroom. We sat down together on creaking flip chairs. I watched the empty judge's dais. The room was like some tawdry, abandoned flea-pit of a movie. I said, "I didn't even recognize you, Toey."

"It's been a long time, Miss Sissy." Toey's large brown hand was still on my shoulder to steady me—another brother, Johnny's boy shadow. When we were growing up, he lived with his mother, Minnie Mae, in the carriage house at the back of our old house on River Street. Until they were fourteen Toey and Johnny disappeared on summer mornings down through the riverbank trees to raise their trotline in the dawn mist. On some mornings the night coal barges with their paddle-wheeled boats had broken the line. On others, I watched while the little leaky john boat they kept on the bank edged out through the river mist. Sometimes in the distance I could see them take a catfish off the line, but not often. The river was too dirty with chemical and coal waste for many fish to survive in it. But they kept on trying. Afterward Minnie Mae gave us breakfast in the kitchen.

On fall nights when Johnny's mind and spirit were fighting the confines of school starting, they would sit on the back porch steps and Toey would hear Johnny's Latin.

*"Amo, amas, amat, amamus, amatis, amant."* Their soft "a's" mingled in the dusk with the dry whispering of the fall leaves. I could hear them chanting from the upstairs window. Toey was an honor student.

Mother would say at the dinner table, "I think it's a shame that Toey isn't taught something useful. A good vocational school . . ."

Johnny, struggling with dinner and Latin, never said a word.

Finally mother said she had to put a stop to us eating together in the kitchen on school mornings. She said Toey would be happier. She started getting up early for the first time in years, and we had breakfast in the dining room. She said it was the least she could do, now that Johnny and Melinda had reached a certain age —but it was Johnny she was watching. Melinda had already been sent to Virginia to school.

I realized Toey had been talking. "If I'd've been here I could've taken Johnny on home," he was saying. "I heard the signal come in about two o'clock, 'Pick up somebody on River Street.' The officer was laughin'. He said some guy was just dancin' down the street, hookin' an arm around the lamp posts and then thankin' them . . ."

Toey's voice veered away. "We have to pick 'em up, Miss Sissy. They git rolled or fall in the river. This jail here on Saturday nights is just a big nursery to protect drunks.

"I never knew it was Johnny 'til I come back and saw his name booked. I slipped out to call Mr. Cutwright but I couldn't find him. I went up to the tank. It was dark in there, only a light from the toilet shinin' through the bars. Johnny was standin' by the iron bench at the back. I could see his face and the white dinner coat, catchin' the light from the toilet. He looked sober then, Miss Sissy. I didn't want to see him in there. You know it ain't the first time. I tried to call to him without wakin' the others up. They was about forty of them in there by then. You don't like to stir 'em up. They's sleepin' all over each other. I whispered out—you know how you do—'Johnny,' and he turned around and seen me. That floor full of men started to roll. Somebody hollered shut up and they started movin' awake, troubled.

"Johnny said, 'It's all right, Toey, quit tryin' to wipe my nose.' That hurt my feelin's. You know, it's funny. Lately he used to talk nigger to me when he was drunk. You know, 'Hey, boy.' He'd put his arm round my neck and talk nigger.

"Well, I come on back downstairs. Figured he was as well off there as anywhere 'til he dried out. They's bringin' this skinny fellah up. Lord, he was coming up them stairs just layin' down the law. Me and two other cops had to cool him down. We knocked him out a little bit, not so we'd hurt him, and throwed him in the tank. Johnny went on lookin' out at that light, never even turned round.

"It was about an hour later, things had calmed down so's we was restin' a little. Saturday night hits a peak about one-two o'clock, then it begins to quiet down. We always know when it's going to be a fight night. Payday upriver—heat does it, makes the women feisty. They start hollerin' at the kids or git on some point and won't git off."

I glimpsed Johnny's night. I could see Melinda, on a point, flashing and flashing her demands. I could see cool Katy edging nearer and nearer. I could hear mother in the Saturday night corridors pacing until the whole house was a silent scream. On such nights the reins hung slack in their hard hands—even the down-river wind whispered against them, panicked the women, aroused in the men a passion for freedom—just once—just a little freedom, to walk more lightly. . . .

"These here Scotch-Irish mountain people, they hear enough hell-far preachin' and they take off—don't like nobody tellin' 'em what to do. Sometimes we have to do things down here I don't figure is necessary, but when the lid's off on a man full of fightin' whisky . . ."

"It was about four o'clock"—I guided him to the dark cell again, with its racks full of men overflowing onto the concrete floor, sleeping like snakes in a cage—"I heard Johnny call me. Heard him call my name," I told Toey, knowing he wouldn't question that I had heard.

"About four o'clock," Toey went on, brought back to that night place, "we heard a ruckus. Near as we could piece together afterward, it had started when one of the drunks—old John Lacey—he

[ 52 ]

comes in and asks to stay when he has twelve dollars' cause he don't like to go home to his wife and he's too dirty for a hotel to take him—he come and booked himself in. Long about three-thirty he woke up and started in to preachin'. Nobody don't listen to him usually. He thinks he's hollerin' but he don't do no more than a kind of singin' whisper. Only at night it gits penetratin' sometimes." Toey's soft-butter voice went on, trying to conjure for me—a natural conjurer like his mother—they had both taught me to conjure, storytelling not in ideas but in colors and sounds.

"He tells Jesus he's a sinner and if he let him off this once he won't do it no more. He just plasters hisself against the wall so the devil can't come up behind him and whispers to Jesus he's sorry and he can see Him and he's saved and ain't never goin' to backslide no more. Nobody bothers him. They got right smart respect for each other's troubles up there. But last night he cut into the skinny guy's nightmares. I reckon he was dryin' out and it was hot and John's preachin' got on his nerves. Anyhow, next thing that happened was the preachin' woke up a colored man who was settin' on an upturned bucket. He said he saw Johnny still standin' there and offered him his seat. Johnny started to say somethin', and this skinny guy, Jake Catlett his name was, he come out a-fightin'—took it out on them because he told us later he couldn't shut a man up was talkin' to Jesus. He swung on Johnny. He said Johnny said somethin' that made him fly red and he swung again. Johnny went down like a sack and hit his head on the corner of the iron bench. Then Catlett and the colored man got into it. We had to hose down the cell. They's forty men in there fightin' and pushin'.

"When we got things calmed down I waded through to where Johnny was still lyin' on the floor. The colored man was lookin' at him. He told me he'd stood right over top of him—kind of instinct—to keep him from gettin' tramped on.

"We took him up to St. Stephens and I reported the incident to

[ 53 ]

your brother-in-law." Toey's voice was formal again. He had traveled with me from childhood back to his uniform and the empty courtroom.

"I been up there this mornin'. They hold me he's still unconscious. They thought I was takin' evidence."

"Hey, Jack." The sergeant came to the door, awkward, trying to be of service. "Here's the keys to McKarkle's car. You follow the little lady up the hospital. See she gets there all right."

"Jack?" I looked at Toey, who had pulled me out of the water when Johnny dared me to swim and said he didn't want a little sister who didn't have the guts to swim the river. "Come on, old Hannah, get in and don't squawk." I could still hear Johnny teasing.

I had jumped in. Toey saw I couldn't swim and came in after me. Johnny was all sorrow and held his arm around me while Toey rowed the john boat to shore, but I didn't squawk. Johnny said, "Look, Toey, she doesn't even cry. Not my old Hannah."

"My name is John Peregrine Lacey. I bet you never knew it," Toey said. "Your ma tole ma she couldn't get mixed up on Johnny and me havin' the same name. She called me Toey after my great-grandmother. Your ma tole me a lot about her. She thought ma hadn't already told me who I was . . ."

I followed him out of the police station, back into the sun.

★　　　★　　　★　　　★

# Chapter Three

THE DAY CORRIDORS of the hospitals are always light. Against that
bright, impersonal, cheerful sun spread across the polished brown
floor, the waiting visitors on benches huddled outside the ward,
whispering to each other, the way people do in church. Sunday in
St. Stephens was the day whole families who were lucky enough to
have someone to visit came, full of quiet excitement and careful
manners, as to a celebration, bringing gifts of flowers, rambler
roses, Shasta daisies, tiger lilies in tin cans or in wicker baskets
with great hoops of handles. I heard the cultic words, stroke, operation, the abstract stomach, the abstract heart, as if these, too, had
been brought as Puritan sacrifices to the polished temple of the
hospital. Against the walls women with bowed shoulders slumped
in their own shadows, their feet splayed out with pleasure at the
outing.

The corridor was long. I could hear my heels clicking fast along
it, but I moved too slowly toward Johnny. Somewhere at the end
of the hall I heard someone's obsessive breathing above the quiet

babble of voices. The breathing filled the hall, heavy, beyond snoring, a slow dragging in and out of groaning wind.

Spud, standing at Johnny's door with Freddie, our doctor, turned and saw me. His round, sad, curious face looked no redder, no more bewildered, than it ever did. Spud seemed to have reached long ago the edge of surprise that his face muscles and his weak child's eyes could register. He couldn't show any more.

He and Freddie moved together, flanking me, shutting me out of the room by the instinct of men to protect the women they have shielded with their lives against any harshness, any truth, hiding from us the backrooms of the world where fact was, until the whole structure of their lives became a reassurance, and no one faced any fact at all.

"Now, Sissy . . . now, Sissy." Spud was rubbing his fat hand across my back.

"Can't I see him?" I asked Freddie Potter.

He too slipped formally into his role. "Hannah, now be prepared . . ."

"Don't go off the deep end," Spud muttered for some reason.

"It may not be as bad as it looks," Freddie told me. "Johnny's in a coma. It's just like being asleep. He's not feeling any pain."

I wanted to laugh at the old phrase about drunks—"he's not feeling any pain," used to comfort me, as if it were an ideal end for a shallow life or a shallow party.

"Don't be surprised if he doesn't know you. We just have to wait. He may regain consciousness at any time."

Freddie and I locked eyes, forgetting Spud. Beyond the hurt look in the eyes of Johnny's friend reassuring Johnny's sister, I saw a man whose life had to be dedicated to fact. I understood then Freddie's preoccupied, watchful silence as he piloted a silly wife through years of babble and parties, from which he had to slip out unobtrusively night after night to truth like this he couldn't share with any one of us. Despite his careful helpfulness and trained lying, I knew that Johnny was going to die.

[ 56 ]

"Why do you tell me that?" I was furious, trying to get by him. Spud grabbed my arm harder.

"Let me talk to Sissy," Freddie told him.

"Okay, Freddie, you handle it."

We, frozen there, pulled against one another, exchanging child names we never had been allowed to outgrow, three more shadows in the corridor, better dressed, better fed, isolated from the others who were watching us with the patience of poor people used to waiting, watching with interest our impatience, knowing that it wouldn't do any good.

Spud walked back to the door, to the breathing that seemed to lift and settle the noise in my head, drawing me in.

Freddie's hand dragged me to the window. "Don't lie to me, Freddie," I told him. "Lie to the others—they need it."

"Oh, Hannah . . ." I had forced him into silence but not into letting go of my arm.

Once when I was home Freddie, allowing himself to drink too much, dragged me into a corner while the inevitable party passed and repassed in front of us. He kept trying to tell me something that I could hardly hear. People were touching my arm all through it and saying, "Hi, Sissy . . . hi, girl . . . hi, honey . . . hi . . . hi . . ."

"Goddammit, Hannah, did *you* ever try to tell anybody the truth?" I finally heard him say over the babble. "I can tell you who is on the road to dying here—too much mileage, drying up. I can see it . . . do you think I can tell them?"

"Hi, honey." Ann Randolph sailed by and winked at me, thinking Freddie was flirting.

"Hannah, why don't you persuade Johnny to get out of here? He's got more to him than this—nothing to use his mind on. . . ."

He had touched on my hope. Johnny, across the room, was surrounded by mother, Aunt Annie, and Melinda. Mother was telling him something, leaning up to him, her face flirting—cute. I sighed. Johnny was watching her like a troubled nurse. I heard him say,

"Let's go home," to her as if it were a sweet secret between them. She took his arm.

"Be back if I can, Sissy," Johnny whispered as he passed, his face dim.

"Genteel murder," Freddie said evenly to me, watching Johnny's back, "is the slowest form of murder. There's no law against it and no cure for it."

*"Why don't you try?"* I begged his authority as a doctor, furious.

"Hannah, last spring a woman you and I both know came to me for the tenth time in a year with a frozen coccyx. She'd held in her goddam tail so long it had stuck that way. I didn't have time to hold her hand or her tail or whatever she wanted. I had to get up to St. Stephens—there was a woman dying of cancer. I didn't have *time.* So I told her the cure. I told her to get pregnant and the stretching and then her labor would cure her tail. She never spoke to me again. She's in this room and she has Nell and me to her parties. I go, pad along behind Nell. It keeps Nell happy. That woman won't speak to me tonight and she'll welcome the wall right above my head when I go to her house. *Try?* Oh, for Christ's sake, Sissy . . ."

"Where's Johnny?" Melinda swam by in the crowd.

"He took mother home."

A shadow crossed her face, then she saw Spud and disappeared.

"You can't tell anybody until it's too late and the dying has a name—*then* they beg. *Then* they want to know."

I could see little Nell Potter flirting through the crowded room toward us, smiling to everyone she pushed out of the way, her still-pretty Irish girl's face fresh from a distance. She was one of the women who had weathered, not aged. Fine dry lines were like a delicate veil. There was no record, in her skin or in her eyes, of choice or passion. Since the Episcopal Church, which was still like a safe mother to her, told her to, she was entirely faithful to Freddie, as she would have been to any other man of the "crowd," as long as he was patient, intelligent, convenient, and cynical enough to cope with her. She was known as "sweet." She had a depraved view that passed for wit, which would have done credit to a cathouse madam. She understood and talked a great deal about "affairs"—I had heard her ever since she and Melinda, growing up, talked about people on the porch swing, forgetting I was there. Of love she had a complete and clean horror, reducing it safely for herself to two manageable components—sex and secrecy. For those, people should be watched; if caught, punished; and through the years, in incident after incident, she helped without questioning. She bore down on us with her witty, party look in her eyes. Later she would do a shimmy while Wingo Cutwright played a heavy undergraduate piano, his repertoire stopping with the Princeton Triangle Show for 1940.

These two—sex and secrecy—were the only reasons on Nell's horizon a man and a woman should be talking and watching each other as earnestly as Freddie and I were.

She broke it up.

As if we had had a flirtation, because he'd let down his barrier for once, Freddie avoided me after that for five years—not wanting to be reminded.

Leaning against the bench at the end of the hospital corridor that morning, we took up the conversation where we had left off, took it up too late, as he had foreseen, with the sound of that breathing, that pulling air into lungs.

"I won't lie to you, Hannah," he told me. "It's touch and go. Johnny may regain consciousness. He may go out this way. Somewhere deep inside him, where we can't get to—can't help—he's working it out. If his body is strong enough to stand the strain he may make it, but Johnny's been pretty hard on himself."

"Can I see him now?"

"Come on, honey." The door was the second from the end of

the corridor; through the first open door an old woman propped up in bed in a pink bed jacket pecked at us with her eyes as if we were her favorite television show.

"I *have* tried, Hannah," Freddie apologized, whether for all the times he'd tried with all of us and been repulsed into the safe, pleasant, hand-holding doctor he had become or for Johnny at that moment, I will never know.

For a point of time, when I walked into his room, I saw Johnny as a separate, broken, self-used, unknown man, his repulsively blank face white and glossed with sweat, his mouth stretched catfish wide for air. He lay in the impersonal hospital bed, his arm strapped for glucose feeding, tapped like an inhuman tree. His left ear was bandaged, his face, in that deadly repose, only shaded darker under his left eye. Saliva channeled down a scar I didn't know about beside his mouth. He seemed in a perpetual pause. His only movement was his slow sucking in of air, down his loud throat until his lungs could stand no more, then letting it out in a long, noisy, despairing sigh. With his dead stare and the laboring of his chest he could have been blind drunk. An early, polite "Fall Arrangement" stood beside his bed, red and yellow daggers of gladioli, fat, fleshy-petaled, among the impersonal white enamel paraphernalia.

His eyes were open. He looked someplace else, like an evasive painting, never on me, as I moved toward his bed. He watched, meeting no demands, pure or impersonal, answering for once in his now ebbing tide no life, no lust, no wishes. None of us could read what we wanted there.

Then the person the man was, my brother Johnny, whom I carried as talisman-mentor in my mind, rushed into me and refocused my watching. I saw his eternal, to me, face, his boy's face. He became again the brother owned and demanded by my fixed heart.

I took, then, the indifferent hand and begged him to live.

"Johnny," I whispered, trying by will to wake him for me.

"Johnny, please. Oh, don't do that. Don't do that." My voice was petulant. I could hear it, involved with his hauling in of air.

"Sissy, honey, he can't hear you. Come on, come on now." Spud had slipped in behind me and now apologetically took my arm.

"I've tried, Sissy . . . God knows, I've tried," he whispered, echoing Freddie in the beginning of all the apologies we would make, in our ways, for Johnny. His hand was shaking on my arm. Shock had brought out the central wound. I knew what he would say because he always did, as if touching his heart could only touch one aware place in it.

"Sissy, you know I haven't had a cent from my father yet. I paid for the house Melinda wanted. Not anybody in town knows I paid for it." He hardly knew what he was saying. Everyone did know. He kept telling the open secret. He had for years. In the hospital corridor, that morning, it was not irrelevant at all.

The after-church visitors were walking through the shining halls as they had marched toward the churches, ladies stealing peeks into room after room for someone whose eye they could catch, recognize, and lightly cheer.

I could hear nothing but Johnny's loud breathing.

As I walked back out into the sunlight of the steps, two of mother's friends pushed through the crowd of ladies with great purpose. I had known them all my life, and I realized with a jar that I couldn't remember either of their names. They pinned my arms. Shock had cleared my eyes too much and I saw them.

"We wanted to see a member of the family," one said, gracefully, quietly, so the crowd couldn't hear and stare. "Oh, my dear, what a terrible thing. Pity that dear boy . . ." Then, without a change of breath, bright curiosity took over her sad voice and it glittered and probed at me. "What *really happened?*" She would never in her life believe that her consciously kind eyes could be that hard.

Under her soft, parchment skin I saw something that Melinda and mother feared and lied to with their lives. They had a right to fear it. It was naked and loathsome curiosity for the lives of others, whipping, righteous curiosity without a glimmer of love.

Johnny was giving them, for the day, a holiday. They would take whatever words I stammered out, piece an "inside" story together, their unkissed mouths breathing the smell of cigarettes and coffee into their telephones, making little secretive sounds to each other. I remembered how small termite mandibles were, and how, if you lean close and pinpoint attention, you can hear them, how their combined tenacity can crush a building. These women were moving close to trouble, chewing at it because they had, that week, none of their own to feed the others with.

"We think," I spoke officially, "Johnny's going to be all right." Then I lied, as easy as breathing. "He stumbled and fell last night. One of those stupid accidents anybody could have." I even managed to laugh a little. Their knowing eyes seemed to meet each other's through my lying skull.

"We'll just *peek* in." They were away, up the steps.

"You can't. He can't have visitors . . ." I begged after them.

"Just a peek," one called back and smiled. "What a blessing it isn't too serious. My, we were upset."

I couldn't stop them. No one had ever stopped their feeding in their lives.

Toey still waited, sitting strong, relaxed, in the authoritative police car, elegant in his blue shirt and black peaked cap with the brass polished almost white, a man of great physical pride. He didn't turn his head, as if he knew I would come down toward him and lean into the open window.

"Jack," I said, to draw his head around. "He's still . . ."

He didn't turn, just went on watching the distance down the tree-lined back street. When he spoke, he only began aloud from someplace else, where he was thinking.

"Miss Leftwich ain't in there, is she?"

"I wouldn't recognise her." We were murmuring.

"I seen her followin' him at night along the street, seein' he didn't git into no trouble. She never said nothin'—just followed along. Every once in a while he'd turn around and see her. When he did she'd stop, like an animal. She a saint's face. She never moved 'til he went on. Then she'd follow him.''

"Jack," I said, "why? Why didn't they . . ."

His mind jumped to the next place. "I don't know, Hannah." He still talked to the road. "Seems like everybody wiped Johnny's nose. It was there to be wiped and runnin'. He never asked and he never thanked. He only thanked people he had to court. Melinda and your ma, the only ones he wasn't sure of."

"Jack . . ."

"We watched you-all. Just watched you. Every Negro in this town knows what you ofays are doin', and you can't even tell us apart. It's like you was always movin' and actin' in front of our black houses. Didn't even know we noticed, no more contact than through a glass. You just dancin' around and what the hell."

"Jack, for God's sake, don't go nigger on me right now. I need you too much." I was so angry with him my voice rose and touched two mountain women. They stopped still to watch and listen, completely calm-faced.

"I've got to go to Egeria."

"Honey, watch your pa."

I was surprised. No one had mentioned or thought of father.

"It's mother . . ."

"Jesus, I hate that woman." Jack was completely at ease, telling me. "Have you ever been looked at as if you wasn't there?"

"I just have—oh, Johnny . . ." I put my head down on the car window frame. My shoulders were heaving. "Jack, let me alone."

"I used to know Christmas was comin' when her eyes started to focus on me. She stopped me believin' in God. If there was a God she would have died when you and Johnny and poor little old Miss Melinda were kids."

One of the mountain women came over and took my shoulders and held them, saying nothing. Her contact was the first impersonal blessed act that morning. When I straightened again, she turned away and walked toward the hospital door.

Jack was looking at me. I couldn't tell whether his eyes were bloodshot because he was a Negro or because he'd been crying, but he wouldn't, or couldn't, stop his mouth.

"I tell you somethin'. She *liked* Johnny's drinkin' like that. She *liked* it. That way he stayed guilty and he stayed home. When I'd take him home her face would melt with affection like butter and she'd take him over. If she could have carried him upstairs like a little baby she would have. Once she turned around under his shoulder and said, 'You have to understand, Toey, gentlemen act like this sometimes.' She didn't want no man. What she did want I don't know. Jesus, it was terrible . . ."

"I've got to go," I told him.

"Miss Sissy"—his thick black hand touched mine—"I'll be here. Wish I could go with you. Now drive careful."

"I've got to know *why*." I couldn't leave his hand. "Where's the man who did it?"

"We moved him over to the County. Charged him with malicious wounding, for now."

"Can I see him when I get back?"

"Sure. I don't know why though." He watched me. "Okay, I know why. Now remember, go easy with your pa."

Without another word he started the motor and drove away, as if the car were part of him, down the Sunday street. The light on the top of the police car turned round and round, watchful as a lighthouse.

How could I "go easy" with my father—a man whom I had never seen separately, as you see, in a split second of love or even horror, in all my life? Christ, I knew a two-day lover better than I knew my father.

★　　　★　　　★　　　★

# Chapter Four

Johnny's Porsche smelled of dogs. It drove loosely. I had the
same twinge of fear in handling it that I had of him, though until
the shock of that morning I had hidden this all my life. The
wheel swung as if it had been used recklessly. In the back seat was
a check lead that had been there the year before. The Chipp straw
hat had been flung down beside it; a few quarters had rolled out
on the leather seat. When I stopped at Minelli's garage to have
the car checked for the drive across the mountains east to Egeria,
George Minelli came out and touched the fender. His dark face
was sad and veiled. I wanted him to speak, to give me a clue, as
much as I had wanted the women to shut up.

He filled the tank and checked the oil without looking at me.
I searched in the glove compartment for Johnny's credit car. The
compartment was jammed to the brim with the life he carried with
him, the secret life, as a turtle carries its shell: a map of Ohio, a
sterile package of condoms, an address book, matches from the
Wayfaring Stranger and the Mountain View Motel, cigarettes, a
dirty glass, a flask I had given him one glittering Christmas, a blank

order book; hidden under them all, a prayer book. I couldn't find the credit card.

George put his hand into the car over my head and took it from the sun visor. "Sissy, honey, you be careful," he muttered and turned away.

I drove fast through the new valley road, lined all the way to Beulah with hot-dog stands, drive-ins, red and blue neon signs moving in the sunlight, rolling spirals for the motels, the beer joints. For twenty miles, marked by the deserted skeletons of the wildcat tipples bridged over the road to the river, past the chemical factories with their small towns of brick and iron and great silolike vats, I never glimpsed the river, a meadow's width away from the road.

Beulah's familiar hills swept past the slip stream of my concentrated vision. Once, driving to Egeria alone, I had stopped to see the "Mansion"—a deserted house, twenty miles "upriver" from Canona, crouched forgotten below the huge eight-lane ramp that arched over Beulah Valley as if it were in the way. At the end of the ramp I had turned off the highway, and back up the old valley road, to sate my mind with a place that had become for us a dream, a part of mother's touch-point, forever gone, forever yearned for, where life was ordered in dignity, and days were lovely, and there was no change.

A huge billboard stood in the tall dusty grass in front of the house. The wind and rain had half-stripped its signs, and the sun had dried what was left in curled fragments, so that a faded pink convertible seemed to be disappearing into the stomach of a girl in a bathing suit. One foot, arched in a spike-heeled shoe, was left, hiding a cupola at the end of the porch; her head was thrown back, and her faded blond hair streamed down almost at the other end of the house. Its upper windows, gray with coal dust, were half-hidden by the top of the sign. Behind it, I walked along the rotten boards of the veranda, my feet making a hollow noise. The lower

[ 66 ]

windows had been boarded. By some neglect, an old swing still hung in the downriver cupola. I sat in it in the half-dark, swinging a little, afraid of falling.

I guess, in that borrowed memory of children, the kitchen at Beulah was more alive for me than any other room. When I read *Kenilworth,* Aunt Annie told me she'd read it with her feet almost in the kitchen fire during the coldest winter she could remember in the valley. The copy of *She, the Enchantress* still had darkened spots on one of the pages where boiling fat from the great iron skillet had popped out and burned my mother's arm.

So after I had sat in the fragile swing on the porch behind the billboard, I jumped down into the high weeds and pushed my way through to the kitchen ell. The back porch had fallen; the square wooden columns looked as if they had been chopped down with an ax. Their stumps jutted up beyond the flat slates of the porch floor. I could barely see into the window.

At some time the kitchen had been used as a canteen. Thick cups, dark with dust, littered the window sill inside. The fireplace was dead, stuffed full of rubbish. Part of its iron grate had tipped forward and lay against a pile of cardboard cartons. Something moved out from the cartons and streaked along the floor, the shadow of a huge river rat.

It was too late to stop and seek out the Mansion roof, too late even to slow down. The ramp swept me over it at sixty miles an hour. I caught a glimpse of the tops of tired wooden, deserted miners' houses, the crests of trees, a few well-kept roofs, and at the top of the valley, on the little rise we knew as Old Fort Hill, the deserted, half-ruined red-brick church with a few sunken neglected graves left behind it.

The sun fell slowly behind me. I drove east as if the whole river valley were in the way of my going.

The mountains rose higher and the valley murmured. I did not dare to think of Johnny for fear of crying. The sensuous concen-

[ 67 ]

tration on the road was a relief. The last plant's smokestacks were as tall as cathedral spires throwing out dark red flashes like pentecostal fire.

Beyond the factory the air cleared as if it had been freed. After the heat it was a blue, bright fall afternoon; the road broke toward the river. Beyond me the great falls fanned, throwing swaths of spray into the clean hunter's day.

The water above the falls formed a wide, deep lake where huge island rocks rode like proud keeled ships. Around it the mountains stood, sheer rock cliffs, impassable until the rock was blasted to expose cross sections of limestone and the graves of great forests that made black coal seams shining in the following sun. I left the valley and could feel the car under me strain on the hairpin curves of the mountain rise.

It was as if my father met me, as he always did, at the first curve —at least all of him I could remember as a man, the gesture of his hands, the cringing of the lower eyelids in his still face against small, distracting blows, the training which isolated him and made him seem, with a little fear under his measures of success, perpetually preoccupied with my mother. He had a kind of mountain watchfulness, underneath the golf tan and the well-cut clothes mother insisted on, prepared always to follow her if she walked or catch her if she fell. He would sum it up by saying, "We better get mother to bed," not as a man of his wife but as a father of a constantly ailing child. I don't think she demanded his love, but part of her did live on his almost singular concern.

"You leave the Neills in the valley, Hannah. Now, you're in McKarkle country." He had said it so many times by habit; as a child I remember my mother twitching beside me, as she did when he repeated things. He didn't seem to say it to me, although he used my name.

I saw the first sign, *Prepare to Meet Thy God,* whitewashed in a sprawl across the cliff face. Hung over it, the sumacs, the first ripeners, dropped bright blood leaves. My senses, trained to notice the coming of hunting time, of good scent, quickened and sang until they brought back Johnny, not condom-carrying salesman, genteel, small-town man actor, but the escaped one. The woods up the first mountain hollow vaulted over a rough nave where a creek flung itself down against the stones and tunneled under the road.

I could not think of Johnny and still drive. I turned on the car radio, forgetting it was Sunday in the mountains, the McKarkle country.

Thin voices sang a nasal song, true-pitched, into the car—a single line without harmonics.

" 'I've reached the land of corn and wine,' " they whined, echoing in some space beyond the microphone. The car passed under the last gaunt flayed tipple thrusting out from a slag-dark hollow. " 'And all its riches freely mine' "; the voices began to fade professionally behind the homely cracker-barrel intimacy of the radio preacher.

"This is WRIM. The Bible hour is being brought to you folks on this purty September Sunday by the courtesy of the Cherokee Milling Company. When you make that Cherokee cornbread and eat those real, homemade butter-soaked Cherokee biscuits I jest want you to remember what day it is, folks. Hit's the day of the Lord, the Sabbath. Drive careful."

The voices rose again, tinny in the fast car. I piloted around the swooping mountain curves. The owner of WRIM drove a Porsche too.

" 'Oh Beulah Land, sweet Beulah Land, as on thy highest mount I stand, I look away across the sea, where mansions are prepared for me . . .' "

A mouth that knew every nuance of the microphone swelled through the car, arresting my speed. "Brethern and sistern, I want to talk to you a little bit today about a little verse from Isaiah

[ 69 ]

three." He was close, almost licking the microphone; he stepped back and let his voice echo in the studio. The sound blared through the tubes of the car radio:

"'The mighty man, and the man of war, the judge, and the prophet, and the prudent, and the ancient,

"'The captain of fifty, and the honourable man, and the counsellor, and the cunning artificer, and the eloquent orator.

"'And I will give children *to be* their princes, and babes shall rule over them.'"

He came back to the microphone as I drove past a sunken dirty white clapboard filling station perched on the mountainside. There were a few cabins sagging in the back, little bigger than beds. A chipped, painted sign read "Mountain View Motel." With what wild urge had Johnny driven the mountain, who beside him, to bury his need, secret and ashamed, in that drab place?

Johnny, suspended in my mind, mingled with the flirtation of the preacher.

"Now listen to that, children; we're all children. Listen to that, little child.

"Did Jesus Christ have a education? Was Jesus Christ a lawyer? Was Jesus Christ a captain and a mighty man? You born-again Christians know the answer."

He stepped back. "NO! If you was goin' to put CHRIST on your payroll would you keer what kind of education he had? If you git to lookin' at one of the sinners and wonderin' if he's saved, do you git him a good lawyer? NO. You don't give him nuthin' but Jesus *Christ* to *face* his shame with.

"He don't wear no fancy clothes. He don't go to no fancy hotels. He ain't got no money in the bank. He don't drive no Cadillac.

"But He's here to save and judge us all. I seen a well-dressed banker with tears a-rollin' down his cheeks. I seen the owner of a three-car garage throw away them cigarettes and lay aside that whisky bottle, and I seen a good lawyer forswear bad women and them a-kneelin' down in agony, beggin' me, clutchin' at my pore pants they wouldn't put on their fancy legs and *a-beggin'* me to save their souls from *Hell Far!*

"Jesus," he lapped the microphone, "come to them sinners in their hour of need. All He asked for was their bad habits: all He asked for was their fancy livin' and their dirty bodies . . ." I could hear him swallow spittle.

I managed to turn off the hate-filled ugly voice and pull the car to the roadside. Ahead of me the indifferent mountains rolled. I knew I had to stop shaking, get the perversion of that shameful, professional envy in God's name out of my head, that terrible use of part to prove the whole. Johnny and I had heard the verses from Isaiah before, more mournfully used, but as wounding.

An arrow pointed into the woods. It read Lookout Rock. I walked toward it, trying to drift away, for just one long minute. The air at the mountaintop was kind and clean, and a sweet breeze shifted through the nearly ripened leaves of the tall trees. A path with a log railing had been built out to the rock where it was said that George Washington had once stood as a young surveyor and looked westward.

The flat table rock poised over the deep circling gorge of the west-flowing river was etched with wind that seemed as old as the world's beginning, bending the young trees downriver and fanning my face. As far as I could see upriver, the mountains rolled green and endless, walls now, not furrows as I had seen that morning from the plane. Far below, a miniature freight train traveled east around the great curve of the opposite mountain. I judged as easily as breathing a hundred or so coal cars, open-topped and black. That far away the grainy grunt of the warning diesel whistle around the curve sounded like a small hound as the hoot drifted up through wave after wave of air eddies. Across the river and a mountain away from the gorge, the top had been stripped to dead rock and the trees below it had been burned out by some old fire. My face felt damp and cleansed by the healing wind but still I could not shake the voice in Johnny's car.

The preacher had not finished the prophet's words. My grandmother had, and as much for her own purposes as he for his. Somehow, though hers had sounded more sanctified, as she would have said, their motives seemed connected by a tenuous wire of envy.

I had sat, huddled, licking my always scabbed six-year-old knee and staring at my grandmother McKarkle's heavy-booted feet. Johnny, an impatient Melinda, and I had been caught by her there on the sunny porch in Greenbrier on a cloud-shifty summer morning, just after we had listened to one of those muted quarrels at breakfast that the grown-ups seemed to take for granted as "ordinary" conversation. When the whole family was there, words spat like the bacon in the thick iron skillet. Out beyond us the limestone pool glittered as the sun came out, then went a sullen gray as the sun scudded behind a dark cloud.

My grandmother's face went dark like that as she turned to my mother at the farm-laden breakfast table.

"I don't see why people have to go and stay at some hotel when they got a perfectly good home to go to," she said over her head, then turned to my father as if she had asked him a question.

No one said anything. It was obviously the end of an old grown-up argument we hadn't heard. As if the last word of the solid old woman at the end of the table eating a mound of spoon bread had pricked her, I saw my mother's controlled excitement, which she always showed when she went to Egeria, go worm-flat and then her face harden.

"I have to go get packed," she said finally and got up. She turned again at the door and looked past grandmother's head. "Children," she said, all sweet with that ire I knew so well, "I'll pack all your things. Remember, the servants know who you are when they open your suitcases." She was gone.

"Servants!" my grandmother said to the spoon bread and attacked it again. "Don't ketch me let some nigger unpack my grip."

Then as we waited for mother to pack and father and Uncle Ephraim wandered out by the huge barn, grandmother flipped open the Bible and leaned it between legs grown wide and relaxed with age as if they had shed all their taught shy woman ways and at last allowed her to set on them aspraddle, as Uncle Ephraim called it. She read the same Isaiah as the tin-voiced preacher—but she went on to her own proving verses:

" '. . . and babes shall rule over them.

" 'And the people shall be oppressed, every one by another, and every one by his neighbour: the child shall behave himself proudly against the ancient, and the base against the honourable.' "

She leaned back and delivered herself of a sigh. I couldn't see her; the sunbonnet she had sewn herself and wore belligerently whenever mother came, and never any other time, hid her cheek from me. The rest of the time she wore an old hat of Uncle Ephraim's.

Johnny exchanged glances with me and winked, but I didn't wink back. I firmly believed what she said. After all, she had taught me to dip in the Bible for the word of God and told me never to do it in front of my mother who didn't know about such things, being a different "kind of people," as she called it.

Mother and grandmother tilted for us in language. Mother called grandmother's square brick house, set in the thick grazing grass of the limestone plateau, the "place" in Greenbrier. Grandmother said it was a farm, it had always been a farm, and so long as Ephraim had breath in his body it would be a farm. She said "places" were for people who didn't work their own land and bought up good pieces of property to spend coal money on living higher on the hog than their people had before them. All this was with a sharp glance at my father, who, she told us, had thrown away a perfectly good education to go into the coal business with "that Cutwright gang."

On Uncle Ephraim's vacations from Washington and Lee, he repaired the old snake fences and rode over the grass pastures among the cattle all day in an overseer's saddle with wooden stirrups, hardly saying a word, but letting Johnny and me ride after him, all flop-legged and bareback. His seldom-heard laugh was as rich as good leather and amber whisky. He had an acre-owning stride, and when we heard him downstairs with the men after we'd all gone to our sun-scented sheets to huddle in the spatial dusk and listen to the whippoorwills and wonder who was going to die, he'd sound as if he lived in an easy kind of joy we didn't know. He would take Johnny hunting but not me then, but at night when they came back he would let me sit on his lap and even hold my head against his tobacco-and-man-smell chest and let me go nearly to sleep. He just didn't have a word to say in front of any size woman. He said it wasn't any use, that it just started them off. He said not to ever flush a covey until your gun was ready, or scatter chickens until you had something to give them to shut the damn things up again.

I knew what he meant, how words could start them. When mother made the mistake of telling us in front of grandmother how, when Colonel McKarkle came home from the War, there wasn't a soul left and he had to put his hand to the plow himself, grandmother laughed and said, not like an oath but like a personal statement about God, "For the love of the Lord, Sally, Gideon McKarkle would whirl in his grave if he heard that. Sounds like he never did a lick of work in his life before." Then she ignored mother and told us why our grandfather was named Ephraim.

"Colonel McKarkle told me. He told me he'd had just about enough. He named him from the Bible because of Jehovah's promise after trouble that Ephraim shall not envy Judah and Judah shall not vex Ephraim. He said there'd been enough bloodshed between brothers."

Johnny asked why father wasn't named Judah then, and grandmother said she named him Preston after her side of the family.

On that morning, after mother had gathered us up and stowed us in the Buick sedan, she went back onto the wood porch where grandmother rocked. I saw, from the flip-up seat in the back, mother lean stiffly down and plant a hard kiss toward grandmother's cheek.

Grandmother never stopped rocking. When mother came back, those small tired tears she never seemed to notice were swimming in her eyes.

On the way to Egeria mother told us, biting at the information and staring at the road to watch father's driving, that there were certain things we must not mention in front of our grandmother—whisky, cards, dancing, and the federal income tax. She said every time she left us there she had to come and pick up the pieces.

I wasn't paying much attention. I was remembering how grandmother let me watch while she sat wide on a tilted stool and nuzzled her gray head into the big wall of the Jersey she kept and milked herself. As the thick fingers pulled and caressed at the heavy mottled udders and the fine streams of milk whistled into the bucket, she gave me advice. There was so much of it I couldn't remember what it was. I just connected it with work, the cow she insisted on keeping as her own, and strong disapproval of everything that wasn't hard as a rock and as clean.

I saw my father smile slightly in the rear-view mirror, but mother seemed frozen solemn with annoyance and a kind of ashamed hurt she picked up as she entered the gate of grandmother's farm and then shed two or three miles down the road toward Egeria Springs.

There, on Lookout Rock, as the freight train disappeared and the trees sighed over the magnificent, stern, indifferent gorge, I saw my dead grandmother again and recognized for the first time how she had always defeated my frailer mother. She bore a mark of suspicious, shy pride, her simplicity a protective rock-ribbed Baptist arrogance that trusted cows and children and Ephraim, whom she called her "least one," but never what the wind blew in from downriver or across the eastern mountains to runnel her hard righteousness. Seeing her, I felt lightened, shed of her, and sensed in the tensile fault in mother's ore that could be touched, a shame of joy that ran all the way through to a salesman's sex and made him keep condoms hidden in the glove compartment of his car and sneak over dark mountains to cheap motels to act. I raced back through the first fallen leaves to Johnny's car and threw the condoms over the mountainside, partly so mother wouldn't find them.

Suddenly the absurd vision of John Knox in his great testimonial anger traced to a sterile Rexall condom hidden in a Porsche sports car in the Allegheny Mountains made me want to howl my laughter back at the mountain wind.

There is a time when even sorrow and wondering become unbearable and fade away for a while. I felt rested when I started the engine again, as if the guy-ropes of all the family burdens had been cast off to let me glimpse a freedom from their heavy love, just for a little while.

The sermon was over, the radio clear. I twirled to jazz and drove like a fugitive across the long mountain plateau toward the Greenbrier levels. I sped through Shiloh, Sunday dead and mine dead. The stores of the main street, catering to coal miners, were boarded, their windows grimy and empty. My body swayed to Sidney Bechet. Around the road through Zion Corner my knees loosened and I sensed the way of the machine. I passed the sign to Dead Man's Cave, the two-and-a-half-hour mark into the mountains of Canona. It was three o'clock.

Ahead, the levels of Greenbrier lay, a great natural savanna of grazing land with limestone rocks jutting above the green meadow, dented with pools and springs which disappeared into hollow caverns like Dead Man's Cave, where Uncle Ephraim had taken us, and I, afraid to enter the huge grinning mouth, had clung to the broad safe back of my pony and cried, while Johnny and Uncle Ephraim exchanged patient man looks over my coward's head. It was another one of the thousand acts of blooding.

Away to my right, its neat, elegant split-wood fences half a mile along the road, lay Uncle Ephraim's "place." It was now so classic it made me grin to see it.

In the year after my grandmother McKarkle died, when Uncle

Ephraim was forty, after the first stunned months in which he saw no one and hardly said a word, his strength flowed back from where he had always found it, from the land. It spread and burst beyond the pastures and downriver to pick George Minelli's black-eyed, smooth-moving sister Rose for a wife and take her back to Greenbrier. All the secret caches of his pleasure opened, and he began to enjoy being a man as sanely as he judged horses, raised cattle, and hunted. Mother had a sick headache the day of his marriage, but as word began to come back from Greenbrier that he was what she called "remodeling" the house, which meant setting columns in front of a square farmhouse and taking the yellow and brown linoleum off the wide boards of the floor to please Maria, she began to let the McKarkles creep into a place in her careful conversation they had never had before.

It was from there that Johnny called on rare Saturday nights when he had flown that far. I would know from his voice at once where he was.

There was not time to stop and tell Uncle Ephraim, or perhaps I didn't want my parents to face his hard, demanding questions. I drove on by, into the round valley of Egeria, surrounded by mountains, like a little Eden.

On both sides of the road perpetually blue-green golf courses lay under the hot Sunday September sun. Walker's Creek ran out from the mountains, as groomed in the valley as the grass. It no longer swept past high crowded rocks where golf balls could be lost, but purled over a pretty sandy and white-pebble bottom, widened into still pools of water, tunneled under pretty rustic bridges, curled around the smooth green mound which was said to be an Indian grave, and now was a hazard making a dog-leg fairway on the sixteenth hole. Over the green fairways, clumps and pairs of figures strolled, at first glance as if they had been there since the last time I saw Egeria, as perpetual as the carpet-soft emerald greens with their bright flags, white linen people stopping here and there, even the body arc of their drives and their huddled putts slowed down and formal as I passed behind the insulating glass of Johnny's car.

I still had joy left and the twinge of excitement I had known ever since I was a child and went to Egeria for the first time with my parents. In my memory, it was a place where everyone walked more easily through old quiet paths under the last virgin trees, or down muted high corridors that filled my child's eyes full of wonder and made my mother call me down, embarrassed at my staring. Voices were muffled there by the rotunda of the ballroom where not even the table silver made much noise. Egeria's smell, from the gate on into the rooms, a smell compounded of expensive secluded mountain air, hand-ironed linen, polish, huge, glossy, well-fed plants, and thick notepaper, I recognized later wherever I smelled it, and it brought me back to Egeria Springs. It was the clean, crisp new smell of protected American money.

The avenue ran under trees around the near hill. Down in the valley below me, the sunken temple that covered a spring which had once been the center of Egeria still stood under its painted Roman statue. Now it was a place we were taken to see once, to say we'd seen it. After that we raced past it, past faded, frail, disused cottages, to the Nile-green pool with its scarlet umbrellas or to the black tennis courts. Mother said that the temple still had its original wooden columns, but Uncle Ephraim told us they were about as original as grandpa's ax which had had five new handles and four new blades.

As I stopped Johnny's car I glanced up across the huge white Roman façade of the hotel, jutting out between the broad dining-room porch and its balancing twin that opened off the ballroom. My eyes stopped. The Chippendale railing, unchanged, quiet in the shade, held me suspended in the driveway. Johnny was back, his heavy breathing in my head, the danger which had been there so long with him and now was pinpointed on a hospital bed, as if, for a second to split the brain, all his roads had led to it. I remembered, self-protecting, the expected beauty of the first dance I went to at Egeria.

We were in the bedroom in the Laurel Wing. It was night. Faintly, far away, I could hear music. Mother fussed behind my worried, frowning head, picking at my first long green organdy dress ruffled off my bony shoulders. Under it my knees shook, and my feet hurt in new shoes. I was at that clear, exposed fifteen when a girl is first conscious of herself as moving awkwardly across endless alien floors, only knowing later that that self-consciousness had its special grace—expectant, when every frightened walk down wide stairs to these first dances was an ecstasy of fear and hope, a dreamed-of meeting with some Sebastian-eyed boy whose hidden, nameless grief only one's self could cure, for in 1945 the ideal boy had a lost look about him.

So in front of the mirror I forgot what night it was, that it was all for Johnny, home at twenty-one from Europe, on his last leave before his release from the service. Mother had planned it all because she said we had always been so happy at Egeria. Johnny watched us as if we moved on a screen in front of him, making no contact, even with me, his eyes as stony as a cat's with a dead anger I couldn't understand.

Mother was saying, fidgeting in the pink bedroom, as she had said over and over behind Johnny's back when he disappeared into the Wayfaring Stranger to sit with Charley who had been in his company, "I think the best thing is to treat Johnny as if nothing has happened. We'll make it just like it always was. I think that's the best. Just put it out of our minds."

Once I heard him stumbling up the stairs to his room in the middle of the night, crying. Once he screamed and woke the whole house, but in the morning he said he'd been asleep. I could hear mother telling about it on the telephone, excited at her glimpse of war.

It was October. Outside the windows and along the walks, I

could hear the bright leaves swishing as they were harvested by the wind.

There is only one time when the form of dancing and light comes as true as the dream, and that is the first time one sees it, as some fledgling might see the swallows swoop and know it needs only courage to follow, and falls all feet and wings from the nest, then either gives up to the dog's mouth or learns to learn; only one time when fear and beauty together meet and swirl through one's senses. For me, trained from the time I "dressed up" and smelled the musty, dry-grass smell of stored silk, and found my mother's old scuffed satin slippers and put them on my five-year-old feet, it was my first dance. Evasiveness and delight were for me, for a little while that night, as instinctive as an animal scent.

The door into the ballroom was at the end of a long corridor covered with dark red flocked paper and lit dimly by electric candles in crystal sconces along the walls. I was literally borne through it. Ahead, under the glowing chandelier, the dancers whirled past the door, dresses swaying as if the fall wind had entered the ballroom and was swirling them like leaves. On the edge of it mother and I stopped to watch before we plunged in. They all were strangers, swinging and whirling cloud skirts, kept from flying away by tall men in black or in uniform, tree-trunk colors. They played that year and that minute "Sentimental Journey."

I stood for those few minutes that stretched to hours, wanting to be taken into it—part, for the first time, of the ancient ceremony of woman waiting. Then my father caught me and piloted me around the floor, in and out among the dancers. They took on their own faces, became familiar, and I was part of the whirling, the dresses, the heavy billowing of the red velvet curtains as the wind pushed in from the open porch. My father stopped to talk to "Uncle" J. D. Cutwright by the bar, where a mass of men had gathered in a still center of the dancing, and I hung onto his arm, dancing inside and watching.

I wanted to find Johnny to tell him how beautiful it all was—to tell somebody about the excitement that poured into my eyes and ears, into the rhythm of my body, and surged through my veins. He wasn't there. Kitty Puss Wilson floated by, singing into my cousin Brandy Baseheart's ear; he looked pink with pleasure and handsome, for once, in naval uniform.

Then, out beyond the moving curtains, caught by the pale drifting light from the ballroom, no longer glittering but lying in soft fingers across the porch, I saw Johnny. He was standing against the white Chippendale railing, watching the dancers as calmly as if they performed for his judgment, drinking his drink. I could hear the ice tinkle in his glass as he jerked it down from his mouth, never stopping that cold judgment.

Behind me father was saying to Uncle J. D., "We sure managed enough whisky for the boys. Boy, it wasn't easy," as if the whole United States Navy floated on whisky so they could have only a little, and that with guilty pleasure.

"We sure did that," Uncle J. D. told him as proudly as if they'd made it themselves.

I raced out to Johnny, forgetting the long dress. It made me move so slowly. I pulled it away from my legs and heard the skirt tear.

Johnny saw me coming but he didn't do anything. He just stood there, drinking and watching. I forgot what it was I was going to tell him. His face, now in profile in the pale light, looked worn and noble, just as it should. I hitched my bottom up onto the railing under the green organdy, imitating him, trying to be as cool, watching the dancers, ashamed that my heart still thumped at all the movement under the blinding star shower from the chandelier.

"All those soft, fat, pretty shoulders," Johnny muttered. "It looks so goddam *fat*." He put one hand up to my protruding shoulder and jerked at my organdy ruffles.

"All that *crap*, Sissy . . ." He seemed to be talking to himself but accusing me at the same time. He wasn't looking at my eyes but at my neck, under my hair. His fingers bit deep around my collarbone, just for a second, then he turned his back on me and threw his glass as hard as he could. I heard it crash against a tree.

He said, "It's like a bad dream when you wake up in the morning in the same place. It's the same place and it isn't because you have the bad dream inside you. It's behind your eyes, you know, so it can't be the same place . . ."

Johnny knew something I didn't and couldn't know then. He had the hard, unforgiving eyes of those whose bridges have been burned behind them, by somebody else.

Then he said, quite calmly, looking at the dancers again, "Jesus, Hannah, it's just like it always was."

I didn't dare tell him that it was, after all, the way mother had planned it.

Released from the pull of the dancers, one dark figure swayed in the doorway against a haloing light that made her face and her wide skirt a dark shadow, kept on swaying, trying to get her balance by grasping the lintel of the door.

Johnny sighed an exhausted sigh, then raised his voice. It soothed and flirted, faintly teasing. "Honey . . ."

Kitty Puss swayed from the lintel to Johnny. Her face was glossy, her teeth clenched.

"Honey," she mocked him, "come here and let me rehabilitate you." She giggled. "Mother says . . ." She leaned forward deliberately into his arms and slowly sank her teeth into the shoulder of his uniform. They were together, rigid. I could hear them breathing. I wanted to run. The party changed focus—was ugly, loud, too fast.

"Get back inside, Sissy," Johnny ordered over her shoulder, but he was looking at her hair. He twined his fingers in it and began to pull her head back.

"Hurry," he whispered. "Hurry!"

His face was concentrated with a cold, hard joy. I had seen him look that way before, when he hit the boys on the shoulder playing airplanes, when he shot, deliberate. When he sensed my minding, it would make him tease, annoyed. "It's only a game, Sissy—have some sense of humor." I was crying, but they were locked together and couldn't see.

"You damn prince," I heard Kitty Puss behind me whispering. "Where can we go? Where can we go in this goddam fish tank?" She sounded as if she hated him.

The floor was too bright to hide me. People clogged my way. I got through to the dim corridor, and mother caught me there.

"For heaven's sake, Hannah, pull yourself together. Carrying on like this. Can't you appreciate what's done for you for one evening of your life? I knew better than to let you come. I *knew* better," she was muttering, half helping, half dragging me toward the elevator so no one would see.

I was sobbing too hard to look at her or answer anything she kept saying, but I could hear the band still playing "Sentimental Journey."

My father had seen us and come up behind us, just was there. "What the hell is the matter with Sissy?" he asked mother.

"I don't know. I can't get anything out of her. Where's Johnny?" The elevator door opened, and I got away from her.

"Let her go," my father ordered as the door closed.

How much I cried, and even why I cried so, I didn't know, but at last in the darkness of the bedroom I drifted off to sleep. There was murmuring outside in the corridor, then it was words, low, urgent quarreling of people who wanted to hide it. I could tell by the dry taste in my mouth I had been asleep a long time.

Something had happened, something that had stripped away the masks tense between Johnny and my father and mother, their voices were naked with each other, a sound so rare it made me go cold again with fear.

The voice of my father with that phrase he used at the end of long, long built-up silences, broke through the door. "I've had just about enough, Jonathan. Your mother and I have tried to be patient with you. God knows . . . no son of mine . . ."

I heard Johnny murmur.

"That will be enough out of you. We've spent a thousand dollars bringing you up here. Your mother has sat and listened for her son to come home drunk every night. You don't know what she's been through, waiting for her son to come home."

Mother interrupted; she was urgent with protection. "What right have you to talk? What right?" She was spilling, "*You* made a damn fool of yourself the same way. He made a fool of himself," she begged Johnny.

Father turned even on her. "I don't care what he's been through, the boy's going to have to learn some respect for his mother and sister."

"Well, I just can't stand any more." I heard mother's door slam.

As if their monitor had gone, the two men, for a minute, treated each other with as much politeness as if they were strangers, thinking no one heard.

"I'm sorry, son," father said. "It's been too much for your mother." Johnny answered as gently and formally, "I'm sorry, father."

"Son," father told him, "I don't know what to say. You bring it all back. I remember that on Armistice night in Paris I thought I knew the answer to the whole thing. I did too. It just didn't hold up. Didn't seem to fit. Then finding you in a car, using that sweet young girl I've known all her life like she was . . . I just want you to know I won't say a word. You can trust me. After all, we *can't disturb the women*." He said it as if he were saying one of the Ten Commandments.

Johnny started to laugh. He pushed father away with his laughter and went on laughing.

When father could answer that sweep of laughter, he had backed down to his own door. "You might at least try to comfort your little sister." I heard him, dimly, as his door closed.

Then my door was being tried. A shaft of light followed Johnny inside. I saw his dark shape move over to the window. He snapped on a small lamp, and the light made my eyes sting. He didn't turn to look at me. He watched himself in the black glass of the window. I could see the dark reflection as he stared at himself. Beyond the window a branch in the night wind slapped at his reflected face.

He knew I was awake. "For Christ's sake, Sissy," he asked his reflection, "you too? What do *you* want? What do you all want from me?"

I wanted to bury my face in the pillow, shut out that man who watched himself so coldly. I wanted to cry, "I want my brother," but there he was at last, standing in the muted light of the room that was all rich and pink with little roses on the dresser and all the polished mirrors, not off in some dark place I could only imagine, some lost place I had prayed every night for him to come back from.

Finally he sighed, the same way he had sighed before Kitty Puss had been aware that he noticed her. With a last look at his reflected face he turned, his shoulders sagging a little, and came over to sit beside me on the bed.

"Now look at that dress." He picked up a torn ruffle I'd slept on.

I began to feel warm and safe again. It was too soon. Johnny turned away and clasped his hands between his knees and looked beyond them at a space that was toward the floor, but he wasn't watching anything in that room. What he said rippled out then without stopping, some plug in his mind pulled by memory and trouble and whisky and the night. He didn't seem to stop to breathe.

"I can't do it. Jesus, I can't do it. I'm too tired. You people don't know what it is to be tired all the way to your gut. You think you're tired when you go through a day and then go to bed. Pretty high on the hog bed, out of a solid day into a solid night." He went on without waiting, swam into whatever it was, relaxing.

". . . what they call perfect English, with a broad *a*. There he was, standing in the woods, easy, like a hunter. He said he had been waiting for somebody he could recognize as a gentleman before he came out of the woods. He said he had to surrender honorably.

When he stood there in front of me I *admired* him. I *admired* the fact that his uniform was fitted and his boots were polished. I admired the fact that he had the Iron Cross and a goddam shave and some personal pride. We recognized each other all right. We"—his voice faltered as he told himself, trying to find the word—"we . . . reflected . . . each other. You get that way, respect for your own kind. Respect for his cool eyes, clear without any crap. I'd seen tears and wailing faces and cringing bodies and crazy heaps of dust and rubble and trash flung all the way across the damn country until I was sick to death of them." He pounded the bed, once. "I was sick to death of them."

I watched all the pictures of him in the pier glass on the bathroom door, in the mirror over the pretty dresser, his head, now down, in the black window, heard his voice muttering like water dripping, as if he were replacing tired tears with tired words.

"We walked through a wood. There was no undergrowth. Sissy, you could have hunted through it and seen a dog point way ahead under those cared-for trees. It was spring. You know, that tender yellow-green. We had come over the hills like this, wooded, with polished valleys between. It was so peaceful, so pretty. We walked through the beech woods, slow hunting pace, slow, guns alert, slow. He came through the beech woods from behind a tree, easy. Then he put his hands up. After our honorable exchange, one of the men in the company took him back to the rear.

"That's what they have around Weimar—the prettiest beech woods you ever saw. We even stopped and chewed branches. Weimar was so pretty—the people were like people at home. Nice people. They were clean and polite-looking, woods and trees and those neat, cared-for houses after all the rubble and shit and blood and fear."

He remembered I was there, huddled behind him on the bed. "You'd like it, Sissy," he said gently. "Goethe lived there, and Bach and Schiller.

"North of Weimar we found it. You know what it was called?

The German for beech wood, because it was built in the beech woods and they didn't bother to change the name. We just went through the pretty homelike country, and there it was. They called it beech wood—Buchenwald. One square mile of dead space . . .

"Thousands of them, thousands. White as limestone skeletons all bleached and dry in that bright April sun. Did you know that when people are nearly dead and still walking they sound like paper blowing and they all look alike? Men and women all look exactly alike. All they had—the ones alive—was this thin sigh of life in them.

"They pressed in on us, they stank. Jesus, they were . . ." He watched his face for a long time. The wind whisked the windows. "They were unattractive." He used the final aesthetic word calmly. "One of them asked for a lipstick! I didn't even know it was a woman. I was ashamed of being human.

"When the nice people from Weimar were made to come and see it they whispered, 'We didn't know'— *'Wir haben nicht gewusst'* —it whispers, doesn't it? Thousands whispering, *'Wir haben nicht gewusst,'* and thousands whispering back, 'We told you'—*'Wir haben Euch das gesagt. Wir haben Euch das gesagt.'* " Johnny whispered, the wind outside joined him, whispering at the window, the branches scratching like fingers.

"That day I saw the gentleman, the honorable soldier. He was sitting with his black boots still shiny, still honorable feet on top of a huge pile of dry white bodies in the back of a truck. We made the Elite Corps bury the dead—it went on and on and on . . ."

Johnny looked at himself in the glass of the dressing-table— carefully, inspecting his face.

"I was his parody and he was mine. We both looked sensitive and did what we were told. . . . We are what we'd been taught and what we held dear: God and Country and Virginity and Christmas and Dogs and Chocolate and Obedience and you don't fuck nice girls. Weimar, the parody of home so urgent it had made my throat hurt. It didn't end there. I came back here, and this has become a parody of Weimar, even the pretty girls protected from ugliness, the same round shoulders, the same well-fed bodies, the same lipstick and motherly care. There you could 'get engaged' for a few weeks for a bar of chocolate—same clean living room, smiling mother. Here it costs a fortune." He slapped my rump and laughed. "Look after it, Sissy," he told me. "It's worth a fortune."

I had a dim sense that Johnny hardly knew I was there, only that I was listening. After a silence he murmured, *"Wir haben nicht gewusst."*

At some point I must have slept while he was still talking. I woke, surprised, to daylight. Johnny was gone. The morning was full of October sun on the lovely woods, red and yellow sentinels over the hills around Egeria. Johnny, I remembered, played golf and was his old self again. It was as if a burden, shared, had slipped from his shoulders. He had banked at least the unbearable excess of his memory with me, and, blessedly, I began to forget, or bury, as the officer had buried the dead, what he had told me. He never mentioned it again.

In the new year Kitty Puss married Brandy Baseheart. She got on a laughing jag at the reception.

★　　　★　　　★　　　★

# Chapter Five

A MAN was standing beside my car, his soft hands on the rolled-down window, leaning a huge feminine body down almost as if he were bowling. He had the exaggerated politeness of Southerners who hate Jews and Negroes and think women fools and yet have arrived at pride and enough money to learn the wisdom of silence.

"Lady," he said with great deference and patience, "would you mind moving your car out of the middle of the driveway?" His face was florid and veined, his eyes hard. On the lapel of his large Madras jacket he wore a yellow ribbon rosette, four inches across. In gilt letters at the middle of the flower were the words, "Fuel Association: J. P. Twilby."

I knew the formality of smiling an apology and letting him see a masculine, protective self in my eyes.

"Oh, I'm sorry," I said and tried to start the car.

He leaned, heavy on the window, assuming the expression for a pretty girl. "You want me to park it for you?" His manner sounded contemptuous.

I shook my head. He stepped back from the window and forgot me as I moved.

A bellow sounded over the car roof. "Why, Eldridge, you old son-of-a-gun," he was calling to someone on the marble veranda.

From then on, step by step toward my father and mother, I moved carefully. Up the wide marble stairs between the great white dwarfing Federal columns and the huddles of men with yellow rosettes and pastel women, I walked onto the great continuation of the templelike marble floor. Ahead, the double stairs curved out to make a bowl for a little forest of green tropical trees standing in pots in front of a mirror to the ceiling behind them, which doubled the plant forest and made an infinity of the foyer, reflecting the columns and the tree-studded sweep of the front lawn. I had forgotten how many mirrors there were at Egeria, as if the vain, more often the insecure, could check themselves forever, their walks, their greetings, their place in the green and marble world. I glimpsed myself, a slight, thin, easy-striding girl, noted with the care of habit that the dress of the reflection still moved with a scarlet dot of grace through the inhumanly high room, even after the flight, the trouble, and the drive. I smoothed my smooth hair with the checking, secretive dandyism we were trained to have; to hurry in that great space would have been as impossible as running against a strong current.

At the top of the curving stair the huge lobby broke, gilt catching the faltering sun and swinging the space of the room so that the loud crowd of men seemed fishlike in movement under reflecting water. When I saw rosetted Brandy Baseheart coming toward me, his arms outstretched like a politician, I was as shaken as if he had walked out of my fifteen-year-old recall.

"Why, Cousin Hannah, baby!" He covered both sides of my hand with friendly paws. "Hey, Kitty honey," he yelled. He engulfed me, asking no questions, drawing me into one of the clumps of rosetted people. The noise in the room was deafening. I floated in shade and noise, too startled to break away and try to explain.

Brandy had widened with the years; the questioning cheerfulness he had had as a boy had turned belligerent, as if he lived within a plastic bubble of good fellowship he warily guarded against breakage. Kitty Puss detached herself and turned toward me. She had grown muscular, the promise in her plump, pert girl's face fulfilled into the immobility of a woman who drank hard, played and thought hard, had learned secretiveness in her new smaller eyes against the constant buffeting of Brandy's loud good humor. She looked as if all caring had been burned out of her face, leaving it smooth with a dead indifference. She had weathered brown in the sun that had covered her skin with a mask of lines as she marched across innumerable golf courses, disdaining protection. She simply had honed down, hardened and survived.

"Sissy, come here and meet these people," she yelled back, casual and not caring. She had a cigarette clenched between small teeth and she grinned around it. "I don't know who they are." She had, through years, perfected a breezy carelessness that allowed her to be rude with enough gesture so that people covered for her and she didn't have to bother. She waved her drink around a little group of strangers.

One diffident man was embarrassed into speaking. "How do you do. I'm National Gas and Fuel," he told me earnestly as we shook hands. I smiled my way out of the clutches of the strangers already bored with one another in the four o'clock dullness of the Fuel Meeting that had gone on too long.

"I have to find father and mother." I tried to move away from Brandy.

He went on holding my arm, suddenly solemn. "I think your father took your mother up to lie down," he said. "They're in their usual suite." Brandy glanced at the strangers to see if anyone had noticed what he said, trying to impress as habitually as he breathed. "I think your mother was a little tired," he apologized.

"Tired!" Kitty Puss threw her head back and hooted; the cigarette bobbed up and down. I backed away to swim through

[ 91 ]

the roar of people, knowing Kitty Puss had drunk enough to spare no one her easy, loose, tough tongue.

Through the polished, hollow bowl of the ballroom, deserted in the afternoon, I walked beyond the noise. By the elevators beyond the dark red corridor, I found a house phone to warn my father.

He hardly let it ring once. I could hear anxiety in his quiet voice, naked on the telephone, when he could not hide his tone with the withdrawing gesture of his mouth.

"Father," I said once and stopped the urge to cry.

"Why, Sissy honey!" He sounded pleased and surprised. "Where are you?"

"Father, I'm downstairs."

The silence between us lasted too long.

"Why, honey." At last father tried to breach it. "You better come right up." He paused again. "Knock on the living-room door, fourteen-fourteen. Your mother's asleep. She has a little headache. Oh, honey . . ." He was trying to tell me he was glad I was there, but he couldn't bring it out. "Come right on up here."

From the elevator to their rooms the long tunnel of the corridor stretched on and on, muted, empty. I made no sound on the thick, soft gray carpet. The great labyrinthine acres of purple rhododendron that covered slopes of the wild mountains with its dark glossy leaves, mazes for lost hunters, had been imitated, sentimental and controlled, in patches of pale green leaves with huge blossoms of mild lavender over the walls and ceiling. Down the luxurious corridor, through arches of safe, painted mountain rhododendron, I walked to tell my parents about Johnny.

At the turn of the wing, far away, I saw my father already half-gesturing for me to be quiet; before he could hide it his mouth smiled, wide with pleasure, the kind of smile let loose rarely from a man who still wants the love and approval of a boy but has learned to fold his mouth against expecting it.

I was sickened by the pity I felt for him. The corridor seemed so long, what I had to say too heavy for me to do the thing my body urged—run toward him, comfort by being his daughter.

"Why, honey." He put his arm around my shoulders and whispered, then caught the tension as he touched me. His smile left and his mouth shot its tiny lines across his face as he asked, life gone from his question, "What's happened?"

"Oh, father." I tried to crawl up his shoulder, hide the child who had kept quiet so long.

"Shhh! Honey, shhh! You'll wake your mother," he said, trying to stroke my heaving shoulders as he led me inside the room and eased the door shut behind him.

I stepped back from him. I stood as I was taught to and had to fight to do, on my own feet, halfway across the room from him.

"It's Johnny," I told him calmly.

"Oh, damn Johnny." All the memories of his annoyed disappointment went into the oath. "What's he done now?"

"He's had an accident. I drove up to tell you and mother. Melinda didn't think you ought to just hear it by phone. He got knocked down."

"Is he dead?" Father shot at me, needing facts.

"No. He got knocked down. He's in the hospital." I had to get through his bland, stern wall of annoyance at the interruption, his disbelief in its importance. "He isn't expected to live."

Father turned his back on me. Perhaps he too couldn't stand what he saw between himself and his children. He walked to the window and looked, not out at the trees, but at his own reflection, as Johnny had so long ago.

"How did it happen?"

I slapped at his back with the words. I couldn't stand any more retreating. "He was drunk. He got picked up. A perfect stranger hit him. He fell against an iron bench. He was just standing there. A perfect stranger."

A perfect stranger—that word for an unknown man, an absurd shadow with a fist to hit Johnny and nearly kill him for no reason

—was between us in the room. The air-conditioner hummed. That was all, except the cold and space between us.

My father's shoulders began to sag, then bow. He was crying, not the tears of a woman with their evocative, relieving sound, but the completely silent tears of a man who had waited too long to cry, to tell, to ask one thing of us. He staggered into one of the pink chairs and hid his face. After a while he asked a question.

"How did it all go so wrong, Hannah? Oh my God!" He knew there wasn't an answer that could be given all at once, for the answers between people are daily and are told in a lifetime of gestures. He put his head down again on his hand, hunched forward, shy. I had never heard him use the word "God" before, except at eleven o'clock in All Saints when he muttered responses, one among three hundred voices.

At last he straightened up. They were his last tears. He disappeared into the bathroom. I heard the toilet flushed, then water running. He was splashing cold water on his face.

"Hannah," he said, standing straight in the doorway again. "We have to be careful with your mother. You know she isn't well. I haven't told you, tried to keep it from you." He tiptoed toward the bedroom. "You know she's been through so much." It was a phrase as habitual with him as "we'd better get mother to bed."

He put his head around the door. I could see the drawn shutters of the half-dark room beyond him.

"Sally . . ." He spoke softly, as if he were waking up a child. "Sally, Hannah's come to see us. Can we come in?" he cajoled.

"You can come in if you want to. I don't give a damn," my mother's sleepy, harsh voice came from the bed.

As we tiptoed in she heaved her body over, away from us. "I don't give a damn." She belched and buried her head in the pink pillow, legs spread and body flaccid under the ruffled tester of one of Egeria's Confederate beds.

It was all coming at once, how they had always prepared, both

Johnny and my father, so I would only half-know. I remembered the times I'd called to come home and been put off, the preparations as we drove down the hill from the airport. I had thought it was something unseen, a walking in wariness. It was concrete. It was one of their protections of me as the youngest—the hiding of this harsh, stripped woman, pretenses thrown away like clothes, lying spread-eagled on her pretty bed. They all had lived with it; it had straightened Melinda's back in her uneasy, demanding pride. It had caught Johnny's pity and wrung him dry. It had formed the apologetic face of my father.

"It doesn't happen often, Hannah," my father misread my shock and told me, "just when things get too much for her. And it doesn't take hardly any. Only one or two."

"Oh, for Christ's sake, shut up, Preston," my mother grumbled from the pillow; then she lay flat on her back, watching me, her drunk look completely honest, hiding nothing.

"Hello, Miss Hannah, who asked you to come down here and tell us all where to get off? Look at her, Preston, she's as right as your sainted damn mother."

"Sally . . ." Father leaned over her. "Now take it easy. This might be hard." He seemed to be sponging her with tenderness. She just lay there, looking up into his face, without love, without hate, cringing rather in her dry white skin and looking like the wreck of a fifteen-year-old girl. She waited, hardly breathing, keeping her eyes on his face. When he didn't, or couldn't, answer she switched to anger, cold, but without moving, only sinking farther away from the head hanging over her.

"What's she done now? What have any of them ever done for me?" She pushed his shoulder and sat up, crouched back against the sleek mahogany, and looked at me as blankly as she had looked at father.

"They taught you every damn thing you'd take. You've been to Europe. Staying up there in New York not doing a damn thing.

You know what they taught me? You know what I learned?" The accusation was chased from her face by the new thought, melting and changing its lines. "I read poetry and I was pretty as a picture. Wasn't I, Preston? Wasn't I pretty as a picture? They said I was like a Rossetti." She grasped his hand without looking at it or letting him answer. "You know what I learned? I learned to dust." She pinned me, awkward and long-armed, in front of her. She seemed to read some judgment in my nearly blank, sucked-out mind.

"We sent you to Sweet Briar! What more could we do?" she cried at the wall she saw in me.

She hunched there, her thin body jackknifed in the inevitable yellow georgette nightgown she always wore. Her short gray hair, brushed awry by the pillow, stood up from her gaunt white childish face. Her lips were so pale they were almost invisible, her skin as transparent, as frail, as fine broken bone china. She lashed out at me and "they" as if she, incapable of being mother, were flinging words at last at a luckier sister. That's how I first knew about the wound she carried. She had never shown it naked and bleeding before that day—oh, unconsciously in her genteel protections and her barbed tiny spurts of envy, but never as flung back in time, reliving it, to a listener without identity or even a true connection with her. If she drank to forget what it was, drink had not worked with her. It had only exposed her, impaled her on an irretrievable, unchangeable time of freezing and recognition I couldn't know then, as if some longing pointed like an iceberg and all the liquor in the world would not melt one sharp freezing barb of it.

I would on that day have found this rift of blood in the brittle armor of her bodily dignity unbearable had I not faced it once before when, in a hotel room in Paris, I had seen her sitting alone on a straight chair, a thin, begging girl, her eyes moving to one after another of ignoring, noisy, faceless strangers, her sad, begging smile trying to connect with at least one indifferent passer-by. It was the only time I had ever pitied her, and that was after a vivid dream, halfway across the world.

Father and I waited for her to quiet.

Suddenly, in one of those surprising spurts of sense, like a break of blue in a cloudy, drunken mind, she looked up at father and said quietly, "Preston, you better tell me."

"Honey!" He sat down on the bed beside her. They had forgotten me, he fathering her by old habit, she drawn back from him, afraid and starving. They seemed caught there, never to speak.

"It's Johnny," father said at last. "Now he's been in an accident . . ."

Her face shrank as if he had hit her. "Is he dead?" She trusted him to tell her.

"No, honey. It isn't that bad. He . . . stumbled and fell on the stairs. We think he's going to be all right." The lies caressed her without his even noticing what he said. "We better get packed and go on home."

"Not again. They're not going to do it again." Mother dissolved back onto the pillow. "They can't do it to me again." She didn't ask any more about Johnny.

"Now, honey . . . now, honey." Father stroked her damp gray hair until I thought she was asleep.

She opened her eyes. "Hannah," she said as soberly as if she had just waked from a nap, "get your mother some coffee, will you, dear?"

I ran to the telephone, and as I ordered I could see her pulling herself together, beginning with her voice. She began to take her own shape, hiding the woman again behind the lady.

"Get us some food, Hannah. Must eat something," father told me, still watching her. It gave her a chance to react to a familiar sound.

"At a time like this . . ." she answered formally. But it made her lips purse and take on color. She pushed father aside and eased her feet to the floor. She lurched, her body drunker than her

[ 97 ]

mind, toward the bathroom. We heard the bath running. She called with a quavering sigh through the shut door, "Hannah, you better help me."

"You better go help her," my father echoed. "She'll be all right. She hadn't had much of anything. It just gets her when she's tired."

In the bathroom mother's frail naked body was an arc over the basin. Her legs were like crinkled paper, her hands talons, holding her up, her elbows trembling.

"I don't like anybody to see me like this," she begged me as she stared into the bathroom mirror at her sweating head. I couldn't bear the suppliance. I wanted to reach through her old body to grasp the fifteen-year-old girl by the smooth arm, be true with her in time to save us all, but when I touched her wrinkled seared elbow she jerked it away and climbed alone into the tub.

"You *know* I can't stand being touched," she muttered to herself.

I knew as if she had told me that she was straightening her back, preparing for the long, long exposed walk through the endless romantic halls of the Egeria Springs Hotel, and on and on beyond it.

I drove back blankly, fast toward Johnny, into lowering evening and then black night. After the tense heat of the valley the rain swooped down. I went through a black, shining tunnel of water, water swishing under the car wheels, pounding the padded top like night rain falling on a tent roof, sweeping against the windshield. There were only the steady rhythm of the wipers and the path of my own lights reaching ahead of me, reeling around the great curves. Nearer Canona the neon signs in the wet night left long, glistening images shining in the stretched road, running with water like a river. In the tiny, powerful car, I left father and mother far behind me.

The visitors had all gone from the hospital. In the waiting room under the strident fluorescent light, a few of the truly vigilant sat exposed in their waiting. There was a silence so deep that when I stepped into the dark corridor to Johnny's room I picked up the slow, grating labor of his breathing as if it had never been absent from my brain. I tiptoed to keep my heels from sounding like shots on the dark floor. It was dark except for two muted lights in isolated pools, one over the nurse's desk, the other at the end of the hall over the wooden bench. I saw two vague figures waiting under the pale circle of the night-bulb, one a bowed woman, the other leaning against her, comforting.

I must have appeared, going so quietly in the edge of the dim light, like a ghost. One of the women lifted her dark head. It was Aunt Rose McKarkle, George Minelli's sister, Uncle Ephraim's wife, who sat with her arm around a wan blond girl, her face like a young *Pietà,* as still as a stone virgin. Rose held hard to her shoulders as if she were trying to will life into her.

Rose said, unsurprised and not explaining, "There's been no change," as if she spoke of the whole world, unchanged by Johnny's decision to live or die. We stood there, three muted women, attendant only on his breathing. Rose got up then and came and hugged me, giving enough for both of us to draw from, and drew me down onto the bench. It was then I knew that I had gone too long and too far since morning and my body was parched for rest.

"George called just after you left. He said he saw you at the gas station," I heard Rose say. "He said you were probably going to tell Sally and Preston."

"Where are they?" The blond girl roused herself from her despair. She was much older than I had thought.

"They followed me. They'll be here in a few minutes," I told her, surprised at the shadow of panic I saw.

The girl stiffened, got up as quickly as a flushed bird. "I've got to go."

"Tel, stop it," Rose told her shoulders. She towered dark and strong over her. "You'll do no such thing. You have *some* rights . . ."

"Please take me home," Thelma Leftwich asked, not begging but stating.

I could not remember having seen her since she and Johnny had sat together in the airport canteen. Her name had never since that time been mentioned in the house.

Rose looked at her for a long time. "Goddam their little souls to a small hell," she said calmly and took Tel's arm.

They turned to go down the corridor. Tel drew away from Rose and dragged herself back to stand in front of me. Her face was hallowed with forgiveness.

"If you need a place to come to in all this . . ." Her eyes were great dark blots, sunk with a despair far older than the night. "Rose knows where I live. You might . . ."

She turned to go without waiting for me to answer. Perhaps she saw I couldn't. In the blank eyes of that good woman's face, fed and nurtured on old sacrifice, was a condemnation of me and of us all beyond any hell that life-loving, strong Rose would ever know. It was the condemnation of old indifferent grief, of a face hungry with the kind of nobility that could only be sated by suffering.

They receded out of the light and disappeared from the unchanging world of our waiting. The corridor was filled only with Johnny's breathing and my stretched, loose calm of fatigue.

Then father and mother tiptoed into the lights' periphery with Freddie. He must have been watching for them to come. He had one of mother's arms, father the other. Behind them came Father MacAndrews, tall, stooped, and moving awkwardly in time with the occasion. Mother was dressed in tragedy and black linen; she moved with the procession of her world of comfort around her into Johnny's room. Her head was down and she was almost smiling, her face prepared through the long ride to love and help the son lodged safe in her mother-mind, waiting, needing her in the stark hospital room.

The night light showed obliquely on Johnny's face, caught in his blank eye pools and his gaping mouth, and softened the room around him with shadow. A nurse sat beside the bed, professionally watching. When she saw us she rose and tried to fade back against the darkened wall, out of notice.

Then, just for a second, as I had, mother saw the man in the bed. Her gaze sank and shifted; she looked at him as coldly as if he were a stranger. I saw the stranger sink from her eyes, the boy she most needed replace him; I knew by her voice as she walked, crooning with an element of humor called up to lighten what she said. As if she were waking him up in the morning at the boy-time of his life, she said, "Now, Johnny, come on. Come *on,* Johnny." I could hear, as if the boy had answered, the voice I remembered from school mornings. "Oh, mother, let me be. Let me *be,*" and hear her seldom light laugh as he rolled over to sleep again. It was in the years that I, growing to ten, eleven, twelve, heard that lightness in her most often. She would say, proud and joking, "Johnny, you look just like a statue I saw once—a statue of an angel." Or, suddenly stopping whatever she was doing when he sauntered through the high, dark living room of the River Street house, she would pour her praise after him, letting him hear. "He'd make a wonderful hussar, wouldn't he, Hannah?"

Later, as he tipped over the balance of sexless beauty into his escape to manhood, she would follow him with disappointed glances when he would disappear from the house, as if one sad look could reel him back, caught on her lifeline like a fish. As the door behind him slammed she would say sadly, tinged with worry, "I *don't* know what happens." From time to time she would see flickers of what she had lost, see only that in him again, let her worry change to wonder and live again, as she did when she found the Bible on his bedside table and told Aunt Annie in front of Johnny, "He's *very* religious . . ."

She touched the hand that lay along the brown hospital blanket. His body, aloof in its coma, rejected her; she let the limp white hand drop.

[ 101 ]

"He doesn't know me. He doesn't know me," she cried to father. For once, he didn't notice her. He too was watching the impersonal face, his lips trembling. It was Father MacAndrews who took her shoulder and muttered, "Sally, do you want me to pray?" He was gruff with embarrassment, but when she nodded, dumbly, he expanded, laid his hand, as professional and strong as the nurse's had been, on Johnny's head, over his staring eyes. He knelt; mother knelt beside him. I felt myself sinking down with them, and heard father, behind me, sigh and creak as he got down to his knees. Only the nurse, ignoring us, went on watching Johnny's face and the instruments that were connected from his dying to the world, as if we were not there.

"O blessed Redeemer . . ." Father MacAndrews spoke softly into Johnny's unhearing, bandaged head. "Relieve, we beseech thee by thy indwelling power, the distress of this thy servant."

I, alone in my praying body, seeing darkness, begging toward his prayer, heard my mother sigh and change her position.

"Release him from sin and drive away all pain of soul and body, that being restored to soundness of health . . ."

Were we praying for Johnny or for his fragmented reflection in each of our eyes, the need and dependence of each separate man that gaped and yawned in that night room? Could God have answered the corrupting demands we made there—father for son and heir of his way of living; mother for angel-boy, conjured up innocent and dream-pure to her dictation; I for mirror-brother holding my hand, twin-flying, his legs free in the air before his fall? Did anyone pray for the man who lay there, essential, unknown, unrecognized?

"That he may offer thee praise and thanksgiving; who livest and reignest with the Father and the Holy Ghost, one God, world without end."

We murmured Amen. Then there was only Johnny's breathing. We moved all at once, mother like a blind child treading dark womb-water toward me, the nearest in looks to him. Stripped of loyalty or wisdom, she was wandering toward me as his replacement, not for him, but for what he had been to her. Her head came to my shoulder and lay there.

"I'll have to take her home," father said and detached her from me.

". . . in case he wants to tell me something. I'm sure he'll tell me something." She ended her hope to father, wanting Johnny not to keep even his dying secret from her. I could hear them as they left, Father MacAndrews tensed beside them to catch their need. Father said, "They'll let us know when he comes to. Now you sleep."

"I'll sleep. I have faith," my mother told him, obedient.

Then between Freddie and the nurse Johnny became sick body and duty again. Freddie consulted the chart and gave the nurse new orders. I sank into the armchair at the foot of Johnny's bed out of sight of their work, in the dark. I didn't know Freddie was leaving until he touched my hand.

"Hannah," he said, "why don't you get some sleep? There's nothing you can do here." I shook my head without looking at him and he was gone.

The night stretched on, as flat and dumb and cold as Johnny lying between the nurse and me, staring, staring at the ceiling, unseeing, disconnected from any of us, the incessant drawing in of air like a huge gadfly caught between the walls. Once he moaned, and the nurse and I both jumped up, but the lamp was still reflected in his unwinking eyes. It was only an animal moan from somewhere deep in his body.

In the language which is as deep as myth and does not lie, "patients" do sink, and they are patient. Hour by hour I watched Johnny sink, his face blood ebb without returning, his body flatten, heavier and heavier, sinking into the bed, patient under the burden of dying. He no longer fought for breath but allowed it in, faintly, delicately panting, not breathing enough to keep a bird alive.

I must have slept again, as I had only the night before, waiting for him to call. I remember hearing the clock on the Coal Trust Building strike four o'clock, hollow over the sleeping valley.

At seven o'clock Melinda was in the room, and the new sun drenched the sheets and her brisk blue linen dress. She ordered me home to bed. "We will let you know if there's any change for the worse," she said abstractedly, already slipped into hospital character.

As I went away I could hear her questioning the nurse about the state of Johnny's faintly but steadily ebbing body in her must strident, efficient voice. Later, I waited in my own bed without sleep and watched the flowered and latticed cage of the wallpaper. Far away a power mower ripped the Labor Day air. Mother had revived and was moving about downstairs, insisting that Minnie Mae let her dust.

"I like to do it myself," I heard her say. "It takes my mind off things." Furniture rolled across the living-room floor. There was a dry tinkle of glasses being put carefully away. At eleven o'clock the telephone rang. Its shrill call shot through my waiting. At the top of the stairs I leaned down over the banister to hear what mother said.

"Did he say anything?" she asked calmly and then crumbled in a little heap on the green hall rug, her dust rag still clutched in hand.

Johnny had finally escaped whatever kind of love we were capable of offering him.

★　　　★　　　★　　　★

# Chapter Six

Iᴛ ᴡᴀs late afternoon. I could hear the blinds sucking and sighing against the downriver afternoon breeze. I opened my eyes. Oh, damn him, Johnny was dead somewhere, lying in the same flat way on an impersonal narrow cot, all tension gone, sexless, leaving me high and salt-dry. A fly had been buzzing, maddeningly, before I slept. Now it had escaped and the room was vacuum empty of its insistence. I remembered that I had lain across the bed, dull, trancelike—that's all. I had been alone then. As I breathed awake I saw that there was a white hand with polished nails in front of my eyes. I looked up. Melinda sat on the bed edge, waiting. I had never seen her so still. She sat in a parody of the repose she had never known. We shared the dead blankness of the room and beyond it of the house, the unbearable, stolid brutishness of loss, anesthetized in it.

Nothing moved but the blinds, not the trees or the muscles of my heart. I lay, relieved of love, dullard-bodied. A howl began, tiny, and grew. I was slapped awake as if I were new-born, with all the anguish of a dirty trick played after the promises of safety, into the alien hard air of what had happened. I had been tricked by Johnny; that obscene, ludicrous death he served up, damned fool, unforgivable, shutting off so that he would not even be there to forgive, let live, let breathe, allow whatever we had been supposed to do, damned Johnny, self-sufficient sufferer, dirty trickster, giving me nothing in the past to recall and face death with. He had served us with a final flippancy, a mute stranger, an inanimate iron bench to crush his delicacy of brain and leave his body to fade down dying, go out, leave a blind sucking, a day like other days, damned with indifference, that most pure damning.

Sounds entered the room at last, dulled. I could hear mother in Johnny's room, looking for something. A drawer thudded on the floor.

Melinda jumped up. "I told her not to. I told her she was supposed to stay in her room." She wandered over and lifted the window blind, letting in the late afternoon sun.

"I'll go and see." I sat up, full of weight.

Melinda stopped me. "Wait a minute. I've got to talk to somebody."

I couldn't see her face, only the blind cord still swinging in her hand. She'd forgotten to drop it.

"Haley's answering the door. Ann Randolph's writing down people's names . . . close friends . . ."

I realized then that the downstairs hummed with people, tiptoeing, whispering.

"We have to go down. Mother has to stay in her room. She shouldn't see people, except of course a few close friends."

"Have you made a guest list?" I was empty, drained of everything except disgust at the beginning of the inevitable formalities as the selected hid the body, the hopeless fragment of Johnny, as the rules for death took over. The guests of death in Canona moved slowly and lightly, those who wrote names at the door, those father would take into the library for a drink, all permeated with the solemn embarrassment which was our dry substitute for mourning Johnny's soul.

And we would be watched to see how we were taking it, calm demanded; no embarrassing show of grief or knowledge, except in a still face where seemly feeling, controlled, could be read and commented on as the cars started outside; no one to disobey the rules and take our hurt hands.

"Oh, Jesus!" I got up. It might have been a cry of prayer, even dimmed as I was, but Melinda took it for swearing.

"Hannah, please, don't *do* anything." Melinda turned around. I saw that she was afraid and that her face was drenched in tears, calling me to her. But when I went she moved away and sat holding her own hands hard, perched at my dressing table. Her slumped back pushed me away.

Mother shut Johnny's closet door.

Melinda cried out, "Make her *stop!*" Her tight fist crashed down among the "old" perfume bottles mother kept and called my "collection." "Spud's down seeing to—he's down at the funeral home." Her mind leaped for safety, her voice scrabbled at it, clutched. ". . . Bess Everett is there taking names. She's new but she's all right. They ride. They go to Aiken. They're nice. Business people go to the funeral home, and church people that you know in church but don't have much in common with . . ."

Finally I burst out of the stupor. "Melinda, shut up!" My mouth began to stretch. "Don't do anything. Don't say anything. Don't rock the boat. You talk like you don't even know what's happened."

"Be quiet, Hannah, there are people downstairs." Melinda's voice was sure. She didn't know how to deal with words—she hadn't heard mine—she had heard only the tone, and that was too naked, too loud.

"Don't you want to know *why?*" I pulled at her arm.

"I don't want to know anything. I have to live here," she said calmly, the most honest words I had ever heard her say. She smoothed her black dress and frowned. "It's a Trigère dress. Do you think it's too . . . ?" She submerged the neural touching of her mind and left the knowledge only in her small, fearing eyes, and walked out of the room, shutting the door behind her.

The world had put one tentacle almost into the door. It caught her in the hall. I heard a woman's voice. "Somebody ought to sit with the mother."

"I think mother would like to be alone for a little while," Melinda said coolly. The tentacle receded down the polished stairs. The woman had not been one of the tacit list who could be "brought in to speak to mother." Her rules for death had had that damning subtle difference—in our set nobody "sat with the mother," nobody "viewed the body," nobody cried, nobody got drunk, and nobody stayed over fifteen minutes. Nobody rocked the boat.

Melinda went into Johnny's room. What happened between them I don't know. The door reopened as I opened mine. Melinda was leading mother toward her room. Mother was shuffling in a flat, calm doldrum, to sit queenlike in her room with the beams of Canona's kind of mourning focused on her, insistent.

"I was only looking for something," she explained, her face and voice dry and matter-of-fact.

"We'll find it for you later. Now come on." Melinda steered her firmly across the hall.

Mother balked at the door. "I don't want you. I want Annie," she told her and pushed at her body with tired flat hands.

Melinda's hard eyes weighed on mother until she willed her to sit down on her flowered chaise longue.

In the living room the wake went on and on, with little bursts of careful conversation, led by Melinda, obediently followed by the rest. She covered the silence when I came in by raising her voice, letting it flow, panicked, as she had in my room, telling the inevitable listener, Haley Potter, about a woman on a boat—she'd traveled on it and so had a woman whose friend she knew and the woman married a duke. No, they hadn't traveled at the same time, only on the same boat; the story reverberated among the silent women. What grief Melinda had I could not weigh, touch to heal, as one can honest grief; it had simply set off a chain reaction, as if she drew a possibility of life only in vague connections. I heard her behind me, starting the story again to a new woman about the friend of her friend who'd married a duke and had traveled on the same boat—no, not at the same time. She seemed, as they say at such times, to find comfort in it.

When I turned I saw that the woman was Kitty Puss Baseheart. She watched Melinda, not listening. When she saw me she brushed Melinda aside.

"For God's sake, Hannah . . ." She didn't say any more. We stared at each other, each reading the other's grief, the room as poised as if a bomb were going off. Finally Kitty Puss said, trying to grin, "How's life in New York?" She sat down beside a woman on the sofa, who whispered, "Oh, Kitty Puss, can't you forget about sex at a time like this?"

Kitty Puss put the cigarette into her teeth that she seemed undressed without. When she lit it I read "Mountain View Motel" on the dirty book of matches she threw down on the table beside her. She didn't answer.

I had so forgotten that obsession of frigid women that I didn't connect the remarks then. Melinda rushed over to them and asked Kitty Puss loudly and sternly about the Fuel Meeting. It was only one of her thousand acts of shoring up tears or words. She was willing the days to Johnny's funeral to be savagely correct to make up for the obscene manner of his dying; the manner of his dying was the only truth we had that was his own. I managed to get out of the room.

At the library door I heard father say, "Thank you," to a man— that sad shutting-off thank you to someone who had come too near to sympathy.

"Come on in, Hannah," Plain George called out softly. "Can

I get you a drink, honey?" He led me over to where a small bar had been set like an altar on the library table. There were vaster patches of silence among the men. Silence had sustained them through all the labyrinthine training which had brought them to the library to swing ice in glasses over Johnny's memory. It kept on sustaining them, except when Plain George spoke quietly to father, and I knew that what had happened was a little nearer the surface.

"Do you know anything about the man?" His whisper carried through the room.

"Some redneck poor white," father said. "Out-of-work miner . . ."

"It was an accident," Uncle J. D. Cutwright said as if that was the end of the matter.

"He'll get ten years," someone said at the bar.

"He'll get ten years," someone else said as if the words didn't still hang in the air.

I could find no whys there where none were asked. Only Jack had told me any truth, and I had to find out why.

I ran into the kitchen. Minnie Mae sat huddled and crying, like a child in my world, but in others like any human being melted by grief and pity. I, starved dry, watched her, jealous, not knowing how to do that.

"Minnie Mae, have you told Jack?" I held her shoulder.

"Toey," she corrected me gently, reminding me where we were.

I reached for the wall telephone and then remembered, cold with exposure, that I didn't remember his last name. I looked mutely at Minnie Mae; she read and answered.

"It's Lacey, Miss Hannah."

*My name is John Peregrine Lacey,* Jack had said.

Mother had told me how they took anybody's name, usually the people they had belonged to. She had told it so often she had blotted the name out of my mind.

"Is he on duty?"

Minnie Mae nodded.

"Jack . . ." I found his voice at last. "Do you know about Johnny?"

He was as hard as justice. "We've changed the charge. Involuntary manslaughter."

"What's the bail?"

"Ten thousand. He couldn't raise ten bucks."

"It's that high?"

"Lot of important people mad . . ."

"I'm coming down . . ."

"Don't."

"You made a promise."

He didn't answer for so long I thought he had hung up. Somebody, without listening, had started to dial the telephone someplace else in the house.

"You can come down. I still don't see—oh, maybe I do."

"I'll be down as soon as I can get away."

There was a little pop of an "oh" where a woman had been listening.

Melinda was waiting for me in the hall, still a sturdy, golf-playing Horatius, still holding the middle-class bridge against the untoward.

"Hannah," she whispered, "Kitty Puss picked up the phone and said you were making a *date*. She told *everybody*."

"Sure, Melinda," I whispered back to her, "there's nothing like a fuck at a funeral." Since both love and death in any undress were the only obscenities she knew, she shut up long enough for me to get out of the house.

It was five o'clock, silent tea time; the trees were yellow in the last warm daylight before blue evening, a calm time when people were in their houses or on their lawns and the neighborhood children caught the drift of day ending and rode their bicycles quietly. Far down the drive at the end of the trees a boy balanced on one foot from his bicycle, staring up at our house, the evening paper folded in his hand, wondering how to deliver it where there was an unusually muted house front and a long line of cars, but no noise of a party. Finally he laid the paper reverently in the center of the driveway where the cars would run over it.

I found Johnny's car. I could not remember driving it home at first, then I remembered Melinda telling me to.

My father ran out and clutched at the car window before I could maneuver from among the shining line of large cars parked up the arc of our driveway. He said, using the words he'd found the last time he'd given me an order, when I was sixteen, "Young lady, come back in this house. Melinda's . . ."

I tried to shake him off. He opened the door and got in beside me.

"Do you think it's easy for any of us, Hannah?" He didn't look at me.

It was my time to say sorry, my time to carry through with the expected, asking nothing, making Johnny's death even more absurd and useless than it was already—his double death, the one of son, brother, lover, friend, and the one of secret Johnny.

"Johnny's dead. I don't have to keep quiet any longer," I told, not my father, but myself.

"There are a lot of ins and outs, Hannah"—father choked and cleared his throat—"that you don't understand."

"Make me understand."

"Young people always expect . . ." He began again. "None of you women know what a man goes through . . ." I thought he was talking about Johnny, but he wasn't. He was talking about himself. "I tried to tell, but it wasn't a damn bit of use. Don't try. Don't be a fool." His face was harsh. He had turned away from me. I could hear mother's voice, so long ago, in the corridor at Egeria: *He made a fool of himself* . . . As if, still trying to be heard at the point where he had been shut off, had paid with silence, father said, "When I came back from the war . . . It was Armistice night in Paris . . ." Then he sighed, gave up, as if it were finally too late to say any more.

Like Spud's mortgage, Armistice night in Paris came always to the surface of father's mind in bad times. He remembered it as a great awakening for him, but that in him which clung to it as a rebirth and a homecoming had never fed on any other event. Sitting in Johnny's car and trying to bridge a great gulf from then to now, to me, even to death, was too much for him. The hurt and disappointed boy's eyes of that aging man, sunk in a weathered, apologetic face, remembered without words the youthful Armistice as one remembers having found all the answers in a dream, and on waking can't remember what they were.

"What can we do?" he asked finally.

Two ladies gave us a little fragile white-gloved wave, and we watched them church-walk toward the door.

I wanted to ask him, just for a moment of need, to be father, speak the word only, do what he had never tried to do since I was born.

I could hear Father MacAndrews muttering through the years, " 'Speak the word only . . .' " We muttered back, " '. . . and our souls shall be healed.' "

But I said, "You people might just begin by giving a damn."

Another pair of ladies church-walked out of the door, looked back tentatively, and went toward their car with their heads down.

"You always thought we didn't, Hannah. Your mother and I . . . you and Johnny. I've seen your mother's heart break over and over . . ."

"Your heart only breaks once. Once! Once! What you and mother thought was heartbreak was disappointment. For most people disappointment and embarrassment are the strongest emotions they ever know."

He had led me into impersonal abstraction, the last stronghold against the buffeting of Johnny's death. "When you care—oh, not what we did, but . . ." I tried to draw him back.

"We . . . I can't tell you anything . . ." Father's body was old that minute; he moved crabwise toward opening the car door.

"You could try," I begged, cold as ice.

"Has it ever occurred to you we don't know how?"

"You could learn. It's hard to learn." Tears sheeted my face and my father's face. We put our heads down like two conspirators when the door opened to let out two more ladies.

"Why didn't you ever say anything?" I was in my father's arms. I'd thought he was a big man, but under his jacket I could feel his ribs like bars and his heartbeat and his breath-sighs that didn't move the hard bars.

"Once you gave Johnny a present not like a Christmas present or birthday, just a present he didn't expect. Once you did it, unexpected, and he called me in California to get me to thank you—just to thank you. I was in California. We didn't have any words—there I was in California on the run and he called me all the way there."

Father's hand moved over and over my bowed head.

"You wouldn't say 'Hannah,' you would say 'no daughter of mine,' as if I were two people, so we were always two-faced. We had two faces, one for home, hearth and home, and one for whoever would take it for a little while. Oh, dear Christ"—words and tears flowed down father's darkest suit and over his thin legs—"we laughed once. It was just after I came home from, oh, whatever trouble it was that time you never wanted me to bring with me, it belonged to the other face so you and mother could behave as if it hadn't happened; that innocence that blankets everything, that nice-people way of not giving a damn. We wanted to stay home for once. It was a cold night. You retreated and mother thinned her mouth so no one would mention anything. Then it was too heavy and she said, 'I thought you children were going out.' We remembered we'd cleared the evening ahead of time by lying. So we had to go without any place to go. So we went to the Wayfaring Stranger. There were some kids from Slingsby Creek in the booth behind us and one of them had been arrested. He was telling the others, all quiet, about how he'd been caught. I don't remember even what he'd done. Oh, some arrogance that we're all bred to. After he'd finished the truth, somebody said, 'What did you tell the judge?' After that, Johnny and I, when we'd tell each other anything, would always end it with, *What did you tell the judge?* Two sets of stories to keep the peace. Anything to keep the peace. We had a rule, 'Thou shalt not get caught.' Hey, old Johnny got caught at last, didn't he?"

I watched my father's shoes, waiting for him to give some small absolution of understanding. Even if he'd demanded strength, called me "boom brat"—his name for our scurrying, evasive, self-pitying little generation—blasted me, I would have felt absolved.

His body creaked when he sighed. I knew it would come. I knew it would come, like his hand on my head. "Oh, honey," he said, "these things work themselves out."

I don't think he even knew he said it any more. I straightened up to wait for him to get out. What he had known no longer served him. He only looked exhausted and surprised.

"We, your mother and I . . . always gave you everything we wanted. To the best of our power, Hannah." He didn't hear his mistake—his confession. He got out of the car so slowly, so defeated, life in him so too late, not wanting me to stir him ever again by begging or by trying to help. He had seen the face of me and of Johnny that he hated and feared, and slowly he was trying to get away from it, back into the only soft safety he knew, where things took care of themselves and families loved each other. I had asked him questions he couldn't admit existed—much less their answers. I had asked too much of him.

"Father, I'm going down to the jail."

"You *can't*. A girl . . ." He tried to grasp some reins again and turned to forbid me.

"I'll be back soon. Nobody in there will notice," I reassured him. "Don't tell Melinda and Spud."

For one point of time there was a meeting of a daughter he hadn't met and a father I had suspected and yearned for but had so seldom seen—his other face, of a man who could make a fortune and run a mine but couldn't bring that part of himself home. It was the face of a man's private life. I knew then that it was mother's green, graceful dream we were living, not his. For peace or out of fear father had taken his false part in it, as we had.

"All right, girl, find out. You go find out." He tried to smile.

"Everything is going to work itself out," I said solemnly.

"Come back quick, honey. I need you," he told me and wandered toward the house. He had the awful walk of a man growing old among demands he was literally dying to ignore.

So I set out to ask why, the traveling word, the dream-splitter. I drove slowly off between the thick green planted lawns of our manicured hill and watched for the wet-haired children who, after swimming in parent pools, played and darted under the groomed trees before dinner, free of being organized for the little while of the cocktail hour, to play the play of generations, loose and wandering, taking sides, touching, fighting, hurting honestly.

A small boy squatted on the sidewalk, fastening his skates at the wrong time of their child year for skating, just to skate by himself through the amber time of evening. He stood up, found his balance, and looked around him as if the world had just been created.

★        ★        ★        ★

# Chapter Seven

THEN IT HAPPENED. I knew where I was going, I was setting out
on a whole trail of cleansing whys, beyond the jail, beyond Johnny's
death, beyond one small valley. I caught the child's wonder and
rippled off, leaving death behind, passed by the houses one after
the other that I knew as well as my own, high-tailing across the
river hill where the beds were too short for a man to stretch himself and the covering narrower than he could wrap himself in,
where too many sons had died while they were still sons, not men,
not father yet, not even old Adam, except in secret. There was not
an envied ivied front with its safe rhododendron religion where
some man did not have to change his face as he changed his shirt
when he came home to dinner, where sex sang no good ways to love
and live daily but sneaked and whimpered in pipe dreams or hidden places.

I was off to find Johnny's faces before they all faded, hum-
drummed out of the minds, and see if there was one face of his
and of mine, because death too soon was a serious business, a
plague. The blood price for the standard we lived in was getting

too high. Where the search would lead me I didn't know. It seemed at that point to lead through the man in the jail if he would let me in.

Down at the hill point overlooking the bridge and the dark river, I slowed to enter the town. After the small cluster of hill homes it looked big, unknown, full of people whose lives spewed all along the narrow banks, forgetting us, bigger than we were, knowing something I didn't. I crossed the bridge where the western sun made the water shine.

At the jail I had expected to find a shirt-tail hill boy, slim and mean as a rattlesnake, a Saturday-night hell-raiser, a car-roller, nigger-hater, tire-stealer—that would have been easy, fitted the pattern. But what I saw was a tall, quiet man, neater in movement, slower.

Jake Catlett leaned on the jail window sill, watching downriver through the bars. He had a patient waiting back. When Jack opened the cell door he didn't look around or speak, even when Jack said, "Somebody to see you," and then, "Catlett, you got a visitor." I saw his back arch as Jack walked toward him.

"Let me talk to him by myself," I whispered.

Then he turned around. He had black eyes under heavy brows, the hate or grief in them so deep it could have been mistaken for aloofness. His face was gaunt and made without fat, his black hair fell long on his neck, the sideburns made his cheeks hollow. He needed a shave. He was spare-boned, straight, skinny as a rake, his head jutted forward as he took me in slowly, then Jack, and said, low, like a man not used to speaking, "I ain't got nuthin' to say to nobody."

I was afraid Jack would ruin the calm, make the man retreat still further into the isolated mountain of himself he looked out from.

"Can I talk for a minute, by myself?" I begged.

Jack knew when he was shut out. He made one last try. "Okay, Catlett, you're in enough trouble."

"I ain't gone bother no lady," Jake Catlett told him.

We could hear the rattle of Jack's steps as he went across the iron floor and clanged the outside cell door, stopped within hearing in case I raised my voice.

There was nothing in the cell. Like any other cage, it had bars; the sun drew them in great shadows down the cell block across the sleeping face of a man in the next cell. It smelled of urine and Lysol. I think we stood for five minutes, watching each other, I knowing better than to lead this man, animal caught, wary and still. What had happened did not show with him. He was just waiting, shut away from the river; he kept on glancing at it, clenching and unclenching his long spare hands.

"You from the newspaper?" he finally asked.

"No." I sank down on the end of the rack, becoming small, obliterating anything to rouse his distrust, because he had to tell me what he didn't know himself. I was in an agony of guile, waiting to take him in like a river to begin to find Johnny's death.

"What ye come hyar fer?" His voice came on strong. He was rooted out, ground-hog cornered.

"Catlett, shut up." The man in the next cell turned over and went to sleep again.

"Don't pay no 'tention to him. He's full of sweet lucy." Jake Catlett stared at the man's scrap-bag back.

"It was my brother," I whispered.

He looked at me as he would look at a wounded or frightened animal. I, stone-cold, willed him to it harder, using everything I'd lady-learned.

"I never meant to," he muttered. "I never knowed he was your brother."

I watched him.

"Look, lady. I never meant nuthin'. Why, I'm forty-five years old. I never done nuthin' like taken on to scrap like that since I was a boy. You . . ."

"Tell me!" I had to force him back to the point he didn't know, where it had to begin, like Johnny's living dead men and father's Armistice and Spud's mortgage, the key place, the point, the place where a man stopped and pivoted.

Jake Catlett sank down on the rack beside me and put his gaunt head between strong hands that could work a coal face, hold a woman hard by the shoulders, or hit Johnny. The black hair on the sunburned backs of his fists stood out from their clenching.

"Lady, why can't you git out of here and leave me be? It's bad enough takin' orders from a nigger without no woman after me. You'd reckon at least in jail you'd get quit . . ."

We sat so long that the outdoor sounds came in and surrounded us: the beep of a car horn, across the river the whistle of Number 6 as it drew out to go west. We were getting used to the smell of each other, animal-trusting a little more. The time tightened into the insistence between two people dwelling in the same needs— he to tell, me to learn. I had a dim urge to take his hand because we were growing toward each other while he traveled silently toward that point, the one way back.

I broke the tightning stillness. "I heard he said something."

We sat together, looking at the floor.

When he did begin to speak his voice was gentle, storytelling, thinking. He seemed to have forgotten I was sister, woman. "I been settin' here figurin'—goin' over and over it. He was just standin' there, and that feller kept callin' on Jesus—I figured I had to shut him up, leave me time to think. Gawd knows, I needed it even if I had to get locked up. That old man kept on and on—*he's* just lookin' out through them bars. I seen his face and his clean white coat in the light from the toilet. That was over at the City before they moved me over to the County. This here is the County. I ain't never been to jail before. . . . Gawd, when I think about Mamie and maw . . ."

He stopped for a minute, then came back from his thinking. "I reckon I flew red. Couldn't nothin' be done to shut that old feller up. *He's* the only one I could see. I took and hit him one and he—

you know, when you shoot, a bird hit seems to linger in the air for the longest time only t'ain't more'n a second. I think I hit him twicet. I seen him standin' before he fell and he looked kind of surprised. Then he said, 'Thank you.' He said a real quiet thank you, and just sighed down on the floor and hit that arn rack. I figured he was jokin' when he said that. I never hit him hard. Just blowed off the last of my steam. I figured he's makin' fun of the rest of us . . ."

"How long had you been standing there looking at Johnny before you hit him?" It was such a curious question, not what I had meant to ask to draw him to what had exploded behind his fist—not one jug of red-eye, but the power behind that.

"Jest about all my life." He looked at me then.

I began to laugh. It insulted him. "You hit the wrong man," I said. I managed to stop laughing.

"Y'ought to be ashamed of yourself. Settin' there grinnin' with your brother not cold in his grave. I can sure see you two are brother and sister."

"That's the trouble with all you damned people who strike out blind. Your fist is packed for an enemy so you hit the first person who looks like him."

"Ain't no use in your a-comin' in here cussin' and swearin'. You people make me sick. When you spit you hawk coal dust same as us'n." He was taking the bandage of wariness and grief and surprise from his eyes, and they showed clear, clean hate—lit up with it—something honest to deal with.

"What got you into it, Jake? What put the chip on your shoulder?" I questioned fast, before he could retreat again.

He sat down. That curious tenderness of quiet men, even with the hate there, made him put his hand on my shoulder. His grip was viselike.

"Now lookee here, lady. I'm goin' to tell you. H'it's too late not to, ain't it?"

"Yeah, it's too late not to." Our hands had the same shape.

"I've jest about had enough. Here I end up with ten thousand dollars' bail and I ain't never had nuthin' in my damned life but a few acres of ridgeland and Mamie's womb and gawd knows ye cain't borry money on them thar. Looks like a man works hard all his damn life and things are goin' along all but Mamie's womb."

He folded his hands in his lap and told himself the story, as he seemed to have told it forever, over and over. "Mamie come to Jesus and got to gittin' sick along about the same time. She had fifteen operations, that purty little gal; she come from up around Beulah—Slavish people. Come here in the mines. Ever' time she'd git in the hospital she'd git purty as she ever wuz. Then she'd come home and git drug down agin and takin' to goin' to bear witness on Wednesdays, gittin' up thar in public tellin' how she had all them operations and come to Jesus and that thar womb of hers must'a had a rock in it that couldn't nobody find start in to draggin' her down again, that thing must'a weighed a ton." He paused long enough to fetch a deep sigh. "Then this July the union ruled you couldn't have no Number Eight fer the hospital unemployed over a year. I'se out of work one year last Saturday, that damn Number Eight wuz all we had worth somethin'. I'se a good coal-face man. I been makin' coal up and down this here valley since I'se fifteen years old." He remembered me and accused, "They ain't a damn thing, ain't even that purty dress on your back didn't come off the coal face and don't ye fergit it. You people puttin' on to ack high and mighty. Lissen here—lissen here . . ."

From his own coal face all the way down his life he was getting to Johnny. But his voice had dropped so low that what he had to say ran out toward the floor and I had to lean almost into his lap. He didn't even notice, for he was no longer talking to me. Some way I had released the beginning of what had happened.

"We're good people. Come from upriver, up around Beulah. Sold out up thar in paw's time. We knowed the coal face better'n anybody. Paw said the seam was runnin' out and we read out to move. Sold out paw's hill farm to the company thirty years ago.

Hit was up behind the Mansion. We'z some kin to them Neills. H'ain't nary a thing left now. They done stripped it. We come down here and paw bought a little piece of property. Old Carver place . . ."

I could see the hill farm at Beulah, the neglected fall field rippling, the lespedeza, the orchard covey wurtling in the air, before it was all thrown away, stripped down to bedrock like this man's face, this distant cousin stranger.

"Things was purty good." He sighed. "Didn't look to us'n like no end to it. I'se makin' a livin'—workin' the farm when I come home. Them ridges around, waren't no people to bother us'n. We had the house white-warshed. I don't know what happened. There wudn't nuthin' wrong with the coal. Hit was fetchin' a good price. We had some labor trouble. Last time we come out on strike, I'se workin' for the Cornstalk Colleries then, last time we come out, the Cincinnati Company and the union got together and sold us out— put in machines. I ain't never been much fer machines so I got laid off. They's eighteen hunderd men workin' fer the mine. Now they's five hundred. They's runnin' more coal out of there than they ever done. We never knowed what hit us . . ."

"Shut up, Catlett." The man on the next rack turned over again. "You been talkin' to yourself for two days in thar."

Jake Catlett didn't pay any attention. He was figuring out; I knew it was the same story, as he went through the facts, that he had told himself as he sat on his front stoop or tended his garden or waited for a squirrel to flirt down a tree trunk, trying to find out what happened.

"Mamie's womb got turble. Five thousand dollars' worth of serious operations at the UMW hospital—that's the only thing we got now worth a cent. Y'ask me why we don't pick up and git out. We got no place to go. Not with Mamie sick like that and maw won't move three feet down the road. I tried to raise a mortgage on the place; they's a feller name of Potter wanted to buy it but maw set her foot down, said she'd moved fer enough. He wudn't goin'

[ 123 ]

to give nuthin' nohow. Figured we never knowed nuthin' about the value of property. Well, what little we'd saved up went. Maw said she'd wish she'd died before she ever seen the day we's on molly-grub again. She and paw'd just set thar in the kitchen and Mamie give up. They'd set thar watchin' the television waitin' fer me to do somethin'. Mamie got so she wasn't even keepin' the kids clean. What could a man do? I went to Dayton and I went to Akron and I rode a freight train to Detroit. They wudn't nuthin' thar. Them folks don't want us nohow.

"I got to goin' down every day, walkin' five miles down to Slingsby Street and five miles back, actin' like I'se some use in the world. Me'n them others standin' around shiftin' nails in our pockets and goin' off to collect a relief check make a man ashamed of himself, a strong man. Wouldn't of been quite so bad but nobody else seemed to bother about it. Wudn't like when I was a boy and everybody was broke so there wudn't so much feeling like you didn't belong no place. I'd stand there, watchin' them fancy cars and them lit-up store windows and readin' the paper over somebody's shoulder about how prosperous the country was. It was like it was all around me and nobody couldn't see me—like I was a ghost."

He was wandering along Slingsby Street where the jukeboxes blared and the stores shone, among the neon lights and the traffic stream. I left him silent until he was ready to speak again. I'd seen and not seen Jake Catlett so often, driven past his country eyes that watched the town as if it were a show, taking no part in it.

"One time some woman come up in one of them cars—last Christmas—with a basket. Maw tuck and run her off the place. She squawked out like an old chicken about us'n not apperciatin' nothin'. Run a tar-ridge right through my plowin'. Maw run her off all right. She run her off with a hoe.

"When you people come up and built that there golf club right in our faces, it was like them fancy cars was chasin' me right to my own doorstep. Not a covey on the place no more. Wouldn't even let us'n hunt squirrels on land we knowed ever' tree on. It wouldn't've been so bad if we didn't feel like we'd been plowed under like a bad crop. Even tuckin' the creek and puttin' it down t'uther way. My kids was run off when they wanted to go a-wadin'."

Beyond the highest green, where the hills stretched away in the distance, there had seemed to be no one. Their houses were hidden along the creeks, nestled in the hollow heads, houses like lairs, where they looked out straight and still, saying nothing, trusting no one.

"We didn't know," I muttered. It made a long echo from Johnny's voice fifteen years ago to a man's fist with its black hairs catching the late sun and me cold with knowledge as a stone. Johnny had said thank you, and once he'd said he was ashamed to be a member of the human race.

Jake Catlett sighed again as if so much talk hurt. ". . . layin' under a tree like hawgs eatin' chestnuts and never look up to see whar they come from . . ." He straightened up as if part of the story had ended and he was a new man.

"It was Saturday night and thar wudn't nuthin' to do, so I got drunk. That's what I done. I taken two dollars out of Mamie's relief money—twenty-five dollars a week. I taken two dollars and bought me a pint, then when h'it got dark and I was damn sick and tard of listenin' to maw and paw and Mamie settin' thar complainin' because the television broke and we didn't have no money to git hit fixed and them snotty-nose kids was a-bawlin' around the place because the truck wouldn't go without no gas and I couldn't ride 'em downtown to see the sights. I taken my bottle and I walked along the ridge. H'it was the blackest hot night but I knowed ever' foot. Only oncet I fell in one of them fool sand-traps and purt near broke my pint. I'se headin' fer a tree I knowed—squirrel tree—I'se been settin' watchin' that tree sincet I don't know whin. I'se a boy. Knowed ever' mark on her—big sycamore . . ."

Like most silent men, Jake Catlett didn't stop once he started. He just went his own way in words, sometimes pacing up and down the cell, sometimes coming back to me and sitting with his chin on his fists, watching the river through the bars, letting his dark face bathe in the gold evening sun.

"I knowed whur I'se goin' all right. Done more figurin' thar thin anywheres else. I'd about got out of yearshot of my own people and into about a quarter of a mile of dark and peace and quiet when I seen the sky lit up pink like a bowl ahead of me and I hyeared music. The light and the music was comin' from the clubhouse.

"I snuck up under my tree and jest set thar, drinkin' my pint and watchin'. Hit wuz the purtiest thing y'ever seen. They'se a big floodlight out ahead of me lit up that big porch like a television show. They's just like butterflies all flutterin' around down thar, different colors in the light. They had them candles on all the tables. Ever' oncet in a while they'd all go inside and you could see 'em just a-whirlin' around in thar dancin' behind that big square glass front. I wish't fer a minute Mamie could see hit. She used to be the purtiest thing, didn't have no religion or nuthin', just purty.

"I never done no figurin' or nothin', reckon I'se plumb figured out—jest a-settin' thar under my own tree drinkin' my own pint. Down thar in front of me this big swimmin' pool was layin' quiet, all lit inside. I'se gittin' purty lit inside too. I must'a been because I fergot everythin' and got to actin' like h'it really was a television. I got up and went and stood in front of the floodlight and my shadow stretched right down across't the pool and along the porch. I had a giant shadow. I puttin' my shadow hands up on both sides of that big square of glass and acted like I'se turnin' hit, only hit never turned. I'se big as a mountain stretched down thar with my shadow playin' with that whole big glass front like hit wuz a toy. Then I needed another drink. When I hunkered down agin they wudn't but one left in my pint. I taken it and rared back.

"Somethin' happened. They all come out in a bunch fer a while. I seen they wuz settin' thar drinkin' enough licker to keep us fer a year and me up thar under my own tree without even a drink left in my damn pint."

The man in the next cell had sat up and was listening to Jake's story without a sound.

"I'se beginnin' to git mad. 'Cause I'se drunk. Whin they all went inside agin in a bunch . . ."

I could see Johnny, neat, handsome Johnny, leading Cornstalk Collieries in, making sex manners for a Saturday night; from Jake Catlett's tree I could see them, small as pretty insects.

"I got up and went down in front of the floodlight agin. I'se lonesome. I wanted somebody to notice me. Hit wudn't nuthin' but that thar. I never wanted nuthin' they had. I just wanted them to know I wuz thar. I knowed that land better'n they done and we'z in the same place, only that glass wall between. I danced that shadow around didn't even nobody look up out the winder."

"Johnny did," I was crying. "Johnny saw you and wanted to . . ."

He didn't hear me. It was his Saturday night and I wasn't there.

"So I run down to the swimmin' pool and lit into throwin' them chairs and mattresses and stuff in the water. Jest run around throwed 'em in and the water wuz splashin' and a hell of a racket. By Gawd, they noticed me then, and some of them fancy men didn't look like they could button their own pants come a-runnin' so I lit out through the woods. They wudn't a one of 'em could of follered me. I come on down to Slingsby Street to look at the lights and jest wander around. Somethin' had broke loose in me and I didn't want to go home and didn't want to figure nor nuthin'. Jest one night, please God, I wanted not to listen to nobody. I figured I'd lay out all night on account of Mamie. She don't hold with no licker. I hadn't backslid for so damn long—two, three years. Then the squad car started to followin' me and I got an idea. Hit wuz like the hand of Gawd, sister. I figured if they picked me up, if I done enough, Mamie and maw and paw could git on the D. P. and A. If they ain't no man hit's the law." When he saw my face he added, "Hell, the state penitentiary's full of men, better for their families they'se in jail, so they tuck and went. I knowed thin hit was go to jail or go home, one. So I found me a brick and heaved hit through the window of the Slingsby Hotel. They wudn't nobody settin' behind it so I couldn't hurt nobody.

"I put up a purty good fight when they tried to take me in. I'se stone-cold sober by thin but I still couldn't take to them layin' hands on me. A man's got his pride . . ."

He ran down and put his head back in his hands.

"What can I do?" I tried to touch his arm, but he drew away.

"You? Nuthin'." He muttered, "Jest leave me alone, lady."

"My name's Hannah."

"So's my maw's. Family name. Come out the Bible."

"Does Mamie know?"

"No, honey, she don't know. She'll figure I'se off lookin' fer work. Ain't no way to tell her nohow."

"I'll phone."

He smiled then, very slowly, and talked to me the way you talk to a fool, carefully. "Listen, Hannar, go back to that thar Cadillac cradle you're livin' in and leave us'n alone. We ain't got no *phone!*" He began to think again, shutting me out. "We had a phone, though. We had one . . . Swear to God, Mamie never got off the damn thing . . ."

"I'll go up there." He was making me beg to help him and I could feel the ire rise.

"Aw, whuddaye want?" He shook me away and went to the window again. This time he put both hands on the bars and seemed to hang there until his knuckles were white. "What's the matter with you people? Hit was your brother. You ain't even got guts enough to hate me."

It was my turn to get mountain mad at that shut-off damn poor white face, arrogant as a dirt-farm mule. I jumped up and could feel my nails biting into my palms, and I hoped I'd stay mad enough not to cry.

"I'm sick and tired of brother," I yelled at him. "You talk about us not giving a damn. You people won't walk across the hollow to help a stranger. Let people ride rough-shod over you and you just back a little further up your hills or take it out on the niggers because you haven't real guts enough . . ."

We faced each other, the razorback bone of the country, me stripped from the topsoil of training down to rock pride too, like the hill farm. Then I heard myself, "sick and tired of brother." I was free of the brother part of Johnny. If it was kinship that held me there, stark-stiff with the whole mess, the crisscross hatreds, if it was brothers that held me loving, I had more of them than a dog had fleas, a whole hard valley of brothers.

"We don't ask nuthin' of you." Jake Catlett tried to shut away.

"You're damn right you don't. You'd rather hate. You'd rather live on your rock-farm pride. You don't even love your people enough to let me . . ."

"Love, Hannar? Go back to the damned picture-show! I'm kneelin' down thankin' God I'm in jail fer 'em, ain't I? What do you want?"

Somebody down at the end of the cell block started clamoring at the bars. "Quit that hollerin' . . ."

Jack came running, yelling, "All right, Catlett, that's enough."

"He didn't do anything." I turned around and hollered at Jack.

"Well, I'll be, Miss Sissy. 'Bout time you got mad." Jack grinned, admiring.

"She sure did." Jake was smiling too when I looked back to go on fighting.

"All right." Jake Catlett came and took my arm. "Go on up and see Mamie. She'd be mighty grateful to ye."

Jack unlocked the cell to let me out. When I turned to say goodby, Jake Catlett stood straight as a man should, wherever he was, and he watched me under the porch of his brows, every inch an old American dream in his strong face. Then he asked one favor.

"You kin find out one thing fer me," he said as if he were doing me a kindness. "Find out if I kin vote in hyar. I don't know what the law is on that, and I sure want to vote. I been a Democrat all my life but *this* time I'm gonna vote."

So Abraham Lincoln Andrew Jackson Catlett stood there stone-faced in the last place he could find in the valley to look after his family, behind the bars of the county jail, and I told him I'd find out.

Jack grinned all the way down the iron grill stairs with me. "Hannah," he told me when he put me in the car, "Johnny'd be proud of you. If you want to come over and sit with me and Irma, ma'll tell you where we are."

The sun had gone downriver when I recrossed the bridge, avoiding the long road up to the hill houses, dark against the evening sky—the Wilsons', mother's, Melinda's, isolated monoliths standing sentinel over the valley, their windows blind. I turned away up the south hollow road, by myself and all alive, up the low road to the country club, to find the Catletts', having no idea what I could tell them. I drove with the face of Johnny, stranger, the man who was killed for the cut of his jib; it was a treasure hunt, the treasure an answer to a ridiculous question of death and train wrecks and all accidents. I knew who had held his spirit. I'd grown up with that; now I knew who hated him for what he stood for, not for what he was.

At the fork of Slingsby Creek the road turned left and began to climb the eroded ribs of Slingsby Ridge among the thin second-growth pines. It was dark under them. My lights put up a grouse ahead of me. I drove carefully up the winding dirt road through the woods Jake Catlett had found to be quiet in.

At the top of the ridge I broke out of the trees; the new golf course stretched across the ridge fingers, a dark silent lawn under the earliest purple of evening. Beyond the highest green I could see the thin pale lights of a deep-country house, appearing and disappearing through an orchard of gnarled old trees. The evening was as silent as after love along the flat top of the ridge where the grass was hard meadow grass, dark bronze in the last light, and the stalks in the cornfield beyond it shivered a little, September dry.

I guess I knew it before I asked. The Catletts' cabin squatted at the side of the dirt road beyond the orchard and the long neat furrows of the fall garden. A pickup truck jutted its rear halfway out of a corrugated iron shack. A long grape arbor of logs, heavy with grapes, led up to the low stoop of a porch across the cabin front. Neatly in front of the house two old tires from the truck had been whitewashed and filled with geraniums. Two small girls darted across the road in front of me, rolling a tire. Inner tubes for swimming hung on a nail on the cabin wall. The logs were huge, gray with age; a single virgin trunk thirty feet long ran under the steep roof. I jammed on my brakes even though I was slowing down and heard a high wail from the stoop.

"You youngins watch whur you're a-goin'." A skinny, bent woman ran out of the house, letting the screen door whang behind her. As I stopped the car and looked at her I saw that she was young enough to be the mother of the two girls, who now stood in front of the corrugated iron shack and watched me without surprise, letting their tire bound off down the hollow. I was surrounded by calm people watching and waiting for me to move. An old woman sat barefooted in a rocker on the stoop. She didn't stop fanning her great head with a huge arm—just watched. Beside her an old man had tipped a kitchen chair against the log wall. I saw that he had one leg. He was in his undershirt, but I noticed that his one shoe was highly polished and that he had a heavy watch chain across his neat pants. He wore an old Stetson hat as square on his head as if it were a uniform cap. His lips were covered by a large white mustache. He sat with his arms crossed on his thin chest, staring out over the hollow. He was the only one of them who didn't bother to look at me.

"Is this the Catlett . . ." I was going to say more, something, I don't know what. Their calm was a solid wall.

"Yes." Mamie Catlett eased herself down off the stoop and

walked slowly toward the car. I had to get out. When the two girls heard the door slam they spurted forward to inspect the fenders.

"You youngins git your dirty hands off'n thar," Mamie yelled at them without interest. The smaller one grinned wide across a square Slav face. Her imp eyes darted up at me.

"I'm Hannah McKarkle," I told Mamie.

She waited, crossing her arms.

"From up Beulah," I called beyond her to the old woman, who stopped fanning and rocking and began, not to smile, but to allow her face to take an interest.

"We're from up thar too," she told me.

"My mother"—I was crashing through the watchers toward the stoop—"was a Neill."

The old man tipped his chair down and peered at me. Only his eyes were snap-black alive; the rest of his face was like the logs, gray and dried out. "You Annie's girl?"

I remembered the language. "No, Sally's girl."

"Well, honey, come on up hyar and set down." Jake's mother opened the way to them without changing a muscle or line of her body. "Essie," she raised her voice toward the little girls, "go git my shoes." The older girl sidled past me in a run, her sad eyes taking me in. She had the thin, high-boned, pale face of an Anglo-Saxon beauty, but circumstance would carve her into an image of Mamie, not of me, though the child and I stood there in the evening in the high pass of the mountains and the only thing that made us strangers was not a deep difference in blood, but an accident, long past, of the inheritance of hill land and the inheritance of bottom land.

Mrs. Catlett went on telling me, "I'se jest settin' hyar gatherin' my breath; me and Mamie put up thirty quarts of beans today." The little girl knelt and put the shoes on her grandmother's feet. "Mamie, show Sally's girl what we done . . ."

"She was a right pretty little thing," the old man's memory interrupted.

"Who you talkin' about?" Mrs. Catlett didn't want to be interrupted.

"Little old Sally Brandon Neill, pretty as a picture. That wuz my cousin Jamie's girl."

"I know that," she snapped at him. They had forgotten us.

"I'se thar the night Jamie died. That girl froze up like to never come out of it. She married the McKarkle boy from up Greenbrier. He done right well fer hisself." Mr. Catlett remembered me. "How's your maw?"

"I have to tell you . . ."

"Well, set down, honey." Mrs. Catlett motioned to the second rocker and ordered me into it. I felt so small before the insistent calm of her great body that I wondered if my feet would touch the floor.

"Mamie, ain't there some coffee left? Git this gal somethin' to eat."

"I don't . . ." I tried to say.

But Mamie had disappeared into the cabin.

"I'm from up Fayette—name of Carver. This hyar was built by one of the Carvers," Mrs. Catlett told me.

"That was 1912. That was two years before I lost my leg. Load of mine props fell on me." Mr. Catlett looked out across the pass where, as far as they could see, the hills rolled in an infinite front yard. "Didn't have no pension in them days. But we had the hill farm at Beulah . . ."

"Jake . . ." I tried.

"He ain't hyar." Mrs. Catlett wouldn't let me go on. "You know your cousin Jake? He never told us'n. He's our least one. Born late. Jake ain't hyar. He's gone off to Ohio. He cain't find no work around hyar. If I told him oncet I told him a thousand times, thar ain't no call to worry. Things gits bad and thin times gits better. Just wait it out. Didn't I?" She turned to the old man to demand that he take her side, as she must have done in that incessant pounding at their dinner table, Jake sitting there, stony-faced as I had last seen him. Mr. Catlett was someplace of his own, the word bad times and the thought of my mother putting him back to the reality of the hill farm and Beulah and old days.

I wondered if Noah's mother had looked like Mrs. Catlett, large, habitual, and immovable, telling Noah not to mind about a little rain, that it was nothing to the rain they'd once had, and had gone on sitting there quite calmly with the flood up to her nose while Noah sneaked off to the Ark feeling guilty as hell. Those two, unmovable and stolid, had been carved by the past for an unsurprising present, a soft time, not like it was, never, good or bad, like it was. I began to see why Jake Catlett got his Saturday night pint.

Mamie was standing beside me, not saying a word. She had a cup of coffee in one hand and a slab of corn bread in the other.

We exchanged the burdens of the old woman's hospitality like conspirators.

"You say Jake . . . ?" Mamie ventured.

"He's . . ."

As if she sensed that something was wrong and didn't want to hear it until she was ready, Mrs. Catlett laid the phrases she was used to between us, cobwebbing over what I had to tell, as she would have used cobwebs to staunch a wound.

"Who'd ye marry?" she demanded.

"I'm not," I fenced with her. What if I had said, "Johnny and I marry? We've done everything but that"?

"That's too bad. Yore gittin' on." I could almost hear the laughter of the cool, refusing generation of my fast-moving friends at the perpetual good-sport Rover Boy I'd made of myself, turned on the spit by this enormous old censor of a woman.

"What do you do? Schoolteacher?"

"No, ma'am." If I'd told that old woman what any of us did, she'd have run me off with the hoe. I wondered which kind friend of mother's had been run off that way.

"We're kin through grandpaw," Mr. Catlett entered in from

where his mind was. "Jamie's maw Miss Liddy was my grand-paw's sister. Show her the pictures, Mamie."

"*She* don't want to see no pictures." Mrs. Catlett didn't have to glare at him. She just stated word-law.

While they waited to see which way I'd jump, a whippoorwill called from the sycamore away down in the depths of the darkening hollow; another answered it. A yellow dog crawled out from under the stoop and stretched along the walk. One of the little girls ran for it and the dog darted back under the porch.

"I'd like to," I said to Mamie. I thought if I could get her into the house I could tell her there.

She walked toward the door and I followed her, coffee, corn bread, and all.

"Show her the knife," Mr. Catlett called. "Come from the hill farm at Beulah."

The deep twilight made the tiny living room like a dark cell. There was a shadow of a door to the other room, dividing the cabin in half. Mamie snapped on a light. Its pink satin shade cast a warm glow as if it had been lit in a cave, and turned the last of the daylight to darkness through the open door, where the evening star and one other, lower, tiny one sprang out in the dark. A lightning bug attached itself to the screen. There was not a word from outside. They were listening.

I set the coffee and the corn bread down on the tatted tablecloth, and when Mamie saw the unconscious gesture she snapped, "Don't ye want it? That's all we got." Her voice grated, bitter, too low for the proud old queen of the mountain outside to hear. I sensed the edge of her perpetual complaint.

Mamie pointed from the light to the fireplace. She looked witch-like, bending over it and casting a great shadow over the double brass bed covered with its crazy quilt and up the wall where the wallpaper had faded to a mild tan and had begun to curl away from the window, dried like the logs and the old man's face.

Two stern, faded daguerreotypes hung side by side in brown oval

[ 135 ]

frames on jutting nails over a stone chimney that must have been
built before the cabin. It was black inside with age. It stood like a
great mud and stone altar, commanding the tiny room. The man
was dressed in a union uniform. He had a full beard. His eyes stared
over it, unyielding, whether because of the way of making the picture or his own sternness, I couldn't know. The woman beside him,
under the flyblown specks of age, looked vague and dim. She
looked straight at me, her head held high above her tight black collar, her hair skinned back, making her ears jut out. She looked still
scared, after all that time.

Mr. Catlett waited until he was sure I was as pinned by the pictures as I had been on the porch, by their stability and the squalid
surprise of kinship having been found by way of a cosmic, man-
killing joke.

"That thar's grandpaw Lewis Catlett. He'z in the Union
Army. He and the rest of them never seen eye to eye. That's what
grandmaw told me. She wuz from east Virginny somewheres. I
forgit whur. Me and your grandpaw Jamie got on jest fine. Mamie"
—his voice changed to an order—"show her the knife."

Mamie met me with a glance of annoyed patience. "I wish't
Jake'd come home," she muttered. "Them two never shuts up fer
a minute. Them youngins won't do nuthin' I tell 'em and I ain't
feelin' so good. I tell you, I'm just about at the end of my tether."
In the pink satin light her hair was still soft and blond, a halo. For
a second I could see the pretty girl. She knew I was looking, and it
made her brush it back and nearly smile, then turn away, shy.

"I'll git the knife," she said.

"Air ye a-gittin' hit?" Mr. Catlett called.

"I'm a-gittin' hit." Mamie slopped into the lean-to kitchen. She
brought it back and laid it in my hands.

"Take hit over't the light," Mr. Catlett called.

The Catlett family silver lay across my hands, its heavy silver
handle nearly black with corrosion. I could just trace the chasing
of a crest. As I brought it closer to see it, the knife overbalanced

and nearly slid out of my hands. The carving blade didn't equal the weight of the handle. I saw that it had been soldered in.

Mamie, over my shoulder, said, disinterested, "t'wudn't always a carvin' knife. Mr. Catlett done that—t'wuz more like a whip but that wore out."

"Grandpaw used to whup his grandsons with it when he could catch em." I heard a laugh from the dark porch that sounded ghostlike. "He said t'wuz a ridin' crop but I dunno."

"Mamie," I murmured to her, "I've got to tell you."

Our heads were together.

"Jake sent me up here. Now wait a minute." Her body had begun to move downward. "He's all right. He's down in the county jail."

She moaned once.

"He and my brother Johnny got picked up Saturday night." Mamie began to rock. "Oh, Jesus, fergive him fer backslidin' . . . oh, Jesus . . ."

"He hit Johnny. He didn't mean to. Johnny fell . . ."

"You two girls come right out hyar this minute!" Mrs. Catlett yelled at us, and we ran like children.

"Now what is all this?" She sat like a Buddha, four-square on great hams. I could see her head etched by the light from the door.

"Johnny hit his head on an iron rack. He died . . ." I was moaning and thought it was Mamie until I realized she was pulling me back into the rocker. Her hands fussed over me.

Mrs. Catlett's face went ash-white. I heard Mr. Catlett say, ". . . hit Sally's boy . . ."

"I'd like to know who he'd a hit been in the valley long enough wudn't some kin," Mrs. Catlett stopped looking at me. There was a pause as dead as Johnny on the stoop.

"I know Jake never meant nuthin'. He's a good boy," Mrs. Catlett told herself.

Mamie was rocking my rocker back and forth. It was the only way I knew she was there at all.

It was so still that I caught a false calm and let myself rock with Mamie's hand. "No," I told the hollow, not caring if anyone heard, "nobody ever means anything. But it happens. Nobody ever stops to *mean something*. That, oh . . ." I let my head fall back against the rim of the rocker; Mamie's hand crawled like a mouse and ran over my hair in little darting strokes. "That would take more caring than any of us give. We're not lazy people. We just have lazy hearts . . ."

We sat there on the stoop as if we'd known each other forever, letting the night fall over us. The first star hung in a royal purple sky, low in front of us. It was beginning. As the star was resurrected every night for the Catletts to watch, a resurrection of care as if Johnny had died to waken it was in me like my blood and I had to nurture it and keep it alive as an obligation for us all. When our pretense was stripped as mine had been by shock and sacrifice, it was the only nobility we had.

Mr. Catlett got up and grabbed his crutches. "I'm goin' over to git Eddie Lacey take me down to see about Jake," he told Mrs. Catlett. She didn't answer.

He didn't say good-by. He slung himself off the low porch by his crutches and went down the ridge road in a long, swinging glide, straight-backed, familiar with the impersonal law and the hard bedrock of a world I'd never glimpsed before. I had never earned the right to know it. Mr. Catlett from Beulah swung away into the night, a man in the way of the big postwar grab, like the topsoil in the way of the coal seam or the forgotten mansion at Beulah in the path of the eight-lane, high-speed ramp upriver, a man who'd learned to wait out change, who had to stay on his own land like the trees, and when either was rooted out the land eroded, eroded into the people Johnny and Mamie and Jake and I and all the rest had become—store-bought people, as useless to a man like him as store-bought bread or store-bought whisky. No one moved to help him.

"That's whur he's a-goin'." Mamie pointed down the hollow,

where away in the night distance a tiny light twinkled that I had thought was a second star.

"I'll take him down," I begged them and started off the porch.

Mrs. Catlett's voice came cold and exhausted behind me. "He wants Eddie Lacey to . . ."

There was nothing to do but go, not home, not anywhere, just off down the road by the now dark space of the golf course to plunge into the black corridor of the pines.

★ ★ ★ ★

# Chapter Eight

I FORGOT for a minute about following Johnny's Saturday. I just didn't want to go home, which was usually the reason for opening the peeled wood door on the riverbank almost under Canona bridge. Its neon sign read "The Wayfaring Stranger," and a smaller sign on the door, "Athletic Club, Members Only." Johnny and I had always called it the Escape Hatch.

The bank downriver from Canona bridge had once been the main street of the town. Wooden houses had opened onto the street and cast their waste down behind them into the river. There had been a blacksmith shop and saddler with a life-size wooden horse at the door, huddled fronts of ex-saloons turned beer joints. They were all gone. All the way up to the Wayfaring Stranger the bank had been cleared for a downtown parking lot, so that as I drove in beside the last of the wooden houses its side loomed up in the green foglights of River Street covered with layers of signs: Coca-Cola girls, a Chesterfield ad. The same long-legged girl that hid the Mansion at Beulah lounged across the top of the little building, half elephants from an old circus sign were almost hidden behind a huge tin Royal Cola bottle, and a red plaque promised quick relief from neuralgia and rheumatism.

Beyond the peeled door a bell clanged to warn Charley as I walked in. It was only a dark hallway: Charley hadn't bothered to spend any money on the hall so it was like a secret labyrinth. I went past the steep dark wood stairs that led up to the bedrooms on the second floor that no one ever mentioned, past the shut door marked "Game Room" which had been the old parlor. Now its window on River Street, where women had once sat to watch life go by them, was boarded up, and a big shaded light shone down on the inevitable green baize-covered round table twenty-four hours a perpetual night. Inside I heard the quiet murmuring of concentrated men.

Lucille, Charley's little, hard-muscled waitress, flung open the back door of the hall to see who it was. She took me in without a word, just put her bony arms around me.

Behind the door, Charley had built a narrow room overlooking the river. It was almost as dark as the night outside. On the few kitchen tables with their dirty cloths he had put candles in small cups of dark red glass that made them look like votive candles. I sat down at the table where I had always sat, then slumped, as if I had, for a minute, come to some kind of home—the impersonal American home from home—all the way across the country. Beyond the big bar doors that Charley kept open in the summertime, the Miller's High Life sign shot its perpetual cross-country fireworks into the black square—a trick of firelight to watch, start to figure out, then keep on watching, not figuring, not anything, just watch as if peace depended on the fine thin spurt of red or green, arching, then disappearing. Over the bar, turned as tan as an old master, Custer took his never-ending last stand. The jukebox was turned low. It played "Honeycomb" over and over. Every time it stopped, waited with its breathing undulations of cheap electric color to be fed, a slim-hipped boy played the song again and then crawled back onto the bar stool and curled his denim legs around it. I saw him because the jukebox was beside the phone booth where at any minute I expected, peace-fooled as if it hadn't happened, for Johnny to turn out of the shadowed end of the bar, hidden from me, and go into it to call me in New York. Time turned back only enough to take us both where we would never be again, in that light privilege, that indifference of the high-stepping, easy cut-out.

Lucille set a drink down in front of me. I didn't want her to see my face, not yet, and she knew it. Her skinny hand retreated under my hidden eyes and I took the drink and leaned back against the screen and watched the overhead span of the bridge, its high steel structure arched across the night, its lights lining its graceful skeleton, as if it bridged a mile in the night sky over the timeless womb of the Wayfaring Stranger. I could hear the water suck and swish, almost at the foundations of the house, as a line of empty barges a city block long slid upriver, pushed by a sternwheel tug that churned the dark river and cast a glow from its pilot house across the water to the bank. It made no sound, slid like a huge dreamboat under the arch of the bridge.

I hadn't even known Charley was sitting across from me. He said, ". . . didn't know anybody would be working on Labor Day." His head was turned away from me, his fat, sad, strong face following the barge, but he knew I was looking at him and he knew what I had come for, to burn the whole thing down to some bone of understanding I could hold, look at, grow from. He added, "I could set here and watch them barges forever. I spent ten thousand dollars on lawyers so the city won't clean me out so I can't watch them barges pass. It's worth it. Lucille, get Sissy another drink."

She was leaning against the inner wall, just waiting. She said, "She don't want it," and folded her arms across her bony chest.

"He called from here," I told them, knowing they knew.

It had begun again, what I came for—the last following I would ever do along Johnny's Saturday-night dream ridge to pick up the pieces.

Any voice seemed to wake the Wayfaring Stranger. A red-headed boy, his sideburns long, his pants tight, his speech a marriage of mountain and television that produced a brat language, said to the boy playing the jukebox as if it had been on his mind and now could be allowed out.

"I'm cuttin' out."

"Whar ye goin'?"

"Dayton."

"Hell, Dayton. Ain't nuthin' in Dayton."

"Anyhow, I'm goin' to Dayton."

"You ain't goin' nowheres." The legs uncurled from the bar stool and "Honeycomb" began again.

Charley lurched up and switched off the jukebox. "You played that damn thing fifteen times. I'm tard of it," he told his two customers.

"One beer and three hours on the jukebox," he complained, coming back to the table to stand with his back to me, following the lights of the disappearing barge.

"Oh, let 'em alone, Charley. They ain't got nuthin' to do," Lucille told him.

"Hell, I'm lettin' 'em alone."

The boys had turned and were staring at me, with the same stone-wall faces that the men would have had for Jake Catlett if he'd walked into the bar of the country club on his fight night.

"I'm in love, I'm in love." The red-haired boy kissed the air without changing expression.

"Cool it," the other one muttered. Then, as if he'd caught it in the air, he went on, "I hear that rich son-of-a-bitch got hit the other night died."

There was a dead silence. The blank eye of the television set Johnny had gotten wholesale for Charley watched us all, reflected in it.

Lucille was between the boys without making a sound. "That's his sister," I heard her whisper.

[ 143 ]

"What the hell's she doin' in here?" They stared over her shoulder.

Lucille snapped the jukebox on, dug a dime from her pocket and let it drop in.

The sound of "Honeycomb" parted us from the bar. Charley let himself down again in the chair and we talked under it. "Sure, he was in here. Sissy . . ."

My glass turned slowly around in my hands, catching the maroon reflection of the candle shade. "People hate us, don't they?" I asked Charley.

"No, honey, just ain't got time for you. That's all."

I had to settle it, there and then. There didn't seem to be any place else to run to. I agreed with the boy at the bar more than he could know—there wasn't nuthin' in Dayton, not there or any place left that wasn't around us and in us at the Wayfaring Stranger with the dark water lapping below. I could see Johnny's reflection, destroyed by the beer can, then the candle reflection destroyed, swimming and reshaping through my tears.

"He come in about one o'clock, all dressed . . ." Charley sighed and began.

"One of those parties, you know, the moon and the stars there," Lucille added.

"He said, 'Charley, what if you'd been asleep for fifteen years and woke up in a blue sateen bunny suit?' I'd go back to sleep I told him . . ."

One of the boys at the bar snickered.

"Of course he couldn't go see Miss Leftwich, dressed like that . . ." I thought for a minute Charlie meant the bunny suit.

"Leave her alone, Charley," Lucille muttered.

But Charley, vague in the distance across the table, great sad face gaping and swaying there like a white balloon, wasn't listening to her, or to me. He was burning out troubles of his own.

"How many times I'd hear you and him comin' in that door like you owned the place. Your voices stridin' ahead of you, just takin' us in fer a while, then high-tailin' off on somewheres, didn't even know we'z alive. Ever' time I'd go home my wife would ask me what you had on. I never knowed. Hell, she'd lay into me then, she'd say I bet it cost an arm and a leg. Yeah, I'd say, whose arm and whose leg? Whaddaya care . . .

"Like them youngins there—they'd watch him when he come in and he never noticed 'em except oncet in a while layin' out to be friendly, imitatin' the way they talked, the son-of-a-bitch." Charley was just mumbling, but the undercurrents of his old patient rage danced to the surface like a slag-heap fire licking out its tongue and then fading away again in the darkness of what he had to say.

"Wife studyin' your picture in the paper and them boys sashayin' around actin' cool."

He had begun it, a long series of reflections, each of what he envied, ending nowhere except within the isolated self. They had watched and imitated us, as we had watched and imitated some vague pace-setter somewhere, now caught in the latest widow, now in a connecting fragment to a richer life, like Melinda's incessant voyage with an unknown woman which had kept her safe from grief in the afternoon with the mourning ladies—imitation of the oppressor as primitive as the cannibal who eats his enemy to gain his strength, the frail armor of the dispossessed, Johnny's Elite Corps, all of us stealing to clothe ourselves in some richer skin, but never, never touching the isolated heart beneath it.

Charley's eyes were glistening with tears. "I don't mean none of this, Sissy, I don't know what I'm goin' to do without Johnny. He changed. . . . We'z together all through the war, only time I ever saw him free. I dunno, maybe all you folks are good for is dyin'. You sure as hell don't know how to live, unless you sneak off somewheres to do it."

Charley's tears were frank and healing. "Gawd, I'm sorry," he said, his head lolling on his bare arms. "I jest been with it so long, worryin' about Johnny." He looked up, his face working. "He'n that pore little ole girl Tel Leftwich would come in here. Johnny'd take her upstairs like we wudn't even here, didn't even notice. She's a nice lady. She deserved better'n that—come from good people. He wouldn't even take her to your family's house—not in all those years. I'd go plumb wild, seein' 'em goin' upstairs. But I wouldn't say nothin'. This here was the only place Johnny had to do what he pleased."

I must have been grinning. I could feel it pulling at me, the grin. Lucille came over and held me hard by the shoulders. I began to tell him.

"Oh, no it wasn't, Charley. Johnny had the phone booth. He had Uncle Ephraim's place, and he had women; he had every place he asked for except the one place he couldn't have." I wasn't grinning; my mouth was gaping because I couldn't control it any more. "You don't know what it's like to have something expected of you and not know what it is except that it isn't ever what you do, it's what somebody else does or somebody else did. You know, don't you, Lucille?"

"No, honey. I ain't got time for that kind of stuff. I got six kids to raise." She slapped me sensible with her rock-hard wisdom. "Why don't you git out and grow up? You two! Gawd, you cain't git nuthin' without workin' fer it." She slammed the door on my wail as efficiently as she would have cleared the table, pocketed her tip, or broken up a fight before it started. I could see Johnny and me and all of us through her eyes, our lives a long, sensitive, attractive, self-suffering wail down through the unchanging years, our flippant suffering a fashion of the time, children beating at a soft, evasive world with silver christening spoons.

"Now I'll git you a drink," she stated, having shut me up.

When she brought it back she said, "Charley, all that stuff about Miss Leftwich. You don't know a damn thing about women. She liked it. She's just another old man on that guy's back." She flopped in a chair between us. "Hell, I knowed that woman. She taught two my kids."

The three of us sat and watched the river now in a more peaceful wake of Johnny's dying, letting the night heal. We sat there until we heard the bell in the front. Uncle Ephraim walked in and took the fourth chair. Behind his God-sent square ugly head the bridge arched as if he were holding it up. Rose had put him into a Tattersall waistcoat, like all the disguises, but she, without realizing it, had only disguised him as himself. He wore his Tattersall frankly, not giving a damn that it was more to her than a pretty vest.

"I been lookin' all over hell for you, honey." He put a callused palm over my hand and held it. "Lucille, get me a drink, will you? I better call Preston." He wandered into the phone booth.

When we closed the door of the Wayfaring Stranger behind us he said, "Leave Johnny's car here and come for a little ride with me—get some air." He led me to his own car as if he'd just thought of it. I suspected that Uncle Ephraim in his slow, sure way was getting ready to say what he had to, but he would say it by telling a story, because he always had, a sort of earth-smelling parable, as if he were laying it in front of me, tempting me to take it, but knowing better than to force it on me. I had once seen him put a newborn calf to a cow, and his hands and voice were as gentle and persuasive as a mother's were supposed to be. He didn't stuff the udder into the calf's mouth. He just gave the calf a chance to live and persuaded it softly that it was worth doing.

He drove me slowly up River Street, down Lacey Street with its same-after-same square houses with begging, open front porches falling behind us, just driving easily, not talking. When we'd driven for twenty minutes and the calf was calm enough for the udder he said, "Sissy, I want to tell you a little story."

"I hate Johnny," I told Lacey Street.

"Let me tell you my story," Uncle Ephraim waited to see if he'd driven the hard words out of my mind, then went on.

"Everybody had two dollars in the bank had to have a horse. You know all that, honey."

I remembered when Melinda and Haley Potter had discovered a new language, new ways to spend time. I had been surprised at

Melinda, who had never cared about animals before and had had Spud's old dog shot one time when he went away for the weekend because it smelled.

"Well, I reckon this begins when Melinda called me up one day, three, four years ago now, and told me. She never asked anything, just told me she was sending the Potters up to Greenbrier to buy a horse. That was all I could get out of her.

"Rose and I had them for dinner and you never heard such going-on. You know Haley—she had taken up horses so damn hard a horse couldn't lay down and rest itself without her going on about casting—we'd go out toward the barn and she'd lay out to tell me about the conformation of every work horse I had. You know how these women go on when they get onto a new thing.

"They had a pretty little youngin with them. Prettiest little thing you ever saw."

I didn't want to hear this story, but there was no way to stop Uncle Ephraim. He spoke so seldom that when he did talk, he usually had something so, to him, worth saying that he'd keep on its track through any interruption until it was finished. We turned slowly out toward the north hills.

"I never could figure out how two awkward-looking people like that big hulking brother of Plain George's and old Haley who looks like a dressed-up farmhand could breed such a delicate little gal, fine feet and hands, little pale heart face, blond hair, good slim head. You can do it with animals, but it sure takes a hell of a sight more care than it does with humans.

"Anyhow, I knew what they wanted, just a mild-mannered little horse for the gal, not more than fifteen hands. I didn't have anything small enough. You know how big I breed. Hell, I don't want to sell a horse I can't ride—so I called up Lester Yunkion. He had a little gelding his boys had rode 'til they outgrew it—they're right good people. The boys and the animals both got good manners. I knew I couldn't turn Haley loose, not with that little youngin having to ride what somebody would maniac around and big-talk into unloading on her. She didn't know a damn thing she couldn't read in a book and never would.

"Well, we went over there to the Yunkion's farm. The youngest boy rode the gelding pretty as a picture. Lord, Haley was sashayin' around there, talkin' about teeth and withers and flanks, Lester Yunkion and me trying to keep a straight face and say nothing. Dammit, I felt so safe with what we were doing. I knew once she and Melinda got their minds set on a thing nothing would stop them.

"They asked me once to come down and lay out a hunt. I thought they'd gone plumb wild and told them so. You can't do nuthin' but fox-chase in these hollows. They just got some feller from Ohio to come out and he took their money. . . . I felt kind of sorry for them. I tell you, there was some mighty sore asses in this valley before they took up bridge again. They wasn't satisfied just to hack and pleasure themselves a little."

Uncle Ephraim was quiet, expecting me to follow. When he went on he was back at the Yunkion's farm.

"Looking back now, I see I should have stepped in. The little gal got up and she looked pretty as a picture, hands down, heels down—but, Hannah, she was scared. You could smell it. Then I realized she wasn't scared of the horse, she was scared of Haley. I could tell it. She watched that big hulking woman standing there, never even looked at the horse.

"Haley was judging her like she was a dog in training belonged to somebody else. She was talking, oh, something about the poor little youngin's seat and way of going, never even reached up a hand to touch the little gelding. Now the first thing somebody gives a damn what kind of animal they're buyin' will do, unconscious even, is touch it, touch its life.

"I borrowed a mount from Lester and took the little youngin at a walk around his horse field. I never said anything, just watched her relax, watched her begin to care about what she was riding. She'd been scared all right, oh, pushed too fast, handled without any idea of what she was like. On a nervous animal she would have been in real danger, but I knew the gelding, knew its breeding, sound, seen it come to maturity, seen it trained, even seen the boys jump it. By the time we'd gone around the field a few times that little youngin had some color and was going well. We trotted and we even cantered, and she was all right without her ma anywhere near."

Uncle Ephraim talked and drove, slowly and surely, taking me back to the long rides, the patience, the watching, that I hadn't known at the time was teaching from him, not hard, imposed form at first, but affection and ease, the caring from which form came naturally, to ride well out of pure spirit and pride. We were back in the barn, brushing and cooling out the little pony, never being told, always being led by that quiet man, Johnny finished first and sitting on the steps to the hayloft, Melinda uninterested, staring out of the barn door across the hill meadow.

"I didn't know any more about the thing; I remember Lester telling Haley not to feed the gelding too much grain, he'd get too spirited for the child, and wishing he hadn't told her that. I just didn't trust her. These big women around horses, they push too hard, push everything.

"Well, two summers ago they had to have a horse show and they asked me and some woman from Kentucky, real hard-looking woman, to come out and judge. Me and Rose had to laugh. There was a big fight ahead between Melinda and Haley who'd put the judges up. I was glad that we went to the Potters' house, partly because your mother and Melinda drive me to drink, always have. Seen Preston and Johnny both . . ."

His voice ran out and he drove on. I glanced at him, but he was thinking something he wasn't ready to say—not directly, perhaps not ever directly.

"I think I was partly glad too, when we got there, because of the little gal. I swear to God, Hannah, Haley had entered that youngin in an open jumper class for children. I just hoped to God the child hadn't had the spirit too knocked out of her to ride.

"That morning at breakfast the little gal came down turned out like one of the catalogues Haley had stacked nose-deep in the living room. She looked like a little princess, but when she slid into her chair for breakfast she couldn't touch her food, just shrunk against the chair back. Haley was going on about champion's nerves, how the youngin was always like that and then rode like a dream. "Don't you, honey?" She kept trying to get her to answer. I can still hear her saying it with her voice edged. Well, she got an egg and some orange juice down the child.

"I didn't like it, Hannah, I didn't like a thing about it. I've been around animals all my life and I can smell fear; anybody can who will let theirself. I was really scared if Haley went on talking the child would faint, but you know Haley. She has to win. She'd drag out every time anybody in the family ever watered a horse and you'd 'a' thought it was the Whitney Stables instead of one little old youngin and a cross-bred Greenbrier gelding wasn't worth more than two hundred dollars.

"Then, by God, she said it. She said it's a matter of honor. 'You see you earn a ribbon from Uncle Ephraim here.' I was so mad I damn near disqualified the child, but I didn't have enough sense to.

"We got to the show. A lot of good coal money had gone into a right nice little stable and ring—good stalls, horses looked fine, pretty little tack room with all the ribbons pinned on one wall, them damn ribbons . . ." Uncle Ephraim was telling the story to himself now.

I had seen it. Melinda and Haley had made it as correct as a whisky ad: the pine paneling, a rustic "early American" cobbler's bench with a few copies of *The Huntsman* which nobody read, a neat row of racks for the saddles with their polished tack hooks above them, the shine and smell of saddle leather. Steel tack caught the light, and, like cheap flowers bursting, red, blue, and yellow ribbons with their gilt lettering were carefully flung across one free wall.

"We all went in and Haley started in on the child again. 'We want one of these,' she said to her. The youngin parked the orange juice and the egg all over her mother's new brown and white pumps. Haley was trying to wipe it off with Kleenex and hollering about champion's nerves again because Melinda came in about that time to find us and Haley was embarrassed.

"I did try then. I said to Haley that I wondered if the child was too sick to ride and she looked at me like she was going to hit me. I know her, she told me, she always behaves like this. Youngin no more than nine years old didn't have no more business bein' pushed half scared to death into any show ring, but I couldn't make Haley see."

He sighed, and I watched his big hands slowly turn the car back toward the river. "Oh Hannah, I still don't know why I come down. I wouldn't have judged at all if it hadn't been for Preston. I knew them women would git after him." Then he added, smiling peacefully for a second in the middle of his story, "It pleased Rose too. Now I like a little harness-racing myself, but the sight of a poor bunch of hacks gingered up, rode by people don't care a thing about 'em don't please me."

The streets were summer quiet. Through open doors lights washed into the street. He was driving so slowly that I could hear a swing creaking on a dim porch and the patter of people's voices dropping through the night as calm as sleepy birds. The streets seemed emptied to receive our wandering. Uncle Ephraim's voice was as quiet as the night.

"It had gotten loose from Melinda and Haley outside. You get yourself a ring and you get you some hillbillies and you got yourself a fair. Come in all sorts of cars, kids running back and forth from a hot-dog stand. I knew the people, way they hollered when a sulky showed with a nice little trotter comin' around in a free-legged dash. It was a pretty sight. I've always been partial to trotters. Used to breed some. . . . Anyhow, pretty soon a couple of niggers come out and set up the jumps, old Haley following them around, bossing—regular hunt course. I could see three, four youngins walking their mounts out by the barn.

"The crowd went kind of waiting quiet, watching the jumps go up—or maybe Haley sashaying around out there quieted even them.

"The class was called and the Potter youngin was first. I wouldn't've known that little old country gelding. He'd sure been manicured, and when she cantered him in for the turn I could see she was holding him in hard—it was her own nerves, but it still looked good, too collected a canter though. I could see that. I could see too that the little gelding had been grained to make him look good. I almost whistled the child out. She was glancing over where Haley was leaning against the fence. Later I remembered Haley's face. She wasn't nervous for the youngin or the horse. She just wanted to win.

"The little gal let the gelding out and he come toward the brush jump. The crowd went dead quiet. We could all see that little pale face, dim scared, crouched up, just as perfect as training could make her. The gelding sailed over. I thought everything was all right, followed along to the next jump. She went over like a swallow —three-foot-six Aiken fence. The turn at the end was short. She come over the chickencoop sideways and faulted—the gelding's hind foot touched going over. I think it was that and the angle and seeing the ring fence loom up in front of her panicked her. She drew the gelding in and he must have caught her fear through her fingers. The next jump was a post and rail. He shied out and turned. She stayed on but I could tell he'd left her behind. She didn't collect him. She just clung on and the gelding whirled and come back toward the fence on his own and sprang. He went over like silk, cleared it by a foot easy. She was still on but her hat went and her hair streamed out behind her. The gelding turned and come up for the stone wall. I had gone over near it to watch her over the last jump safe. I can see her face in the air now, coming toward me, seeing nothing, but the gelding had been schooled to finish the course. Haley had seen to that. He gathered and jumped. I think her body gave up. She just couldn't take it any more. She came off on the rise, just sailed off. I can see her white face plunge like a shot bird against the jump. The crowd oohed like a big gust of wind. When I got to her she was dead—unmarked, just as if she'd fallen as a leaf falls. Her head fell back when Kregg Potter ran out and picked her up, not as big as a minute, her little slim neck had broken and made her head loll and her hair hang down."

He stopped—his point lost somewhere in his memory—and drove down the same tree-lined street we'd kept coming back to—Lacey Street, where mother had once said the kind of plain people lived who went to high school and teacher's college. I had retreated from him when he finally drew me back.

"Later, when the crowd had almost gone—they went gently, Hannah, like people leave church—well, I went to the tack room. The ambulance was waiting outside the barn. Haley and Kregg weren't anywhere around. When I opened the tack-room door he had Haley's shoulders under his hands. She was leaning against all the cheap ribbons, crying. They heard me, and she turned around. Haley had finally earned her ribbon. It had run like a damn big red birthmark all down one side of her face."

He stopped the car in front of one of the blank square houses on Lacey Street and sat there staring down the jade-green arch where the street lights touched the leaves, letting the evening peace come in and gather around us for a minute. He gave me a cigarette. When I saw his face over the flaming match, tears glistened in the deep sun wrinkles under his eyes.

"A man," he told me carefully, so I knew he was touching for me the nerve of what had happened, "he bred the fastest harness horse ever bred in Greenbrier County. He told me every champion has to reach beyond his breeding. A champion horse and a champion dog got more in common than either one has with their breed. This quality—I dunno. I can see it—can't tell about it. There's a place where you quit training and let it take over—little neglect . . . a little trust . . . I dunno.

"You can't make a champion, Hannah, you can only recognize it. That's what those strong-willed women don't know—a little neglect works with animals, works with people. I don't think Johnny ever had an unwatched minute except the ones he hid in."

Uncle Ephraim was telling me his answer, but it wasn't enough. Johnny was no scared child, or whipped dog, not Johnny Escaper, Johnny Flirt. He could do what no animal could. He could pretend to love and still remain untouched. I shied away and let a question come. "What's molly grub?" I asked Uncle Ephraim. He relaxed against the seat and laughed.

"It's what you give folks to eat ain't got a job, honey—like all you people live off the coal face without putting anything back. You live on high-grade molly grub—damn high grade too."

He opened the door and eased his big body out of the car. Then he reached back in and turned off the headlights.

"Now you're going to come in here with me for a minute, honey. Rose's been here with her all day and it's just goddam time one of Johnny's people showed up."

He came around to hand me out. His touch on my arm was a delicate pat of his big hand, explaining no more, leaving me to know where we were going.

"You were the lucky one . . . extra child . . . ran out of models . . . neglected . . ." This was more to himself than to me as he turned away.

I followed him up the stretch of concrete between the hard squares of city grass toward the dull wooden porch of Tel Leftwich's house.

I didn't want to go in, didn't want Uncle Ephraim to make me face the blank humiliation of a woman I didn't know and whom I had ignored all my grown-up life. I knew her as someone in the corner only of Johnny's life and mind. There was nothing of her in his room, nothing in the temple of his private car. To me she had been glimpsed only in fragments, an eye-shining girl at the airport restaurant so long ago, a shadow following Johnny through the night streets, seen by Jack as he rode on patrol, a *Pietà* in a hospital corridor, who had drawn only indifference from mother and Melinda, compassion from Charley to feed his sad hurt, and then a woman swept aside with the broom of Lucille's professional earthy scorn.

She cringed under a lamp in one of the overstuffed chairs, her frail hands folded in her lap in the square, dark room beyond the open window. Rose stood spraddle-legged over her, saying something with such strength that Tel Leftwich shrank from it as if a weight was pushing against her pale, delicate face, framed in blond hair which seemed to mourn down her cheeks in wings, softening her eyes, avid as she stared up at Rose, eyes that fed on what Rose was saying, waiting for some new expected blow as her body retreated.

Her eyes gleamed with a kind of sacrificial lust I had sensed at the hospital. They should have changed. I knew they should have changed with Johnny's death, but they hadn't. They were used to being fed on pain and now they glowed as if what Rose were saying were a drug.

Rose and Tel were so intent on each other that they didn't hear Ephraim and me come in. I hung back in the shadows, fighting through the foreboding and the shock of the small living room Tel seemed hung in as if she would never move again. Rose's dark angry body was rooted, holding the room down. It was cultic in its reflection of my mother's house, forced into a Lacey Street oak square parlor. A gas fireplace with mahogany-stained wooden columns, an inset beveled mirror above it, fly-specked with age, dominated Tel's chintz and glass attempts to lighten the room, defeated sternly the patches of mother's color—cool, frigid green.

Beside her on the table stood the inevitable picture, enshrined under the light in a silver frame, an enlarged snapshot of Johnny at nineteen, Johnny-wandering-boy, his head thrown back, laughing at a joke beyond the picture. He wore an old hunting cap and a dirty canvas coat. I sat beyond him on the fence, almost hidden by his body, a twin profile at thirteen, laughing too. Uncle Ephraim had taken the picture; the joke flooded back, drowning my eyes— it was only that Johnny's dog was trying to charm us into going on when we stopped for a rest. I could see old Nelly running down the trail and back to us, barking.

"I told you, Tel, over and over . . ." Rose broke the spell, threw her head back and sighed. "Thank God for Ephraim. Jesus, I hated Johnny." She turned and leaned against the mantel and the reflection of her dark shining head heaved in the mirror. "I wanted to kill him . . ." Her voice was muffled. I had seen Eduardo look like that—that fury at my light, polite indifference; a hatred as impotent as hating the dead.

I longed to stroke Rose's back and comfort her, the strong one, and tell her that I hadn't understood until that minute that even in the dark corridor of that woman's body Johnny had wandered, ignoring everything but her sex and zest, visiting her body as he visited my mind, only when he needed to. Johnny and I had done the same thing, followed the urge to break taboos, using with our charm the passion, the vitality, of the earthly born, giving nothing except a sex we didn't care much about, silencing anyone who loved us with our mild, wandering insistence, with the cold kindness of the arrogant. Johnny, as usual, had escaped and left me to bear the knowledge that we had strip-mined every stranger who had let us in.

Johnny had had his final revenge on us. He was lodged in our minds as the man we had all demanded. Each in our way had let our love light on him and glow. I saw him, for a second, as dark within, gathering, reflecting our light back to us as what we wanted —a loved one; the ecstatic eyes of Tel, even the correct eyes of the officer in the wood, had reflected on him and found recognition as in a mirror. I thought we would have stayed suspended there

forever, with Johnny fragmented between us in death as he had
been in life, enemy, genteel prodigal, twin, had Uncle Ephraim not
sensed the old neural haunting and broken in by putting his arm
around Rose, who turned from the mirror with a child's trust and
rested her head against his cheek. He held her. Johnny had left her
with him, and he had accepted her as he would have a good animal which had been brutally treated, knowing that there would be
scars.

They were in an oasis for a minute that I saw was new to them
both—a minute that radiated relief. Uncle Ephraim had forgotten me. He said, "I'll get us all a drink," and disappeared as quickly
as such a big man could toward the kitchen, through the black
hollow of a dining room.

Tel had seen nothing of this. She spoke out of her own staring.
"He would have come to me if *they* hadn't . . ."

Rose picked up the tune; the broken record of hatred went
round, turned down so Uncle Ephraim wouldn't hear, the forever, mutual harrowing of women's "they."

I could hear Johnny's voice on the telephone, lighting another
point in his wandering.—"Hell, I don't know, Sissy. I've got on
these damn clothes." Johnny had been dressed in the call-boy uniform of our private, ruthless world. It would have turned on Tel's
patient, suffering condemnation of "they" like a tap.

*He had had no place to go*—no place the size of a man's rest.
Perhaps he had never trusted anyone enough to ask for it.

"I know them, Tel. Christ, I've been through it. They're kill-
ers. Your ass would make them a face," Rose was saying as if
she'd said it all before. "Johnny . . ."

"No," Tel said. She hypnotized herself with her soft voice and
the nod-nodding of her haloed hair. "I can't listen, Rose. I knew
him . . . what he was capable of . . . what hurt him."

"Who the hell didn't? He was as public as a damn privy," Rose
yelled, but she didn't get through to Tel.

"No," Tel said again, and then, "Oh, no," and kept on shaking her head, undisturbed, refusing to give up her sacrifice—a burden of loyalty Johnny had not asked for or deserved. It made her virgin-looking, as if the renewal of it out of her loyalty, her shame, her soft hatred, had taken each day the concentration of a saint, with Johnny caught as her last sheep, not to love, but to follow and save. He had at last become complete, too late for anyone to love him. He had been sinned for, trapped by the righteous, and judged all his life. At least his death saved him from either of the final corruptions; he had not become his oppressors or his disguises.

I had sunk against one of the carved columns of the door when Tel finally looked up and saw me. Her face drained, seeing another picture of Johnny. Her eyes changed then. They softened with a kind of joy. She told me what that surviving, hard-working woman must have wanted to say for years.

"You get the hell out of here," she said sweetly.

Uncle Ephraim made a great noise, blundering through the dark dining room with the clattering glasses.

We all sat and had our drinks politely.

As we drove on down Lacey Street, Uncle Ephraim said, pleased, "I'm glad we did that, honey. It meant a lot to Tel."

We drove back toward the bridge through the dark spacial city between the small centers of Johnny's mourners. The clock on the Coal Trust Building began striking ten as we passed above the roof of the Wayfaring Stranger, over the dark moving water; the sound faded behind us into a last faint knell as we wound up the snakelike hill road toward the tiny protected fortress of the hill houses. Their lights winked toward us among the dark trees. Up above us the indifferent, bright summer stars hung low in the black sky.

★　　　★　　　★　　　★

# Chapter Nine

My FATHER was standing in the doorway with the light flowing past him onto the lawn. Melinda rushed out of the living room, saw me, and turned away in disgust; only Father MacAndrews moved his big, awkward body forward to catch me.

Melinda said to someone inside the living room, ". . . had to drink on a night like this. You'd think she'd spare mother that." She sounded as far as China from my day. I couldn't even mind. Melinda saw what she saw and not even reality would ever change it. She had made the world in her own righteous image, and I could only linger against John MacAndrews' practiced, comforting arm and thank God that I didn't have to live in it. He walked me out onto the terrace, where far below the river wound on westward, and the lights of the city nestled beside it as calm as if they too were under quiet water, moving only as the river moved their reflections.

"Look out there." He made me look, but it wasn't at the city he pointed with the pipe which was as much a part of him as his clerical collar, it was at the stars. "Now listen to me," he said sternly when he saw my head rise up, dragged up as if he had taken me by the hair.

"Right now, six million light years away, a galaxy is exploding apart." He kept his pipe pointing toward the night, not knowing that it was not his words, but the rough tenderness of his arm holding my shoulders, that seemed to keep me from falling headlong down into the river, as inert as sacrifice with the weight of all that knowledge of hatred, like the old man of the sea on my back.

"Man . . ." he went on.

I wanted to cry, "Don't say 'man'! Tell me the truth. Oh, please say 'I.' You don't have any right to say anything but 'I'!"

"Man," he went on, waiting for me to settle into his arm, "can use the balance and order he sees in the stars as an excuse for indifference to other men. He can stay in that until the world refocuses so that he can't see his own feet, or he can come out washed, expecting and seeing some balance in the world."

I had seen the hands of this man, practical, square hands, serve the Eucharist, clean the altar afterward, with impatient housewife gestures, his big feet in black shoes moving like a farmer's under his robes. Sometimes I half expected him to roll up his cassock sleeves. It was with the same hard strong gesture that he turned me and led me over to mother's summer chintz swing, which groaned under us as we sat down on it. Beyond the window of the living room Melinda kept glancing up as if she ought to come out and interrupt, but something—respect for the vicar of Christ's clothes—stopped her. She chewed her lip and said something to Spud.

"Now I'm going to talk to you about Johnny," John MacAndrews said.

He felt my shaking. I'd had enough of Johnny, harrowed the town and my own soul for him; now I was empty, letting go at last. As deliberately as he filled the chalice, John MacAndrews tapped

[ 161 ]

his pipe against his shoe, cleaned it with a knife, filled it, while I watched the safe stars. Finally it was lit and he began to move the swing back and forth, lulling me in its cradle.

"No man was ever made but once, or like any other. That's a miracle . . . God. Johnny turned his back on the miracle of himself every time he glimpsed it, turned his back or let himself that was himself fester, secret and ashamed. He did it partly out of training, partly out of despair, in order to sate every little demanding reflection he met. He chose it. Even in letting go, we choose. You are in danger of letting go of man as Johnny let go of himself. These people . . ."

The pipe pointed toward the window. One of Melinda's feet was drumming the floor to keep away the silence which had settled like a pall over the house.

". . . the ones who brush against you, for God."

I wanted to run away from him and his God and Melinda's tapping foot.

"Oh, you don't know it's God yet. This way you end up no more than a rebel for ideas, words—oh, causes maybe. It's cold comfort . . . just another way to hate righteously." His safe pipe glowed and dimmed.

"You're just doing your job, Father. I haven't even thought . . ." I tried to shut him out and find a shooting star to hold to for that minute.

He sat unmoved in his protected calm.

"You don't see people you've christened and confirmed and run out of your yard and prayed for, *think*. You only . . ."

"Say '*I*.' Say 'I' . . . how do you know?" I was confused. I didn't realize I'd said it aloud until he changed.

"I can only see the way they are going. That's all I can see . . ."

"Who ever saw Johnny until it was too late—if anyone . . . you . . ." I had drawn away from his stolid assurance that fended off my refusal of him like armor, into the corner of the swing, curled up and being rocked.

[ 162 ]

"Honey," he said far away, "he did what you're doing now. I turn my collar backward and you're as suspicious as if I'd turned my feet backward to hide where I've been. He would only have thought I was doing my job. I am." I was nearly asleep. "I'm doing my job right now instead of being at home with my telescope. You try it, Hannah. Take on a job . . . and do it . . . and *then* come back and talk to me.

"There was no way to get through Johnny's lightness. He wore it like a caul. He wouldn't—or couldn't—be born. You know, the second birth is very like the first, same pain, same sense of betrayal, same gasp of fear that let's the life air in, same flow of water. Then finally, so Johnny would not be born—hurt—he acted his parts. You saw him as a rebel because *that's what you wanted to see* . . ." He tapped my hip with the pipe handle at each word.

"Johnny thanked the man who hit him." The memory of what he had said rose out of the lull. Only the swing creaked and groaned; that and the stars rocked my exhausted body.

"Thank God," John MacAndrews said at last, "somebody got through."

"Is *that* all you give him?" I sat up and spoke to him, careful with fury. "Today I saw him killed. All my life I've seen him killed. He died before any of us had the guts to let him live. This" —I drove it into John MacAndrews like a nail—"is a matter of life and death."

He retreated for a heart's pause into the protection of his pipe until his head was able to turn to me.

"Dear child . . ." He attacked quietly as if he were too angry to raise his voice. "Death always happens too soon. It always leaves fury, the 'if onlys,' a plea for one more minute. What would any of us have done with Johnny's one more minute? Nothing! We've been living that one more minute all our lives!"

He put his head down in his hands. I had seen Methodist men pray that way, huddled on big-boned fists.

"I thought my failures would be tragic. . . . I tried, honey. My failures have come from a barrier of nice women shutting my mouth with a million cucumber sandwiches. There was a woman in this town—she was in hell. Have you ever faced the dark night of the soul in Canona, West Virginia? She was a widow, not a very attractive one. After a while, people forgot to go and see her. Naked sorrow embarrasses nice people. I was on call, night after night. One night I was out with my telescope. It was a clear night. I had the best view of Venus I have ever had, pink and glowing. The telephone rang and I didn't go in. I just didn't go in.

"That night she committed suicide. She left money to the church for a chapel of repose—I think where someone else sometime might find out what it was like to be alone without God's hand stretched out through any human touch."

He straightened up and leaned back, looking into the dark. "When the chapel was dedicated the ladies who had helped kill her—and make no mistake about it, Hannah, if you don't give love you kill—the ladies served cucumber sandwiches and talked about that naked driven woman as if she were a saint. I even spoke about God moving in mysterious ways in order to put some damned furniture into one more room of All Saints' Church. If I had said what was on my mind they would have run me out of my church. I simply was not strong enough to bear their hatred. . . . You see, they already knew. That's why they set a wall against my speaking."

The night was kind. The swing creaked on, swinging us into safety as if we both were being allowed, for a stray, unneeded minute, to rest. Finally John MacAndrews got up and stretched his hulking frame, blotting out the living-room light.

"Go in and try to comfort your mother, Hannah. I doubt if she's ever been comforted in her life by a person who wasn't connected by need. You aren't any more, God help you."

"Will she let me?" I still clung to the corner of the swing.

"That isn't your business. Good night, honey." He was almost

[ 164 ]

to the door when he turned abruptly and stamped back across the flagstones and laid his hand on my head.

"The peace of God, which passeth all understanding, keep your heart and mind in the knowledge and love of God, and of his son Jesus Christ our Lord: And the blessing of God Almighty, the Father, the Son, and the Holy Ghost, be with you, and remain with you always. Amen. Hannah, your head's hot. Get to bed as soon as you can."

I saw Melinda catch at him in the hall as he left, before I slept.

Melinda was shaking me, but gently.

"Wake up, honey, wake up," she was saying. "Don't sleep out here. Come to your own bed."

"Where's mother?" I sat up.

"She's still awake. She's been cleaning and cleaning Johnny's room ever since people left. Wouldn't even eat. I can't do a thing with her." Melinda made her inevitable sad cry.

I kissed her. "Go to bed," I told her. "You've had to cope with everything"—which, in the only world she could ever know, she had.

She said, "Why, honey," and rubbed her cheek.

As I went upstairs I heard her let herself out of the front door. Spud must have been waiting for her. I heard her say, "I forgot to ask Hannah if she had a black hat . . ."

Spud answered far across the lawn, "Come to bed . . ."

I could hear the low hum of father's and Uncle Ephraim's voices as they talked behind the closed library door. Outside the cry of fall crickets made an undertone of the night. There was no other sound. I went up the carpeted stairs, avoiding the telltale creaks by instinct and long training. Johnny's door at the head of the stairs was open. The lamp beside his bed was lit. Mother had turned it on as she did every night by habit when he didn't come in.

The room was clean, purged of everything he'd left in it unnoticed in the last fifteen years—the hunting gear gone, the photographs; only the portrait of mother she had had painted for Johnny's sixteenth birthday was left, her delicate face turned slightly away. The sepia print of Michelangelo's *Pietà* that mother had brought to him from Rome hung alone above the bed, the dawn-young face of the girl mother gazing without sorrow or pain at the broken man in her lap. Across the bookshelf, now cleared of the golf tees and the bottles, the shoe-cleaning kit, the silver cocktail shaker from Melinda's wedding, a long line of tiny painted tin hussars marched in neat formation. I had not seen them since Johnny had swept them into his wastebasket years before and replaced them with model airplanes. Mother had retrieved them because they had belonged to her "papa" and put them in a box in the corner of the attic. The only other picture left in the room was a framed picture postcard of a German mechanical organ all red paint and statues and baroque gilt carving which mother had said Johnny loved so as a baby. Johnny was gone from it. There was not even anything left to mourn or save.

Across the hall, my door stood open too, frail, pretty, and waiting in the glow of ruffled white lamps. I stood there in the hall unable to move. The long corridor at the airport, at the jail, the rhododendron-covered hall at Egeria, had led me now to this. I could see myself and Johnny existing only in uncommitted corridors of home and mind and heart, where all the doors led only to a safe and killing past, where a door to the unknown was my only choice if I chose to be alive—not an escape but a walking forward, one step at a time, as men do in battle.

If we can change, change and turn, refocus as if the stains of training are cleansed from our eyes, our lenses polished, sensitive at last, it happened then. Now that I had seen Johnny's death through to the end rather than skirting its edges to avoid the impact of facts on my protecting dreams, I felt a freeing, a dangerous rush, a spurt of intelligence in my brain, a sweetening of my senses. We had been faced with stepping forward, with action, but the ram in the thicket had not been provided for our sacrifice. It had required, in our Egyptian pride, the first-born son.

Something touched my body lightly. It was the filmy white curtain, billowed out in the river breeze, ghost fingers against my arms. Down the hall, where her light stained the carpet outside of her closed door, I heard my mother's voice call, weak and thin as the curtain, "Hannah, honey, is that you?"

"Yes, ma'am," I said to the curtain, caressing it back away from my body. I was ready to listen after so long, to open her door.

She lay propped up against her pillows, staring out of her huge window at the lights of the city. Her face was stultified with calm. She looked up at me and, just for a second, she smiled like a child.

"I heard somebody on the terrace," she said.

"It was Father MacAndrews." Her calm was drawing me toward the bed. Then I was across it, curled up against her, trying to burrow through to her. She stroked and stroked my hair as father had hers and mine. It was our only family gesture of affection. She was almost whispering. "Johnny," she said, "was everything a mother would want in a son. Oh, I shut my eyes to things. You have to . . . but now . . ."

I turned and lay on my back. "The man who hit him was Jake Catlett," I told the ceiling.

"Old Jake Catlett!" Mother's face drew in and went pale.

"He called grandfather 'cousin'—it was his son."

"Oh, Hannah, I'm so tired." Her face softened toward tears at last. "Jake Catlett . . . you try so hard and you're right back where you started."

★ ★ ★ ★

# Chapter Ten

I COULD HEAR the Diesel grunt of Number 2, the George Washington, going east up the valley and knew it was eleven o'clock. Mother melted back into her sprigged sheets and started to sob. I thought at first that it was my news, but it wasn't, not then anyway. It was the Diesel that seemed to break her grief water. I turned over, face down beside her, exhausted, almost touching her, but her muttering barely got to me. It dribbled, like her tears. "I just can't stand those damned Diesels. They don't sound right . . . lonesome . . ." she murmured, and her hand crept out on its own to find mine.

I thought, Jesus Christ, she's going to have one of her talking jags and I can't stand it after looking for Johnny all day; Johnny dead, the sack he came in, which had driven the bored women wild, refrigerating in a drawer the width of a child's trundle bed in the back of the Dodd mansion on River Street. The discreet neon sign, half hidden in the ragged boxwood trees in front of its brownstoned columns said in blue italic type, *Pierce's Funeral Home*. All I would have had to do was raise my head to see it, a tiny blue dot in the distance, down the hill and across the river.

"So lonesome," mother was crooning. Her hand touched mine and gripped it. It felt dry and hard, cold even in the hot down-river wind that bellied the organdy curtains, found our bodies, and rippled over them.

"That night when I heard the whistle of Number 13 I knew right then it was too late. It passed on the other side of the river about eight o'clock in those days. All I could hear was the rumble of empty coal cars away over the night across all that stillness. Of course they weren't running any coal. They hadn't run a ton of coal all that awful October. Now it's all happening again. You think you get away but you don't get away . . ."

"That awful October" was mother's Armistice night, her touch point. I, who had heard it so often, shrank away from that repetitive recital I'd been brought up on, when my grandfather, James Neill, had been caught by the wild bullet from the unknown miner's gun at Beulah.

My shoes dropped from my heels and fell on the wood floor. The hot wind fingered my back. Mother's grip got tighter, as if she were trying to hold on, keep from swirling down into the old minute, sliding toward it, fighting away, losing, an old woman lying in her bed, staring at the blowing curtains as the story came out.

"Not a ton of coal was moving. Beulah was right in the middle of martial law," she was saying, as if she'd never told it before, "I felt so cold that night. I couldn't shake that cold." She shivered in her summer bed.

"I remember leaning against a thin wooden column of the porch, cold under the sailor suit I hated so, when I should have been dressed in my Sunday best and right that minute on Number 13 in the parlor car on the way to Canona. I could hear the hanging swing at the downriver end by the rambler roses creaking," she told me, "forcing its way into my ears when I just wanted to be left alone. Papa must have heard the train and known what I was thinking. I heard him say he was sorry. God help me, I pretended not to hear," she admitted.

I began to listen, alert. She was lightly touching things I hadn't known before, which fitted nowhere into the old Beulah dream.

She was bringing toward me the sigh of dead leaves and the sting of cold on her cheeks, my grandfather, a man and not just a useful legend, apologizing to her back, swinging a little, shadowed by the last of the ragged rambler roses she had always hated so.

"I could hear that stupid whinny of Annie's all the way from the dining room. It was the exclusive-set giggle she copied from the Carvers." Mother slipped into an old language, still picking at Aunt Annie as she had done always. "I knew what Annie was up to. She was looking all googoo-eyed at Broker Carver, who was still lounging at the end of the dinner table where it was warm, close, and all soft lights, bragging and thrusting his glossy boots out where everybody had to walk around them, never taking his hot nasty eyes off the place behind Annie's lace peplum that bounced up and down when Annie giggled like that. You should have seen her. She looked like a take-me-take-me-slave-to-men, asking to be bid for. She wore her hair piled up in a big yellow pompadour with one of those rats. It used to jiggle when she walked. It wasn't the only thing that jiggled about Annie."

My grandfather must have caught, as I did when she told it, her sense of envious loss, shut out from the laughter, because she heard him call her again, softly, in the apologetic voice she admitted he had had ever since she could remember, except of course, mother covered over the admission, twinkling with the safer memory, proud, he was a flirt, "a real flirt," she said, right under my grandmother's crystal-cold, not-caring eyes. My grandmother Lacey had died when I was seven, but I could still see her, with her head held straight, like an Assyrian judge.

"I like to remember him." Mother patted my hand across the body-flattened frill of the bedspread, still making a choice of her

[ 170 ]

memory. "Oh . . ." Then suddenly she laughed, abrasive, contemptuous. "Oh, papa could be charming all right, then he'd get —you know—a little *too* flippant, and we'd all exchange looks, knowing what was coming and that it wouldn't stop until old Ted the colored man locked him in the upstairs bedroom, and we could hear him yelling things you couldn't believe would come out of his mouth. Well, at least he was a man then, a real man. Those times the whole house sank and dried out and everybody listened to everybody else's silence." Then she added, trying to cover over the memory, "He wasn't like that often, though; if I ever knew a gentleman, it was your grandfather. Don't forget it." But it was too late for her to retreat. "You couldn't *force* a word out of him when we wanted him to *do* something. Then all that foulness, dirty, evil, hating us all . . ."

This new truth made me rouse up heavily on one elbow, push back my sweating hair, and stare at her.

She had finished forming the new man with a whisper of new words and the spittle of her fury. She lay, her dust-white face dreaming again, the fine loose skin fallen back, eyes shut, her mouth slack so that her teeth showed clenched by habit, as if she were in pain. One white rootlike leg was thrust out beyond the sheet as if she wanted to be caressed by the wind, if only that. I wondered if she knew, in trying to breed a father again in Johnny, that she had only shown him half a man. My heart contracted at the sight of her and made my hand move forward again to try to touch her, but the touch made her twitch and draw away. She stared at me for a second, hating me too, and then yelled, "Don't look like that at me. I *hate* that hound-dog look. What do you care? Nobody cared a damn bit. He didn't. Just pretended to. He proved that all right." Then she glanced at me again as if she were afraid and turned away, watching the curtains, trancelike.

I could hear my father slowly trudging up the stairs, waiting to see if she would yell again. I heard him pause. She closed her eyes. I thought, or hoped, she was asleep at last and started to ease away from the bed. Father turned and went slowly back down the stairs, still pausing to hear if she cried out.

Without knowing it, she had, in her glimpse of old truth, described the night of shock we now lay in, the dim, muted house, the listening, the awareness of Johnny. I wondered if each drunken retreat of her father's had been a little death for them to suffer through.

She began to talk again, out of the depth of where she was. "They didn't care. Nobody did. He didn't care that mother and Annie and I were just pining to go on downriver." She still said downriver like a charm. "He just wanted to keep that stubborn grip on Beulah, old, ugly, dead place. You had to wipe the coal dust off the plates every morning. It wasn't as if we didn't have a chance. We had an offer—a good offer. It wasn't just a hope like it had been before."

She sighed as she must have sighed that night in 1912, when she was fifteen, making sure her father heard her. When she forced it through the trancelike cage of her ribs, it blew cold and hopeless, and smelled of the hot milk Melinda had made her drink so she would go to sleep. "Well, even if he had just disappointed me to death and it was too late to do anything about it after Number 13 had passed, I thought I might as well go and talk to him. There wasn't anybody else, and he did sound that apologetic way he did so much of the time that year, like he tried to do his best for us all. At least he couldn't tell me to go on inside when he was out there too. There'd been a rumor all day that bushwhackers were coming down out of the hills and that we ought to stay inside. But we were sick and tired of staying inside. The miners had been rampaging around off and on all summer."

She made a little humph. "Broker Carver was still holding forth in the dining room. I could hear that big loud hee-haw. You could have sent him to Princeton for twenty years and he still would have brayed like a jackass. Now you wouldn't know whether he was dead or alive."

I wanted to say, "No, you wouldn't, would you, mother? You wouldn't care if he was lying across another bed in a dirty hotel on Slingsby Street, crying out his scarecrow heart because Johnny is dead." But I didn't. I was trying to listen her toward sleep for once, not goad her into waking up. But dammed-up talk was flowing from her, relevent and irrelevent together, as if she were at long last sluicing her mind.

"When he deigned to notice me at all, he called me colty. He looked like a big bay himself, shining with money like sweat." She giggled. "You know, like horses sweat and men perspire and women glow. He used to have a lot of what I like to see in a man —pride of ownership. But when J. D. Cutwright rode upriver he put him in the shade. He'd been to Princeton too, and it showed, even if he was born in Cincinnati. Oh, you should have seen J. D. then. He moved through rooms like a prince before he got fat." We smiled together to think that Uncle J. D., father's partner, Melinda's secure-bodied red-faced father-in-law, had ever looked like a prince. "Of course Princeton in those days was the be all and end all. I could just see all those men in a gray-spired town, a Prince town like it said, full of lean hard princes of the money blood."

Then she made a little confession. Her face went soft and she smiled away from me. "I had the biggest crush on J. D. When he rode up the hollow to the mine, I'd wait all day for him, and just convince myself he was going to take me up on that big black he rode and take me downriver, away from all that tackiness and not having any money. Then he'd come up the walk and speak to me as if he couldn't quite remember who I was. Oh, I acted so silly about it, honey, but I kept it a secret. If anybody had known they would have been unmerciful." She was remembering tenderly, her child self. I hadn't known until then that the dry hand over dry bones that scurried away, or clutched at me in attempts at arid empathy throughout the story had been as dry already at fifteen, virgin-dry, paper-dry with fear she had confused with taste. What I had always taken for granted had happened when grandfather was killed had happened long before.

"Once papa called him a damn fool," she went on about J. D. Cutwright. "It made me ashamed when he was so embarrassingly courtly to his face. I could never stop seeing the little streak of fool in him, though."

She twisted against her pillow to release her nightgown, drawn too tight over her flat breasts, and admitted, still ashamed, that they had been sore that night under the camisole that she'd outgrown because she had what she called little buds that nobody had noticed enough to give her new underwear. She told about the smell of her father's after-dinner cigar mingled with the sweet scent of the tea roses. She said the thought of J. D. Cutwright was pulling her toward the dining room like a magnet.

"I wanted papa to say something, anything, to keep me from going. I had more dignity than to go and sit there ignored." The lanced hurt in her voice made me turn and stare at her, but she didn't see me. She still was mesmerized by the blowing curtains.

"Papa seemed exasperated with me that night. I hadn't done anything. I was the one who'd been disappointed, but I didn't care. I just wanted cold words. I didn't want anybody to sweet talk. Don't you get tired of that, honey?" she asked me but didn't wait for an answer. "Papa used his softest voice. He said, 'The whole world can't stop in its tracks for you to be amused, missy.'

"I told him it sure seemed to have stopped, and it had. There wasn't a light anywhere except away off at the depot. The houses were all empty because they'd moved the miners out when the trouble started. There didn't seem to be any town there at all, all the Jenny Lind shacks gone."

I could see the senseless scrawl of railroad tracks crisscrossing the bottom land, scribbling over it in dirty black lines, the film of coal dust on the trees, the slag ground into the dirty lanes that was the town of Beulah.

"It was all gone," mother said. "Nothing but silence all the way to the river, as if everybody had hidden, waiting for the bush-whackers to come down out of the hills. I shivered. I could imagine them all on the hills behind us with Mother Jones crouched up there with them ready to pounce on us all. Papa told me not to be sassy after I'd even forgotten what I said. He said it didn't become me. But I fussed at him. I reminded him for about the thousandth time that he'd promised. I couldn't get it out of my mind. Then he said what he always did when he was fed up. He said, 'Good God Miss Agnes, I didn't paralyze the valley!' That's as near as he ever came to swearing except when he was sick." She used the word "sick" delicately, with a little pause.

What the promise was she hadn't told me. Every time she mentioned it she seemed to veer away from it. "I just didn't want to be reminded," she said as if she were answering me. "I didn't want to think about the promise and I didn't want to go into the dining room and I didn't want to think about Mother Jones and scare myself to death. So I sat and gathered strength. I used to do it by practicing my gestures. Did you ever hear of anything so silly?" she said to her child self, amused and fond. "You know what your Uncle John said about me the first time he ever saw me?"

I knew she wasn't waiting for me to answer, but she always told it with a little air of surprise, as if she'd never told it before. She called him Mr. Baseheart in the story, ignoring the fact that he had married Aunt Annie and been her brother-in-law for forty-five years. The first time Uncle John saw her, when she was fourteen, he told grandfather, letting her hear, that she reminded him of the "Annunciation" of Dante Gabriel Rossetti. She took on the shutting-out, frightened gesture of the girl like a coat. It was the only joke Johnny ever allowed himself about mother. When the temperature went down and she turned her head, suppliant and withdrawn, to show how moved she was, Johnny would make the word Rossetti with his mouth at me, and she would catch me grinning and punish me with her silence. She never saw him do it. Because of it Uncle John was set in her mind as the mentor of all the culture she'd crammed into her young-girl head and left there like an old scrapbook she'd stopped adding to long ago but still used. I always wondered how much of what mother called her "ideals of life" she had pinned to Uncle John Baseheart, just because he was born in England and ought to have had them. He and Aunt Annie were physically comfortable people. They shared a complete disregard for foolishness of any kind, in which they included music, painting, books and the scrapbook of mother's mind. They also shared a decisive, homely wit, a kind of elegant fatness, and the ownership of Number Eight Mine.

But to mother Uncle John Baseheart meant money, culture, and control. From her father, with Mr. Baseheart always there, agreeing and sharing, she had a picture of the court at Dresden, and Paris and operas, and, in her words, all the important things of life.

She told proudly how grandfather had used these things to flog her brother Jim when he came to the table in his work shirt, all wet muscles and still smelling of the horses, leaving dung from his riding boots on the carpet. Once he yawned in the middle of one of her father's stories about Dresden and she said her father told him to dine in the kitchen with the servants. He said dine in front of Uncle John, and he drank in a courtly way.

"You know," she went on, "I just love that word 'dine.' Papa would say it in such a sardonic way. Nobody is sardonic any more. I guess they don't have the time. And it takes manners too."

She shut her eyes, her face peaceful, and I thought, after a few minutes of lying still, hardly breathing to keep from jarring her, that she had gone to sleep at last. I moved inch by inch from the bed and tiptoed around to the lamp on her night table. When I looked at her again her face was wrinkled and pink. She was crying like a weak child. I sat down beside her to catch and hold her until it was over.

She gathered herself in my pity for comfort and stammered through her tears, "Why didn't he take me? Why didn't he? You think it didn't matter but it did matter." It was not the death of Johnny that had reached her at last. She was taking from me the pity she had craved for so long for a child's disappointment, as if the first wound had to be healed before any later wounds could even be felt. Her hands were flat against my breasts, making mother of me as she had made father of Johnny. "Don't you see?" she muttered against me. "It wouldn't have happened if he'd done what he said. None of this would have happened. We wouldn't have even been there that awful night. We would have been on Number 13 in the parlor car and we would have gone to the park and I would have sat in front of the big gold and red mechanical organ and just let the music half drown me and watched the carved angels beat drums and blow trumpets and the ballet-girl statues dance around and around and the Hermes at the ends would be almost watching me under their grape hair and the music of *The Chocolate Soldier* would be playing like it had the year before when papa took me . . ."

"Never mind, never mind," I told her dry gray hair. "He couldn't help it, now could he? The train wasn't running and it was too dangerous."

"That's what he kept telling me. He could have found a way." She was calmer, curled against me. "When I heard that music I could just feel the elegant hussars papa told me about with their red coats and their kid pants so tight they put them on damp, all young and gay and ready to die in their purity."

She looked up at me; her face streamed with tears as the music must once have streamed over her. For a second she looked blessed, with that unquestioning light in her face, by the thought of a mechanical organ. Then the light was gone. She wailed, "All *I* had was Brother Jim and Broker Carver to tease me. I wanted to see papa's face shine again like it had the year before. All the way home on the upriver train he told me about the court at Dresden and how the chandeliers glittered and the gold braid and the lady's jewels. We sat close together on the labor train and he held my hand while we sang "I'm Just a Chocolate Soldier Man" and kept time with our feet. Then he sighed and wouldn't sing any more, and I knew he was going through the disappointment of not seeing his way clear to sending me abroad or east to school or at least to eastern Virginia. Several other nice people whose money had run out were going there to school. Nowadays, well!"

She seemed no longer to need the comfort of my body. She turned away and plumped a pillow behind her and drew her legs up, talking matter-of-factly, forgetting the tears before they were dry. "He made another promise that very night. He told me he'd take me to New York next time he went. But we both knew he couldn't. I was embarrassed for him and looked out of the train window and didn't talk to him any more. That shadow was back on his face and all the shine from the park was gone from him. He went to Philadelphia and New York a lot, but he always said he was going on business and I wouldn't like it. Brother Jim said he wouldn't let anybody go with him because he spent all his time waiting in offices, trying to lease out more land for the mineral rights. Northern men who came down and accepted our hospitality made him cool his heels and stay in cheap hotels. In those days a land-poor place like West Virginia had to go begging. Papa always said nobody cared who or what was on the land's surface. They had to dig down a little bit nearer hell to get what they wanted. He always said he would take me to stay at the Plaza Hotel." She sighed. "Think of the number of times we've stayed at the Plaza Hotel! Well, *that* doesn't settle a thing, does it?"

She looked exhausted. Gradually her feet slid down and she nestled in her pillow, almost contented. I thought she had made her whole relieving confession. The rest I knew, how grandfather had wandered that night down to the bottom of the garden like he did when he wanted to think, and someone had seen him move and shot. No one ever knew why, I was told. It had been such a wild night. Some of the miners had been drunk. There had been sporadic shooting all night long in the hills.

"Turn out the light and stay with me while I go to sleep," mother told me, and she watched me as I leaned forward to touch the switch. She looked, for a second of the last light, cool and relieved. In the pitch dark I felt my way around the bed and slumped down again beside her.

The stars and the river light far below us sprang out beyond the wide picture window of the bedroom. The room itself seemed suspended in black space, drifting in the air away above the flowing riverbed below us. Somehow what she said didn't matter, there above the slow flowing river, long before and long after us, moving like vein-blood west through the river valley, too deep for any sound, after the arterial spurt away east in the mountains. The only sound in the distance was the swish of late cars along River Street, whose lights were like a flung necklace, shining along the opposite bank. Upriver to us meant east to school, to mother's dream of a Dresden that no longer existed except in her borrowed memory, to her "things that mattered." Downriver meant going west to cold cash, as if money floated down the Kanawha like silt, gathered in the Ohio, and deposited itself in the fuel companies of Cleveland or Cincinnati, and then was sent back neatly to meet our going price, to buy up the source again, labor, love, and land to strip. It was the market the river provided, for mothers to try to marry their children off to awfully nice fuel companions from Cincinnati, who'd been to Princeton, just as Crawford Kregg had come from the James River to western blood, selling his daughter Lacey across the mountains to a Neill like a filly at Keenland. I had wanted to laugh at mother's tender romance with Uncle J. D. Cutwright. I wondered if mother had ever had a passion that couldn't be traced back to safe money. She once described a girl as "having such nice money" when she meant manners, and

Johnny had started to laugh with the rest of us until he saw that there were tears in her eyes because she had been teased.

Then, in the dark, over the running river, mother told me the rest. She told it as if she didn't really have to "face" it, but just let it happen aloud in her mind. Like the drift of the room or the current of a waking dream, she told me what she could not tell in the light of any day. For once she let me, and herself, hear something of the truth, at least all that fifteen-year-old angry eyes could see, or rejecting ears hear, through her isolated discontent. I was rocked in the darkness and her voice. Parts of it I missed, nearly asleep. Parts of it broke through as clearly as if they were happening to me.

Mother couldn't know, never taking her eyes off the river, that gradually as she talked the lighter darkness filtered into the black room. In light all the way from the stars, mirrored on the river and thrown back swimming on the ceiling to reflect on her face, the shadow of her that I saw looked as she must have thought her soul looked. I saw a sad, retreating, young virgin face.

But her face was still hidden when she began, letting the story drift into words I could hear. "You know, I'll bet Jake Catlett hasn't entered my mind for thirty years. All this time I'd forgotten he was there that night, but he was. I remember hearing that deep slurry voice of his. He talked like he didn't care whether anybody heard him or not. I couldn't tell how long he'd been standing by the path, listening to papa and me. They all had that way of moving, sneaking up like snakes across the grass and there they'd be standing watching you, you wouldn't know how long. I guess they got it from hunting squirrels. He said something to papa and papa moved over in the swing and asked him to come on up and sit down. I can still hear his new boots scrunch across the board floor, big old lace-up boots from the company store. He and papa sat there for a little while. They always did whenever they got together, very quiet, before they started to talk about whatever it was on their minds. Papa slipped into a different way of talking

[ 180 ]

when he was with those men. He seemed to change shape and size, and he had that way like he ruled the roost. Of course it was only habit. Poor papa didn't have an ounce of authority left, but none of them seemed to pay a bit of attention to that. Of course mama said papa was never happier than when he was with the white trash. When he said they were his people and depended on him, she just laughed, one of those sharp bitten-off laughs. Mama said there wasn't a Catlett or a Lacey left to amount to a hill of beans, and she'd been named after a better branch of the Lacey family herself.

"They did depend on him though. That night I heard Jake Catlett ask him what he thought they ought to do about things. Papa said he didn't rightly know. He just fell into that way of talking and rared back in that tacky comfortable way whenever he was with that awful bunch of Catletts and Hunkies and rednecks.

"Jake Catlett told him there wasn't a miner left on company property. He said that Giovanni Minelli had been the last to go, only he called him 'that Wop Minelli.' Minelli had told the mine guards his wife was pregnant and couldn't stay in a tent. I'm sure she was too, she always was. They were Catholics. Jake said the guards had gone up that morning to dispossess him. He said they took his truck and threw it in the river and hauled his wife down the porch steps like a sack of potatoes. Of course we knew better than to believe half those stories, but Jake had that quiet way that made you believe he wouldn't say he saw something he didn't. He told papa that Minelli had seen red when they laid hands on his wife and started to fight, but there were too many of the mine guards and they just hog-tied him and threw him into a cart and took him off to a little temporary jail they all called the Bull Pen. He said there were sixty-seven men from our side of the river down there in a little shed not ten by twelve feet.

"I guess Minelli was the only one of the Italian miners I knew by name, and that was because when Brother Jim and Annie heard what Mr. Baseheart said about me looking like the "An-

nunciation" by Dante Gabriel Rossetti, they purposely got it all
wrong and said I looked like one of Giovanni Minelli's youngins.
When you think we're even connected to him now. That," she said
delicately, "was Rose's father." Mother went back to the old night.
"Well, anyway, I didn't care. After all, nobody English or stylish in
those days would have said Annie looked like anything but a cheap
picture postcard, all peaches and cream and kittenish, and too fat
and laughing at everything like a hyena. I was the one who had style
and dash. Papa said so. Well, some way Jake Catlett must have
made papa mad, because he just snapped at him that Minelli
had signed a yellow-dog and ought to abide by it. Jake sounded
as mad as papa. He reminded him, as if he didn't already know
it, that most of the foreigners couldn't read or write and that nobody had explained anything to them. Then he really hurt papa.
He said half the men thought they were still papa's houses and that
he had something to do with them getting thrown out because of
the strike. Papa said Jake knew goddam well that wasn't true. He'd
forgotten for a minute I was on the porch. He said he'd told the
men when the houses were leased to the mine that there wasn't a
damn thing he could do. To all intents and purposes they belonged
to the company, and he pointed out again, almost like he was comforting himself, that everybody knew that yellow-dog contracts
specifically stated that if a man left his job he didn't have any
claim on a company house, that the relation was just like a master
and a servant. It was the law. He might as well not have spoken
for all the attention Jake Catlett paid to him. I guess he'd heard it
too many times.

"He just went on telling about Minelli getting thrown out. He
said he started to say something but that one of the mine guards
had said that the first son-of-a-bitch that moved would get his
brains blown out. Jake said he didn't know which was worse, coal-
company thugs or union thugs, with the people that really belonged there just sitting in between, hauled into fighting first one
side and then the other. Then he got up and went over to the side

of the porch to spit tobacco. He came back and folded himself down, a little easier. He said he'd told his wife 'Hannar' that no-body couldn't kick them off the hill farm because they owned it. He said she got all riled up about it.

"Then papa remembered I was there and told me to go on in the house. He used that man's excuse they used to use, you know, talking business, when they wanted to shut you out. It wasn't business they were discussing and I knew it. I knew they would just sit there in the swing, complaining, first about the miners and then about the coal-company guards. There was one of the mine guards from the Baldwin-Fells Detective Agency right in the house, living in Brother Jim's old room. That's how Kitty Puss's father first came out here from eastern Virginia. He was at Number 2 Mine on duty that night. Toddy Wilson wasn't any blackleg. He wore better boots than Broker Carver. He'd even been to Harvard. He didn't move down here to Canona until after he married Eliza Carver.

"Papa didn't like him much either. He just never seemed to trust any of those new people. Good God Miss Agnes, what would he think now? It's everybody we know! He said Toddy Wilson was like all those Confederate officers who went before him, who hired out for pay and fought for the Khediv of Egypt and in South American revolutions because there was nothing for them at home any more. He said they could charm the gold out of your teeth and were as ruthless as panthers, coming out to make money in West Virginia west of the mountains, deal after deal on land they didn't care about. I always thought he sounded a little jealous. It was a lesson he never learned. When papa talked about Mr. Wilson he usually ended up talking about money. It would remind him. I can hear him now, saying that word 'money' as if it were a curse, and telling me that nobody won the War but fat Mr. Money. He said defeat made the weak ruthless and killed the strong, and that there were things that a gentleman didn't do for money, but that men like Toddy Wilson didn't know that, that they did a sight more with their honey tongues to kill what we stood for than the North ever did.

"Mama would interrupt when he talked like that and say that ideals didn't fill the pot and that you couldn't borrow money on poor man's pride. But she was as proud as he was and still served dinner at noon and said luncheon at one-thirty, like the Carvers had downriver, was new-rich, coal-baron tacky.

"Papa and Jake Catlett went back to worrying the situation like dogs. When I got to the light of the door I could still hear them, papa saying his hands were tied, and Jake being stubborn as a mule and pointing out that the land was his and when a man owned land he ought to be able to do what he wanted. Papa tried to explain that he had no more jurisdiction, but Jake said Senator Neill had put the houses up when he opened the mine. Papa told him not to talk like a fool when he knew they'd leased the mine out; he said we owned the property but not the rights. Then they both gave up. Jake said it didn't make any sense and papa agreed with him. They ran down and just sat there with the swing creaking in the dark behind me.

"Mama was standing in the door. I can see her hair, the way she used to wear it, like a big furry hat in the gaslight from the hall. I thought she was going to fuss at me for being outside when we'd all been told to stay in the house, but she didn't. She seemed to have given up too. She just asked who it was out there with papa and I told her it was Jake Catlett asking papa to do something. She just laughed that little stab of a laugh and said, 'Your father's cousin Jake ought to know by now he never does anything he says he will.' I knew papa had heard her and gotten up, because I heard the swing creak."

At this point in mother's story I think I must have slept. When I remember her going on she was reminding me and herself of the living room as it had been that October night, and every night for so long, at Beulah. She had told me so much of this before. I don't know, even now, how much she told me that night about

Beulah that was new, and how much, in her exposure, was in-
tertwined with the tendrils of training and the scars. It brought
them all alive again. I wonder now if I hadn't heard much of it repeated hundreds of times before anything had happened to make
me ready to listen, as if, in revelation, I could allow it all for the
first time, as she was allowing herself to tell it.

"Hannah . . ." Mother heaved a deep sigh in the darkness and
said, "Time ruled those rooms in the evening after supper like
that whole house was a checkerboard and people moved on it,
waiting to attack an empty space. Promptly at eight-thirty, grandma
Liddy would look up at mama and begin to roll the string around
her tatting. She would stuff it in her reticule, making little noises
instead of asking outright, and finally mama would put down her
reading and without a word pull grandma Liddy up by her arms
like she was hoisting a cross, and they would trudge upstairs. As
soon as they had gone there would be a few minutes to sit and be
in the parlor by myself before Annie and her men flocked in all
flurry and falsehood and took it over like Coxey's Army."

She rambled a little. Perhaps whatever she had to tell me, and
herself, had to be approached that way, opened up for us not in
time, but in layers, layers of memory or of dreams. But I had a
sense all the time that she was coming nearer, with each small
confession, each old scratch, to a central wound I did not yet
know.

In and out, fading, sometimes clear, sometimes disconnected in
her voice or in my memory, I can hear her night voice: ". . . great
big blobs of red flowers, damp-looking pools, twelve of them," and
then her refrain, "I just *hated* that carpet!"

She seemed to face easily the hatred of inanimate things. She
"hated" the flowered carpet; she "hated" the hooded parlor lamp,
the mossy red velvet chairs, the masses of photographs of relatives
and connections, the brackish-looking huge gilt mirror, the sentimental rolls of music Aunt Annie bought, the fleur-de-lis of dead
baby's hair, my great-grandmother Liddy's embroidered velvet pic-

ture of Leto holding the babies in her arms. She "loved" the portrait of Senator Neill that had been painted in Washington and which hung over the pianola.

". . . oh, I just loved the stuffed pheasants. They were in front of a real painted forest. But of course that was childish, not real taste, don't you know? Oh, honey, I just wanted nice things. I had a game I called playing house. You know I still do it, in other people's houses—you know, when they have oak instead of maple or mahogany in the wrong place because they don't know any better.

"I would sit and I would watch my grandmother Melinda's portrait over the fireplace and I would promise her that someday I would have a room fit for her to hang in; oh, her straight slim nose, and her swan neck, and her dead-white face and her night-black hair, and her delicate long hand holding that rosebud; she always had them in her bedroom at Albion on the James before the War, always buds. The minute they were full blown she had them thrown away.

"Mama wasn't a bit like her. She had the straightness all right. She'd been taught that. But she had a kind of composure about her that was almost defeat. Grandmother Melinda would never have worn her morning dress all day without the energy to change. Of course when the few people mama cared boo-turkey about came upriver to call on her, she always looked like she was meant to look. So it wasn't that she *couldn't* do it.

"They would sit and talk in those silk, low voices women used to have. Then mama would look **more** like grandmother Melinda's daughter and I would study her movements. She never forgot them, but she didn't take the trouble to teach them. I would copy them afterward, whenever I could find a way to be alone: her way of sitting and walking, the balance of her hands. I tried to teach them to you, but you *stride*—it's so awkward. If I've told you once . . ." Then she got nearer the heart of her story, to a part I hadn't known. She almost whispered it to me under the

summer night wind, to the genteel intrigue against reality still going on.

She described how her mother had that imperious way when
she took money from people for staying at Beulah. "Every single
young man that Annie fooled herself was courting her paid to
stay all night. We were what people used to call poor-house
Tory . . ." She cut the words again. "Boarding house," she said,
separately and carefully.

I thought for a minute it was that poor thing she had been trying
to tell me and that she could sleep at last, but she went on. "But,
don't you know, mama could do surprising things, like she'd
waked up and seen us for the first time in a long time. One day
during that very summer"—mother found my slack hand again
and held it, telling me, switching to joy—"mama went charging
into the sewing room on the hottest day of the year. I watched her
hands all day, working over a big mass of tulle, fluting it with the
hot iron that made the room hotter than ever. She made a white,
frothy, girl hat. She wouldn't say all day who it was for. She tore
the white osprey feather from her own hat, sewed it on, stabbed
her white pearl hatpins into it all like she was trying to kill it, then
threw it at me so I had to catch it to keep it from falling. She just
said, 'There. There you are,' and then she marched out of the
room without another word. I had waited all summer to wear
it outside my own room. I knew Annie would try to borrow it and
wear it first, so I hid it."

Suddenly the next thought came, the hate one. It began with a
murmur, buzzed through the bedroom on that summer night, and
chilled my back as I withdrew from its sound and my mother's cold,
grasping hand. Her mouth moaned the sound, and she thrashed
over on her side, so that her eyes stared, darker pools in the dark,
a foot from my face. "Money money money. *You* don't *know*,"
she muttered sleep talk. "Money and men . . . men and money
. . . money money money, women lathering their lips over men
and money. Money makes the mare go. You can't borrow money

on big ideas. Don't marry for money but marry where money is. That house hummed with it. Sometimes I thought I could hear it hum in the gas fire and gurgle in the drainpipes. Mama wouldn't let us mention it though; that was tacky. Once I said that joke about marrying where money was and mama just said, 'I married money,' and papa left the room.

"I would sit in the parlor at night and I would make it all better in my mind by playing house for grandmother Melinda and Senator Neill. There would be cream walls and a clean green rug and a stained-glass window, and I would have a Tiffany lamp with tiny electric lights like flowers—that was good taste in those days—and a Lalique vase with a single red rosebud in it always for grandmother Melinda, and I would wear a yellow georgette dress that fell like a Tanagra figurine's when I moved. Of course I had never seen a Tanagra figurine but I had read about them. They were all the rage.

"So there I was, another Saturday night in my sailor suit," she went on, smiling at her young fool self, and drawing her crumpled yellow nightgown close about her jutting shoulders. "J. D. Cutwright strode into the parlor and never even noticed me. Who'd have thought he'd put on so much weight? Dear God, he and Broker Carver that night! Giants in the earth in those days!" Then she added, her voice sounding duty-bound to include it, "That was the first time I ever saw your father. He was just a shy young lawyer from Greenbrier in those days, just starting, and J. D. Cutwright had brought him up about the offer for Beulah. Annie was giving him her line because he was new. It was Mr. McKarkle this and Mr. McKarkle that that night. To see Annie flounce in you would have thought a summer-long coal strike didn't even exist. She said it was your duty to make men forget things like that. She didn't even push me aside. She just walked right through me and made for the pianola. She was gazing up at your father, running her hands over the keys as if she were really playing.

Your father looked like he'd swallowed a ramrod." Mother giggled. "That's the first thing I really remember about him.

"J. D. Cutwright was standing by the fireplace, and I just took for granted he was waiting for me to be seated because he was such a gentleman and a connection too. Of course Broker Carver was already sprawled all over grandma Liddy's chair, and Brother Jim was laid out on the sofa. Annie put a roll on the pianola and started to pedal. I leaned against the wall, casually, because I thought that was right. Old Annie's throat started to warble and pulse. I rember she was singing, 'Every little movement has a meaning all its own.' " Mother's thin imitation of the Annie girl's way of singing was bleak in the night. "She was twitching her big pink heinie around on the piano stool. I thought I'd just wait there until your father noticed how pale I looked, and willowy." She turned her head without being conscious she was suiting the action to the word. "The men in front of the fire weren't paying a bit of atten-tion to Annie's singing. They were just talking coal coal coal and that offer for Beulah. Brother Jim was bragging like he could change papa's mind when everybody in the room knew he couldn't. Nobody could. Then he started telling some long-winded story about Jake Catlett's meeting a transportation man from New York. I forget. He ended with, 'What I say is, turn some Gatling guns on the rednecks and clear out this valley and get to work,' then looked at the big gold watch he had inherited from Senator Neill so everybody would notice it.

"J. D. Cutwright interrupted him and said it was a little more complicated than that, you know, real calm, the way he would talk at Princeton. He had on polished leggings and beautiful whipcord pants he ordered from New York and he looked like all he would have to do was snap his fingers and all the trouble would be over in the time it took him to light his pipe. He said it was a family fight and nobody outside the state could understand it, that the trouble was that the mountain farmers never had learned how to

[ 189 ]

take orders. He said they came down out of the hills to dig coal and then walked home and washed off the coal dust and came out dirt-farm kings.

"I was just humiliated to death. I knew he was referring to Jake Catlett being distant kin and living at the hill farm and coming around to pass the time with papa like he had every right in the world. I hated Brother Jim for bringing up Jake Catlett and reminding him. He wouldn't ever have known if mama hadn't pointed out to him that we were connections of his through my great-grandmother Leah who was a Cutwright from Cincinnati marrying into the Catletts when they were somebody and lived in the Mansion at Beulah.

"Then J. D. Cutwright sat down. I didn't dare take my eyes off the pianola until the roller moved slower and slower and then stopped and the sound died as Annie let her feet fall from the pedals. I remember the notes swam in front of my eyes and I was scared to death I was going to cry in front of Annie and Brother Jim. J. D. Cutwright hadn't been waiting for me to be seated at all. He hadn't even noticed I was there."

"I got out of that awful parlor and I ran into the dining room to cry by myself. Coffee cups and dirty pie plates were still littering the table under the big dark green shade of the lamp. Papa's place was still set at the foot of the table. He hadn't even been in to supper. I thought then he just didn't care. I leaned there against the sideboard and cried for the day I'd be out of it all, all the heaviness and smell of old pie and loud laughter and tension between people. You know I never *could* stand tension. I vowed right then and there I wouldn't marry at all, with men ignoring you except at that one time when Aunt Toey said they depended like children and you could get what you wanted, the dirty-minded old thing."

Mother made that derisive humph at her girl self. "Oh, I had big ideas. About half the time I was going to marry a sensitive genius who looked just like the big angel on the mechanical organ. We just loved the poets then, papa and I. It was all right then. Everybody did who was, well" —I heard the faint embarrassed sigh that always went with the word—"a lady. Papa read me Byron and the Lake Poets. Oh I had big plans. Dear God!

"There wasn't a place in the world to go. I heard mama's step on the stair; she was coming down like she did when she was thinking, pausing with her whole weight banging down on each step. The front door slammed and I recognized papa's tired trudge. He and mama went into the library, so I couldn't go in there. Wild horses couldn't have dragged me back into the parlor.

"Everybody seemed to be doing just what they always did that night, but the tension was terrible—it made a noise of its own, that silence—like the time Annie got caught sneaking out to meet the Italian who was hired by the State of West Virginia to carve a tomb for Senator Neill when he was brought back to the valley. Mother made Dr. Dodd inspect Annie's body. You mustn't ever tell this," mother interrupted herself to warn me. "Annie cried all that week, but nobody said a word about what she had done. Mama only said the man was unsuitable and made him go to Canona and finish the monument there; then they brought it upriver on a barge, a big stone American eagle coming floating up the river. Annie sat for a week in her negligee by her bedroom window. She was very sweet when you came near her. But that didn't last long! After that week something happened to her and the tension was off the whole house. Mama's face came to life again. Annie went on back to seducing the men, and she'd even been abroad for a year before things got so bad and she hadn't gotten a thing out of it—not a thing. You know, Hannah, I *still* can't understand how Annie caught John Baseheart. She was already twenty-five and she didn't use *any* of her advantages. He didn't tease her or fuss at her like courting men did when they were flirting. Aunt Toey said she comforted him—made her sound like old shoes. Well, she'd been used all right! You can always tell when a girl is no longer, well, frankly, a virgin." Mother let the thought drift between us and gave me a sharp twinge of a look that had long since ceased to bother me.

"The new Slav girl mama had in the kitchen came in to clear the dining-room table, and I half hid behind the sideboard so she wouldn't notice me. She was only nineteen and she'd already had three babies, just dropped babies like an animal. Mama said that kind of people could have babies in ditches, not like ladies who suffered torture. Let me tell you, child, nobody told you anything then. Every time I looked at that girl, I could almost feel my swollen belly opening at my navel, making it a mouth that stretched to scream and let forth a baby in a big bloom of blood, like the horrible roses on the living-room floor." Mother's old body shook beside me, opening her own scar and mine.

I had lain at fourteen with my face to the wall, staring with wonder. When I had run to mother, my hands splayed out with fear, to find out what was wrong, she had pushed me away with cold horror in her fingers and her face suddenly gone childish but drained gray. She had gone to her room and lay staring at another wall, her thin head glossed with headache pain under the tangled mass of the long hair she had then. She wouldn't let me come near her or speak to her.

Now that she had at last spoken of blood, in one of the rifts of gentility Southern women have when they lift the taboos in secret and expose the bawd of curiosity or the old fear, she told me how her own mother had lain in the tufted blue satin bed at Beulah, which was her marriage bed, bought in Washington. She too had turned her pained face to the wall, the braid of her massive bay hair thick and shining as a great snake across the sprigged coverlet. Mother told me how she had run, panicked, to the creek, to wash herself clean, thinking she was dying, and how Aunt Toey had brought her back all wet and bedraggled, and she had stood as one punished by her mother's bed and her mother wouldn't turn her head to look at her.

"I remember mama looked like a little girl," she finished, still surprised, that many years later.

I could see us all, white-faced, marked with the same bay hair, taboo as savages at the time of breaking forth, with our faces to the wall, like one timeless, ashamed, refusing girl, betrayed without comfort or warning, into woman. Once when I was sent a dozen red roses at Christmas she threw them out and called the boy's mother and they had the kind of polite talk she used for women she would never know very well. She said she had done it because florist's red roses were not a fit present for a young girl, but you had to consider the source.

I think it was to destroy the pain of what she had exposed that mother made herself go on talking. "That Slav girl had dreamless married eyes, the kind of slave eyes Broker Carver's intellectual sister meant when she said that for some it was too late for the vote to save them. She really *knew* Carrie Chapman Catt." Mother made a little humph of laughter. "She even had a letter from her. She showed it off to everybody. I thought then it was the answer to everything, the . . . what's its name . . ."

"Panacea." I looked at her old head.

"Oh, you always know the words," she brushed at me, annoyed but teasing. "You know, that very Saturday evening at supper Brother Jim tried as usual to get me started, so he could show off in front of Broker Carver. He said, 'Miss Sally here is our high-browed member of the family. She's against motherhood and she thinks the Holy Ghost is a woman!' Mama said, 'Don't blaspheme,' and shut him up, just stopping it because she was tired of argument and was head of the table. She said, 'I don't need the vote. Aunt Toey's boy Jim does my voting for me.' That quieted them all to think that a nigger was qualified but that an intelligent lady wasn't.

"I went on in the kitchen because there wasn't any place else left to go. I thought maybe Aunt Toey would talk to me, but she was asleep, her old gray mouth folded in where her teeth had been and her eyelids all sunk in wrinkles. The white headscarf she always wore was pushed to the side by the back of the rocker. I could see her ear and a tuft of white hair like the lamb's wool I put in my stockings in the dead of winter so my toes wouldn't freeze when I walked across the river ice to school. Her little spindle shanks still pushed up and down on their own in her sleep to keep her rocking. She looked so old that I could believe for a minute that she was a hundred years old like she said she was and could remember Thomas Jefferson coming to Albion on the James River. Mama said there wasn't a word of truth to it, she must have heard it. She said, 'You know how they are, they get things mixed up.' She spoke as if all the Negroes in the world were her responsibility. She said that about other things Aunt Toey told me too, that there wasn't a word of truth, but I know there was. She told me Aunt Toey was eighty-two then, the same age as grandmother Melinda would have been if she'd lived. Toey always belonged to her. Mother treated Aunt Toey as something she'd inherited. Well, Aunt Toey and some spoons were all mama had left. Even Albion belonged to a rich Tennessee carpetbagger.

"And after '98 we didn't have a thing—after all the Senator's money! For a long time the family at Beulah tried to keep up a pretense; mama said it was imperative to keep that up. I used to sneak up to the attic on summer afternoons where the last wicker trunk with the stickers from Baden and Rome and Vienna was pushed into a corner behind baby cots and old piles of bills, to read Baedeker and drape my head in mama's blue traveling veil she'd bought in Paris.

"When the carpetbagger's brother came to Beulah to make a deal for some property, he tried to get close to mama in a way the new people did downriver, by claiming kin in eastern Virginia. You know, 'My brother at Albion . . .' But mama's door slammed shut at him.

" 'I have no connections in eastern Virginia,' she said and put him in his place, the new coal-company squatter. Then she gave me a piece of advice. She said, 'Don't claim kin in front of strangers. Only trash have to claim kin. We don't.' But she'd claimed kin herself to J. D. Cutwright. Mama wouldn't let papa lease Mr. Potter an acre when they needed the money desperately. George Potter's father never forgot how she'd treated him." My mother smiled as if it were still a family joke. "Look at them now. Good God Miss Agnes!

"I waited and waited for Aunt Toey to wake up but she wouldn't. There didn't seem to be a place in the wide world to go."

Then, as if she had wandered into a cold place she couldn't escape from, I felt my mother's body twitch, then freeze. Her voice rose in pitch, high, thin, faster than I had ever heard her talk before. She caught me and thrust me down with her into what she was seeing, caught, unable to move, until it was over.

"I suddenly felt drawn back toward the library. I did, like something calling me. No. That isn't right. I stopped in the dining room, hearing my parents' voices reach through the closed library door. At least mama's did. Her voice was louder than usual, and edged. Papa answered so little she seemed to be talking to herself, dribbling talk, fast, fast. I knew by the tone there was no use going into listen. The sound had that pitch of secrets I knew so well, only worse, much worse. I knew they'd stop talking if I opened the door. They would stare too hard at what they were supposed to be reading and shut me out, like they always did. Damn them, I knew what it was all about. The offer had hung over us all through the week; the men's talk in the living room, that muttering in the library, Annie's sulking; all of us just obsessed with it.

"I knew then that papa had avoided supper and the living room and left J. D. Cutwright and your father to use their sweet talk on Brother Jim. He was already persuaded in his crib to sell anything for money, but he couldn't do a thing to get us downriver.

"I stood there in the dining room and helped mama. I willed at papa's mind as hard as I could to make him decide to stop hanging on by the skin of his teeth and sell Beulah and move our nice things. Oh, honey, the portraits, the fine old furniture great-grandmother Leah had brought from Cincinnati, the blue satin bed from Washington, the two serving spoons with the Kregg coat-of-arms left over from Albion, the carved silver candlesticks that were a present from Chester A. Arthur, the ruby in its heavy gold that mother wore now that grandmother Liddy's finger was too thin to hold it on. That went to Annie. It went to Annie when it should have gone to me. I cared more. It isn't the letter of the law, it's the spirit of the law that counts every time. Oh, I could see it all in a big house on River Street in Canona, just like the Carvers' house, showing the new people with their new things and their new houses and their new families who we really were without our having to say a word. River Street of all places! There's not a soul left there now, but then it was what grandmother Liddy called the bon ton!

"I heard the library door slam. It was like glass being shattered. Somebody had decided at last. I could tell. I just unclenched my will and thanked God. After all that indecision and argument and strain for so long, something had to break. I had never in my life heard either of my parents slam a door. They weren't that kind of people. The crash cut through the house so that even the men in the living room were still.

"Then, honey, I just stood there.

"Nothing happened. The outer door opened. The cold draft hit me all the way through the back hall and then stopped as if the heavy front door had been eased shut. I couldn't move a step. Do you believe that? I was afraid to move, even when I heard mother dragging upstairs slowly. Her feet sounded tired to death.

"I don't remember getting from the dining room to the back hall. I just know I was leaning against the wall, looking through to the big dim mirror in the darkened downstairs bedroom that belonged now to Toddy Wilson from eastern Virginia. I heard it. I heard a light crack from the bottom of the garden. It sounded too light for a shot.

"The men rushed out of the living room and pounded through the front door together. I couldn't take my eyes off my frozen reflection in the dark mirror. I pinned myself to it for safety. I can still see my head thrown back against the dark wallpaper. There were

[ 196 ]

running boots across the veranda. Men's voices were babbling over the scrape of wood as they lifted one of the huge green shutters from a front window. I watched my head in the mirror. It was thrown back against the dark wallpaper. I couldn't swallow. My throat hurt me.

"I heard boots shuffle toward the door. They brought father in on the shutter and laid him down in the front hall. Big Brother didn't even see me against the dark wallpaper; he just ran to the wall telephone and pumped it and pumped it and sobbed out, 'Oh, Jesus, oh, Jesus. Get Dr. Dodd quick. It's father.'

"Dr. Dodd's brother had a fine new house on River Street, the one who inherited the farm and opened the mine. I couldn't move. Big Brother yelled, 'He's shot himself,' as if it were Dr. Dodd's fault. He had papa's little pearl-handled revolver in his hand. I saw my own mouth in the mirror. It was as thin as a blade. God damn you, God damn you, selfish, you're selfish to leave me alone in the back hall in the grip of their hard charity forever, cut off, cut off, hopeless!"

She was yelling at the blowing curtains and the summer night, twisting and turning in the rebirth of the terrible forgotten minute. We heard somebody fumbling to open the door. She shouted, "Go away. Don't come in here!" I held her arms down until I could feel her collapse and soften into sobs under my fingers. The sounds she made were disconnected, then gradually drew together in her mind, first in flashes, then, more calmly, into words.

". . . people running, skirts swishing, Annie screaming, a slap, then Annie crying, mama's slow drag downstairs. That stopped all movement. Her voice was as hard as hate. She said, 'I might have known he'd leave me to make the decision.' She held out her hand to Brother Jim and said, 'Give me that gun.' Then she began to moan, 'Buboo, oh, Buboo,' to Brother Jim. She was calling for him by a name that hadn't been used for years. They walked past me into the dining room, away from father and the others, Big Brother holding her head against his shoulder and the revolver held on her finger like a ring. I never saw it again, and we never told. We had to protect papa's memory, didn't we? Brother Jim kicked the door shut behind them without even seeing me. I couldn't look. I couldn't look at anything but my face in the mirror." Mother's sobs quieted at last and she sighed.

"Then, if somebody wasn't gripping my arms," she said, "you know, hard. I hoped for one second it was J. D. Cutwright, but it wasn't. Wouldn't you just know it was Preston McKarkle, your own father, who tried to steady me with his strength in the dark hall. And you know I was still watching myself in the mirror. When I turned my head a little I *did* look like the girl in the 'Annunciation' of Dante Gabriel Rossetti. I *did*."

Mother smiled.

The family lie had been told for so long it had been turned to truth by Johnny's death, the lies of the parents lived out by their children, as if we were condemned to repeat and reface, not the true past, but its false reflection, until it was exorcised.

She lay there, almost asleep at last, dried out and calm. Then she said, "They're all such babies . . . just little boys . . . you can get them to do whatever you want to, Hannah. I've always worried a little about you. You never *would* learn . . . you're so gullible . . ."

She knew. She'd known all the time. In the very ice wall of her calculated innocence there was something as cold as evil. She would go on, keeping as a safe shrine—because the dead are safe and they destroy no dream of them—a room for a boy who had never existed, except in answer to her demand, as in all the years her father had existed exactly as she wanted him to be, and all the time she would know that she did it.

"Do you think," she murmured, "that they'll put it in the paper? All that business about Jake Catlett claiming kin? After all, everybody has a less fortunate branch of the family . . ."

She had not, in the whole exorcising of her hurt, mentioned Johnny. She was still babbling on when I fell asleep.

★　　　★　　　★　　　★

# Epilogue

THEN I WAS in the dark, dark so deep that it had its own space. Only the dead spongy punk clutched in my hand kept me from floating in a valley of blackness. I was in the hollow sycamore at the old Canona farm, still on the hill as I remembered it before the suburbs were built, hiding, waiting as I had so often, to be found. Its aged angular roots bit against my skin so that I couldn't turn, pricked and held me. Something moved in the dry leaves; I waited for the darkness-snake to caress my thighs. My eyes were bound with blackness.

Beyond me in the steep hollow, through the whole valley, I knew that there was nothing, nothing to scream at, nothing to hear, not even any wind. I knew it was only a game we had been playing all the time, but Johnny was pretending not to find me, leaving me there after the sounds of hide-and-seek had long since died with day, the test of the tease, gestures and jokes, all the games dependent on—not breaking—but a flirtation with trust.

The birds screamed, and I woke up in my own bed watching the two neoclassic Picasso drawings mother had chosen because, after long consultation with Melinda at Christmas, they decided I would like them. She had waited in the doorway for me to notice them, please. "I always believe," she said shyly, "in breaking up the period of a room."

A yellow, still, breathless morning lay in the valley beyond my window. On my blue chaise longue lay a black hat.

For a few minutes the air was as still and empty as my dream had been, as if the past were gone into that black space, and there was only the terrible freedom of the new day.

In the hall mother called out, "Melinda, I can't find it."

"I *told* you, mother." Melinda's voice and her footsteps pounded up the stairs. They disappeared into mother's room and I heard the door slam.

Minnie Mae sounded as if she were dragging herself up the stairs. She stood at the top to catch her breath loudly, then knocked on my door. "You got to eat something," she commanded, coming in with the black dress I had worn the night before, pressed, hanging across her fat arm.

"Your Uncle Ephraim undressed you," she told me. "He said you looked like you'd walked a hundred miles."

The clock said nine o'clock.

"We got to be down there by ten-thirty," Minnie Mae said, waiting for me to get out of bed.

Mother, Melinda, and I sat in the breakfast room, not looking at each other, our white hands stark against our black dresses, drinking coffee as black as cannel coal and paid for by it. Melinda's silver spoon tinkled lightly against her china cup, and I remembered mother's weightless, secret giggle of the night before. They passed each other dry toast with their white hands, white hands crawling along polished mahogany. I could hear mother chew, then little humphs as she tried to keep the toast quiet in her dry mouth.

"Do you know," I stabbed at the embarrassed silence, "that preachers are buried head first and everybody else feet first?"

Mother and Melinda avoided each other's eyes.

"So that when they are raised up on Judgment Day the preachers will face the people," I went on explaining.

The clock said nine-thirty.

Johnny had said, Johnny had soothed, "Don't rock the boat, Sissy . . ."

We looked, in "good" black dresses and black hats, like three provincial ladies having tea at mother's Plaza. Mother cleared her throat.

"Please God, help me to understand them," I prayed. To dress and empower us, to pay for our dresses and our manners, our polite emerald green oasis, the grabbers bit at the coal face, the conveyors carried out coal and left the men unneeded. Johnny was dead so stupidly, Jake wandering a wasted man in his own wasted corridors, two more men in the way of the big grab. Without land to till or people to care for, Johnny had been caught in a parody where the land had shrunk to a genteel suburban house he wasn't even needed to work for, and Jake had been caught by the inertia of change, both with the taproots of their women clinging to the defiled rock, making them stay.

So we sat, the women Johnny had let pull his heart and hamstrings until he was small enough to live with us, we the slaveowners, who had inherited the punishment unto the third generation, that of having to rule, but having no one to rule but each other; need and training turned inward, slave and master one.

Mother sighed and mewed gently, watching my face, "You might try to see some of the nice things in life, for all our sakes. You think too much," she said sadly, asking the last sacrifice to a good life, that it be seen as she demanded.

Melinda joined her. "You won't do anything the way people . . ." She looked scared, embarrassed at the way the sister cat might jump. It was the only emotion she had left that would make her act.

I said inside the silence, "Johnny, I am. I'm going to rock the boat. It's too late for anything else. The cost of using a whole river for our small rowboat is getting too high . . ."

They watched me tentatively, hopefully, as they had watched Johnny for so long.

"Oh, she'll be fine. Won't you, honey?" mother decided. She reached over and patted my hand, misreading my calm face. "She'll be just fine. Everybody watches you," she added vaguely.

All the way down the hill the valley held its breath. As we drove across the river the yellow air began to move; it made the trees sigh. No one said a word. Mother huddled between Melinda and Spud in the back seat, her face smaller than I had ever seen it. She saw no one. She only clutched at Melinda's arm. Beside me, father watched straight ahead as we passed our old house on River Street and the funeral home that had once been the Dodd mansion.

Along the street by All Saints Church, paper bags had been put on the parking meters. They had the word FUNERAL printed on them. It seemed to have nothing to do with us.

At the side entrance of All Saints a strange, thin young man stood, watching for us. As we got out of the car he came forward and touched father's arm. "Would the family come this way, Mr. McKarkle?" He was almost whispering, as if any noise might wake the dead.

We followed him in a straggly line into the Chapel of Repose, all looking at the floor.

"Some of the family is already present," he explained to father. I wondered if he laid out corpses, if he'd defiled Johnny with his long manicured fingers, or if he was just the front man. He tiptoed like a Third Avenue fruit. Johnny wasn't there to see the joke.

Inside the Chapel of Repose the first member of the family to arrive sat, clean and upright, his watch chain glittering on his shiny black suit, looking straight ahead as if he were carved in stone. It was Mr. Catlett, with his crutches beside him. When he saw mother he struggled out of the pew. The man beside him, his narrow face rock solemn because he was in church, didn't look around.

Mr. Catlett swung himself over to mother. "Sally, honey, I ain't seen you for nearly fifty years. Eddie Lacey brung me. I wouldn't of had it no other way." He leaned his old gray face down to look at her.

Mother's eyes were glazed with aloofness, that look which had become poetic in our lazy eyes. I saw for the first time how cornered and cruel it was.

"Why, I'm Jake Catlett," the old man went on to explain.

Mother gave her arm to father and let her head droop away, leaving him stranded on his crutches. He stood in the aisle, watching her as she went into the first pew and knelt to say prayers to some God I didn't want to love.

"Mr. Catlett"—I held his arm—"thank you for coming."

"Eddie Lacey brung me." He looked around at the other stone figure.

The funeral director waltzed up the aisle, sensing trouble.

"I told this fellow," Mr. Catlett whispered, "I wanted to pay my respects."

"I explained to him," the young man said, copying mother's aloofness, "the people of this congregation don't usually view the departed."

I steered Mr. Catlett back into his seat and knelt beside him to hide my face.

"Oh Johnny, get me through this," I prayed. I knew that the funeral would be a correct tribal rite. "Oh, who will beat the tom-toms now that Johnny's gawn away?" It sounded like a jukebox song.

Mr. Catlett whispered to me when I'd sat up again, blank-faced, "You folks Catholic? They ain't nobody in the family . . ."

"No, Episcopalian," I whispered, not softly enough.

Melinda looked around, willing me to drop dead.

"Oh, I thought 'twas Catholic." Mr. Catlett subsided.

Someone's hand touched my shoulder. It was Aunt Annie. Her

fat face looked physically hurt. "Honey," she whispered and clutched my shoulder to strengthen me. Then she looked beyond me.

"Why, Mr. Catlett!" She leaned over and took his hand and held it. Tears swam in her eyes.

"Aw, Annie," he said, shy and pleased.

"Whar's the English fellow?" he whispered when she had gone on down to sit behind mother, touching her shoulder so that she looked around, as grateful as the old man had been.

"He died. Mr. Baseheart," I whispered back.

"He's a right nice feller for an Englishman," Mr. Catlett whispered.

Melinda looked us quiet again.

My Aunt Beulah Neill, as thin as a scarecrow, her yellow face framed in wisps of gray hair and black net hat, slid with infinite care into the opposite pew, speaking to none of us. Beyond her head, the brass plaque dedicating the Chapel of Repose shone brightly, polished by the altar guild:

IN MEMORIAM

Eliza Carver Wilson

Requiescat in Pace

Father MacAndrew's widow had had a brother. I was in the bushes with Johnny, watching Broker splash into the swimming pool.

Mother had said, "I don't know what's happened to Eliza. She's just let herself go. After she got Kitty Puss married and then Teddy Wilson died and she rattled around that big house alone, we tried to find time . . ."

The lights of Aunt Eliza's parties had splashed the river as we sat on the bank where Broker clutched the smelly grass of the last piece of property he had in the valley.

Father MacAndrews leaned down and whispered to father.

It was time.

[ 204 ]

We followed an usher into the church. I saw Johnny's pall-bearers sitting in a front pew—Wingo Cutwright, Luddy Wilson, Charley Carver, Brandy Baseheart, Plain George Potter, and a man I'd met once before in a downtown bar, Johnny's boss, who was in white goods and televisions.

In front of us the empty "family" pew yawned. Beyond it a crowd blasted my eyes. I looked down, trying to pretend they weren't there, hoping for a second of training as rigid as Melinda's that there would be no writing of grief on my face for them to read. I helped Mr. Catlett into the pew beside me. Eddie Lacey followed us.

We sat in a savage, long black row, exposed for once as we were, to wait for Johnny.

There was a rush of people standing up, like wind coming nearer, pulling us to our feet.

I heard Father MacAndrews, far away, intoning, " 'I am the resurrection and the life, saith the Lord: he that believeth in me, though he were dead, yet shall he live . . .' "

There was a whir of little wheels behind us.

Father caught a glimpse of the crucifer carrying the cross high above his head, and the genuflection ran from him, caught by us, until it got to Mr. Catlett, who had not risen.

" 'I know that my Redeemer liveth . . .' " I could hear Father MacAndrews; the cross swam and sparkled in my eyes.

Johnny, hidden as he had been in the midst of life, lay at the foot of the altar steps, his iron-gray steel casket the only reminder of the corruption of his protected body. The casket was covered, as if the church were trying to overlay and hide it in hope, with a huge crossed pall.

Father MacAndrews said, " 'We brought nothing into this world, and it is certain we can carry nothing out . . .' " Uncle Ephraim stood nearest the casket, watching it without hope, the tears running unchecked down his face. Someone sobbed. Melinda glanced over, her face blue under her make-up, to see if it was me.

Father MacAndrews clumped up the altar steps beyond the casket, his eyes set on the back wall of the church, and began to chant the De Profundis, the words as impersonal as all dying, a thousand years of the naked moment, when the church demands, even of nice people, that they face, for once, an unavoidable mystery.

" 'Out of the deep have I called unto thee, O Lord. Lord, hear my voice . . .' "

The response rumbled beyond us and filled the church. "O let thine ears consider well the voice of my complaint . . .

" 'If thou, Lord, wilt be extreme to mark what is done amiss, O Lord, who may abide it?' " Light ebbed away from the altar. The new stained-glass windows went dark. The answering chant was drowned in thunder.

It began to rain, pelting, rolling down the valley, harrowing the church roof. Even so near the altar I could barely hear Father Mac-Andrews read the lesson.

"Cloudburst," Mr. Catlett said to himself. He looked straight ahead still, as if he hadn't realized that he spoke aloud.

I asked Johnny then when he had started to die. I asked him why, but he had escaped us, lay sacrificed in a joke suburban death, and didn't answer.

The rain steadied its pounding. Behind us, mingled with it, the tentative singing of people unused to church except at weddings or at funerals struggled with the old and blood-stained hymn.

" 'When wounded sore the stricken hart lies bleeding and unbound,' " sounded as thin as wind on grass under under the roof studded by rain.

" 'The Lord be with you,' " Father MacAndrews told us.

And we answered, leaf-sighing through the rain, " '. . . and with thy spirit.' "

"Let us pray," he said, and the crowd behind us rustled to its knees. Father helped mother down. We were at last able to hide our faces for grief or embarrassment or whatever moved the black family pew of failed strangers. Or perhaps it was shame, that old cross-bred feeling between a hell-fire gospel and the tentative manners of the perpetually changing American seeking someone stable to copy.

Father MacAndrews motioned to the pallbearers, who shuffled to either side of Johnny's casket. I could see its bronze handles, eighteenth-century good taste, peep out from under the pall. No one touched them. They walked beside them, while the correct attendant rose carefully on his toes and began to wheel Johnny out, following Father MacAndrews and the crucifer. He might have been wheeling a baby carriage.

The rain stopped. The stained-glass windows began to blush with color and the church was filled with their prisms, rods of blue, squares of red and yellow light, flung through them by the washed morning sun. Outside of the church a rainbow arched against the dark cloud carrying the rain downriver. Causeless, my heart leaped at its promise as hearts leap, unprepared always, when being alive unexpectedly lightens the world, seen as the boy on skates had seen it, free for a second, and new.

We drove to the cemetery through yellow water. It roared down the ditches, carrying clay from the scarred hillsides blasted for the road; eroded walls of yellow clay streamed with water. I could see the hearse ahead splatter and part great sheets of hill-laden water as they overflowed the ditches and burst across the blacktop, making it shine in the sun. The sleek black body plowed on, its rear curtains drawn thoughtfully so we would not see where Johnny lay, the *corpus delicti* for so many hidden in death as in life by lazy, easing custom.

I had been "helped" into the front seat beside Father. In the back seat, as if they were playing the quick march to ease them away from stupefied sorrow, mother and Melinda muttered the kind of talk Southern women keep on exuding when they think their mouths are closed, a dripping tap of remarks unmatched by their dim, drained faces. Like the water that rushed upstopped, unchanneled, unthinking, rilling down the rocks of Cemetery Ridge, they reconstructed Johnny.

"He would have appreciated . . ."

"He would have liked . . ."

"He would have laughed . . ."

Melinda said proudly, ". . . the church was crowded."

Mother sounded worried. ". . . there were a lot of people there I didn't know."

I hadn't seen either of them look up.

Melinda explained that they were business people. "You know, a man . . ."

"Oh," mother said.

In a little silence the motor purred on and the hill water splashed under the wheels.

"I always thought it was 'heart,' you know, inside—not *a* hart . . ." Melinda's voice began to ripple again.

"Isn't it? That changes *everything*."

"No, it's hart, like a deer."

"Oh!" Mother said, pleased. "Because Johnny liked to hunt! Oh!"

"Wasn't that thoughtful?" Melinda had moved closer to mother.

Mother began to hum, as she did when she was nervous, to keep silence at bay. She hummed faster and faster and drummed her fingers on the window sill in an incessant woodpecker noise. I thought she was going to fall into talking wisely about God's love, which she usually did on our trips to the cemetery, but she said nothing, only went on humming and tapping.

We turned in at the cemetery gate. The narrow ribbon of road curled and twisted around the family plots and the acres of planted stone in the golf-course green sod of the "perpetual care" section. We passed the Carver mausoleum with its heavy Greek pediment, passed the newer Potter lot, where a flat stone, isolated from the shiny, mottled marble monuments, marked Sally B.'s grave. She had been the first casualty of our "age group," as Melinda called it, in the new sports car Ann Randolph had given her the year the highway was opened.

We wound on up the hill. Far ahead of us I could see the hearse, stopped. The casket was being carried to a rain canopy just visible over the Grecian Urn of my great-great-grandfather and -mother Catlett's grave, moved to Canona from in front of Beulah Church when the ramp was built. Away above it against the sky were spread wings that looked from a distance like a triumphant angel. The road was tortuous on the steep hillside. We wound past the monument of rough-hewn native stone over the grave of Colonel Peregrine Lacey who had died at Beulah in 1833. I could not forget it. Once on a dare from Johnny I had let myself be left there until darkness came, my back pressed hard against the bronze plaque put on the stone by the DAR. It was a bas-relief of a cabin with Colonel Lacey's revolutionary titles under it. When mother saw it, she laughed and said the Colonial Dames never would have made such a mistake as to put one of the old Lacey family in a log cabin.

The car had stopped. Then I saw mother's face, mute and played on as a tree in rain. When father reached for her hand she shrank back and turned her head away so that the hard, etched curve from her thin shoulder to her chin was all I could see, the way she had always had of turning into a dark calm of her own, away from us when we displeased her. Father and Melinda crooned and helped her from the car.

Away down the road behind us, cars had stopped and small dark huddles of people wandered in and out through the tombstones of our family plot. In a long line beside the nearly black fluted pedestal with its Grecian Urn, where a weed was growing, the rest of the bodies moved from Beulah lay under neat gray marble markers. They were washed clean by the rain, the dates ludicrous on the new stones. Mother and Aunt Annie had decided that the other tombs were not interesting enough to move. Our black heels sank in the wet grass. Someone took my arm and I realized the family had walked on. It was Uncle Ephraim. I glanced at him, but as he walked me nearer the presence of people, quiet but not so quiet as death, I watched only the eagle that had looked like an angel against the sky. At the hill's crest Senator Daniel Neill's monument flew frozen in the air, dominating the lot. Life-size figures of Minerva and Justice mourned against a ten-foot-high black marble column. On top of it the eagle clutched in its claw a draped stone American flag.

Uncle Ephraim made me go toward Johnny's grave. There was none. There was not even any soil to cover Johnny. His casket lay on the surface of the ground, its pall turned greenish by the light from the canopy. Then I saw beyond the canopy's shade a mound covered with bright green fake grass, so that we would not be offended by naked earth.

I could not take my eyes off the dull steel that was not covered by the pall. It seemed the only substance there that was itself.

Father MacAndrews began to murmur, " '. . . man that is born of a woman hath but a short time to live.' " I looked away toward the valley. At the other end of the casket from Father MacAndrews, Broker Carver stood, like an aged, unemployed guardian angel in Johnny's cad check suit, standing out from the black around him. He was drunk, his runneled face suffused with peace. The suit and his frayed collar were clean. "Amen, Johnny, amen, old Johnny boy," he kept muttering. Johnny's boss, who had a fat, serious face, red from mowing his lawn, kept jogging Broker with his elbow and sneaking side looks through the prayer with his little silencing eyes, but Broker had been jogged by life far more harshly than that soft man could ever do. He didn't even feel it, just went on muttering with his pebbly voice, "Amen, Johnny, amen, old Johnny boy . . ."

" 'In the midst of life we are in death . . .' " Father MacAndrews raised his voice, sensing the interruption. Broker caught my eye and winked and wiggled his bony shoulders.

In a row across from us Uncle Ephraim stood, looking far away down the valley. Rose was beside him; she clutched at Tel Left-wich's frail arm. Tel looked hypnotized with grief. From the way Rose gazed across the casket at mother's drooped head and held onto Tel, she seemed to have dragged her all the way up the hill. I knew she'd forced her to come. George Minelli stood on her other side, not taking his eyes off the pall, his hat flattened against his stomach. But it was mother Rose was hating with her gesture; she was using Tel as a naked weapon.

Father MacAndrews put his hand back toward the funeral di-rector, who was watching us all so closely for anything out of order he seemed to be counting heads. I could see Minnie Mae and Jack, in his uniform, away behind him by a clump of yew trees, as solid as if they too had roots. Both their faces glistened with rain or tears.

" '. . . and we commit his body to the ground; earth to earth, ashes to ashes, dust to dust; in sure and certain hope of the Resur-rection unto eternal life . . .' " Fine grains of clean white sand fell like salt from a silver vial in Father MacAndrews' hand, making no burial sound, planting Brother Jonathan, Johnny Reb, the old sly boy, in sterile sand where nothing could grow.

Then Father MacAndrews, forgetting us as Uncle Ephraim had forgotten us, looked out, across the wide valley, through the blue air. " 'I heard a voice from heaven,' " he called against the space, as if he had had enough of our smallness measuring the terrible mir-acle of another useless death, " 'saying unto me, Write, from hence-forth blessed are the dead who die in the Lord' "—his voice echoed among the stones and hollows—" 'even so saith the Spirit; for they rest from their labors.' "

The air had paused around us. Someone sobbed. Far down the green slope I heard a bobwhite from the graveyard covey. Father MacAndrews began to pray.

" 'Christ have mercy upon us,' " our voices sighed weakly in the space.

My grief broke like labor; my body drenched with sorrow. It was beginning. Neither the dead nor the living were with me. I was alone. But I knew I stood as politely as the rest, the well-pressed skirt of my borrowed black dress scudding a little in a new hilltop breeze.

It was over, and we were being led away from the awning, and Johnny had not yet been buried. I looked back. Only Father Mac-Andrews and the crucifer, his small cross shining out from the shadows, were left under the canopy. The funeral director had backed away with two strange Negro workmen. Minnie Mae and Jack still stood against the yew tree. On the near side, safe among the Catlett graves, Mr. Catlett leaned on his crutches, with Eddie Lacey's slat-like figure beside him.

I tried to pull away from Melinda. She turned and saw the men.

"What were *they* doing here anyway? You'd think . . ." she muttered.

"I'm going back," I told her.

"You're going to do nothing of the kind. You've humiliated us enough," she whispered at me. Her hand was like a vise.

"At least you never made him one of you," I whispered.

". . . And neither did you," she whispered back, triumphant.

Our hate was a gulf between our close faces, as clean as the air. People walked in a wide arc around the two mourning sisters leaning together in their sad time.

I twisted my arm out of her grasp. She looked up to see if anyone was watching. "Never do anything the way . . ." I heard her mutter as she shrugged away.

It was Melinda's epitaph for me, as cold as if it were etched on one of the stones.

As I wandered back to see Johnny buried, Mr. Catlett came to me, moving fast enough for Eddie Lacey to take long hill strides beside him.

He looked down at me. I had not realized he was a tall man. "Good-by, Miss Hannar," he said and took my hand. His cheeks, since the night before, had shrunk even more. The white mustaches went down below his chin in a horseshoe. I remembered for the first time that day that only his ingrained hill manners made him hide that he, old and dispossessed, had valley troubles of his own.

Behind me I could hear a machine begin to hum as I watched Mr. Catlett going off to a pickup truck parked away from the road, almost in front of Colonel Peregrine Lacey's tomb. I wondered if Eddie Lacey, who had not spoken a word, would see it. I wondered if he cared. All the way out of sight over the hill's edge the dead lay in the last green grass before the suburbs on the southern side of the river. The valley spread out below, covered with roofs of red and brown and gray, its few spires tiny against its space. I wondered if meadows had gone down to the river, or if the dense forest had hidden it. There was no sight of the scars, the stabbed hills, only an innocent town, lying deceptively safe between the hills in the sweet curved valley, hiding its wounded land, its unneeded men.

When I turned again, Johnny's casket had been lowered halfway into the grave. The winch sighed and squeaked as the young man turned it in his pretty fingers. The fake grass cover had been removed, and the earth to cover Johnny lay in the sun, sodden with wet—not earth at all, not even dust, a mixture of clay and shale, which was what we had left on the eroded, naked, treeless hill.

The boy holding the crucifix kept it steady, the staff between his eyes like a cadet on parade, while the Negroes threw the heavy clay against the casket, grunting slightly in unison at its weight. The clay rumbled, loose pebbles danced, beginning to dirty the clean pall.

Father MacAndrews watched until the grave was nearly full, he away from me, I away from him.

"Now, Hannah," he finally said, sounding as down to earth as the workmen's grunting and the thunk of the wet clay, "I'm going to take you home." He came around the grave.

"We'll take her, Father," Jack said behind me. I hadn't known that he and Minnie Mae were still there.

"Well, anyway, walk a little with me." Father MacAndrews led me down among the neat squares of marble. He sighed by Jonathan Catlett, his work with us not yet done.

"Why are you a preacher?" I asked him by Leah Catlett's head-stone—Leah born Cutwright, my great-great-grandmother from Cincinnati. What had she brought us besides cobwebs of kin and an old pride? How far back could the unknown scars go? Father MacAndrews turned up the hill for me to follow him, but I was caught among the graves. Her husband, Peregrine Catlett lay beside her, a jailed miner and a Negro policeman bearing his name. The Senator's father, Daniel Neill, and his beloved wife Ann had helped form me; Jonathan Catlett, 4th Virginia cavalry C.S.A had left his lost gesture somewhere in my blood. I knew then that to find Johnny's death, or any man's death, was more than the work of one spoiled girl in a few days of being touched and formed for once in her life.

Father MacAndrews had turned and stood below the eagle, waiting for me. As I followed I saw his hand reach for his pipe, forgetting he was in his cassock. He sat down on the wide base of Senator Neill's tomb, flanked by Minerva and Justice. Away over his head the eagle soared. He looked so awkward sitting there, with his big shoes and his uncreased pants' legs jutting out from his skirt that it drew me to him and I huddled under Justice, watching him, and took off my black hat.

"Hard to tell, honey. It runs in my family," he told me after I had forgotten what I'd asked him. "At least," he added, "it's a duty to your own people; you can't run a road through or strip the top from or run down the river like topsoil."

Away in the valley, from far down the river, came a fine call of a noon whistle.

"My plane leaves in an hour," I told myself and Father Mac-Andrews and Senator Daniel Neill—"Whose unweening devotion and unselfish service" I read over Father MacAndrews' head.

"You're needed at home," he told me, shocked.

"Don't fool me, Father, just don't fool me." I picked at the grass, and when he didn't answer I looked at him until he had to tell the truth.

"No, honey, you're not needed, any more than Johnny was. But you're wanted. Isn't that enough?"

"No," I answered the grass, urgent. "There's too much to do."

"Do you want to leave?" he asked my head.

"Whoever wants to leave home?" I asked the planted grass. I wanted to tell him that we were made of people who for three hundred years had left home because they had to, and who had had to carry with them that sense of loss, all the way to the American soul, a bleak, tentative place in the spirit we had to learn to cover.

"After all," he told me as if just for that minute we had the same mind, "our country was made by people who had no place else to go . . ."

Not because Johnny had died, but that his death had no meaning that I knew yet; that was the loss—the revulsion against the waste, as I was revolted by the slag heaps, the waste in dead water, the stripped hills.

"I'm going to find . . ." The grass was tattered in my fingers.

"You better find some of the solid guts that were bred into you," he muttered softly, afraid of hurting me.

"Why did Johnny . . . ?"

"I don't know why. Find out."

"I'll find out," I promised him.

Minnie Mae sat, shy in her grief and her Sunday clothes, in the back seat of Jack's car. He helped me in beside her. All the way down the hill and across the valley we clung together in our silence.

When I had almost reached the house I remembered that I had left Melinda's neat black hat on the stone as a small correct offering to Wisdom or Justice, or Senator Neill.

In the living room there was a babble of voices. Ice tinkled in glasses. A sense of relief that it was over permeated the house.

[ 215 ]

Minnie Mae and Jack went into the kitchen and I tiptoed up the stairs, to change my dress and get my handbag, which was all I had brought home.

When I went into the living room, my red dress harsh against the dull green and the black, my father walked away toward the French window and mother looked up and smiled as if I were a stranger. The event had drawn them into life for a little while, and, finding it naked and unbearable, they were retreating, trying to find their safe, dry place again. The ice was familiar in their glasses, their eyes begged for habit, for me to shut up, not make enough noise to wake the dead. Rilke had said that there was evidence that the prodigal returned, but there was no evidence that he stayed. For me, the language of staying had been washed clean from my mind. I had to be born, and the doors to the past were as closed as my mother's womb. There was, simply, no place to go back to, and no more to say.

Melinda didn't speak. Like the prodigal's older brother, she sulked, her face heavy with a kind of perpetual disappointment, shutting me away from the duty she clutched as she clutched her drink.

"I have to go," I told mother and father. "I have a class tomorrow." I lied as I always had and prayed that one day I would find the courage to have one face.

"Hannah's studying something . . . oh, the history of art. Very useful. I forget . . ." Melinda jabbed at me by saying it to Rose, who watched me over her head.

Rose stamped over to me, "By God, you can come to us, honey. Can't she, Eph?" she said to the room, damning it.

"Whoa, there," Uncle Ephraim warned.

"Don't mind me, honey." Rose put her arm around my shoulders. "I can't drink these days. I'm pregnant as a bitch."

I could still hear her laughing when I went to ask Jack to drive me to the airport.

As the plane climbed, the green hills opened out in the distance beyond the valley, their scars shining like raw battlements, their gashes black runnels down to the rivers. Below us, on mile after mile of strong mountains, the sun beat like a gong. There was work to do in the growing back of the trees, work to do in the healing of the earth's wound, work for men as there had always been. We climbed higher, and it was all green, as it had been when it was found by the lost people who bred us—people more lost, more frightened, more unneeded than we would ever be. It looked, so far away, like a new earth under a new heaven, where the former things could always pass away. Except in tiny spots distance hid where the exploited ground had turned to overlay us like a sleeping giant, clay and shale without topsoil thrown over our wasteful faces. We had cut down its trees, and the water had poured down its naked gulleys and swept itself clean. We had stabbed too hard, and in those places it had shrunk back baring its rock teeth. Arrogance and lack of care toward its riches had grown into arrogance and lack of care for each other. The crash of the grabber at the coal face had exploited, grabbed, as we had grabbed. We had left a residue of carelessness, and the hatred that grew in it had made a fist.

We had sat so lightly through the blind days of our building that our ruins already glistened in the tiny black defiles below me, ignored by the miles of indifferent trees; we had forgotten our frontier, the same frontier that we had always found, a frontier of indifference, whether of trees or men—not in space now but in inheritance.

We banked northeast and crossed the faint white bandage of the ramp over Beulah. Slowly, under our leaping shadow, the small wasteland of the hill farm turned like a dead bird nestled in the green new sea.